The Crocodile Masquerade

Quig Shelby

ACORN BOOKS

Contents

The Crocodile
Masquerade

Chapter One

Oxford

Felix, the nurse, stepped back from the corpse on the bed, a pillow in his hands. The patient looked no different in death than life, with grey thin skin, and gaunt cheeks. Felix was trembling, cold sweat sticking the tunic to his back. But there was no guilt, only relief it was over. He returned the pillow underneath Arthur's head; sunken eyes shut for the final time. Felix picked up a silver backed comb, brushed his victim's course white hair neatly into place, and then slowly pulled up a sheet, smiling.

'Sleep tight,' he said.

Felix looked around the bedroom at the faded flowered curtains, an upholstered high backed chair, and one hastily arranged wardrobe. There were model aeroplanes, newly painted, taxied on the window ledge. Many in old age revisited their youth.

A favourite wooden jigsaw lay on the dresser, carefully arranged on a dining tray, but with one missing piece; a hawk's beak. Felix searched his biro stained side pocket, before lifting out a small irregular shape. He snapped it into place.

Satisfied there were no signs of a struggle, Felix flicked off the light. Quietly he closed the door, and made his way down the narrow corridor, passing the small half lit library. He entered another patient's room, checked she was asleep, and then swiped a handful of mint toffees from a tin atop her wardrobe. In the corridor he threw one in the air, and caught it in the palm of his hand, without breaking stride.

'Felix, thank God,' said Julia the day nurse, dark circles shadowing her eyes.

It was seven-thirty in the evening, half an hour before his shift began. Julia sat slumped in the office chair with her shoes off.

'You're early,' she said.

'That's because I care,' said Felix un-wrapping a mint toffee.

His loose fitting tunic couldn't hide the emerging spare tyre, spilling out over his belt.

'Well I won't hang around then,' said Julia, struggling to read a scrap of paper on the old mahogany desk, brimming with tea stains and indented scribbles.

The lightshade was covered in dust, and the walls stained dark yellow, like much of Greenpastures nursing home.

'Mary had a fall in the morning, Henry's still refusing his food, and if you could be a darling Arthur needs a new dressing on his leg ulcer. It's all in their notes.'

'Sure,' he said, watching Julia hurriedly shuffle out of the room in her mules.

He pulled Arthur's file from the overhead shelf, an obituary, and studied the photo of his victim pinned to the front.

Felix stroked his balding head, before twisting the remaining strands of hair around his finger, the roots tugging tight. Something brushed against his leg. He looked down, and winked at the ward's newly adopted cat; a stray that had wandered in, like the residents.

'Where have you been hiding?' asked Felix, lifting it up.

The striped moggy purred in his lap, stretching a paw towards Arthur's file.

'Now don't go telling anyone,' said Felix, grinning like a Cheshire cat.

It was half an hour before the two care assistants arrived. Felix hadn't moved from his seat.

'Nothing to report,' he said, and an already sleepy Doreen and Ivy relieved the remaining day shift.

The carers wore their own un-pressed clothes, and soon charged around searching for residents, who once cornered had tea and stale sandwiches thrust into their midriffs like bayonets. Some patients were more with it than others, though all could wear a look that said it might be my turn today but soon it will be yours.

Ivy knocked on Arthur's door, and took in a cup of tea and one jam sandwich, but he was dead to the world. Felix feigned his surprise, did a few cursory checks for the sake of appearances, and then rang the on-call doctor.

'Respiratory failure,' said the Doc 'but he went peacefully in his sleep.'

Felix said exactly the same on the phone to Arthur's son.

The night stole more hours of their lives, with Felix for the best part scanning the replies to his lonely hearts ad. One image in particular caught his eye; that of Dela Eden Obi. At forty-two she was ten years his senior, but had a look of hidden deviance he found seductive. She cut a pretty figure too, and he was intrigued by her interests - voodoo and restraint. Now who in their right mind would put that he wondered? She sounded perfect.

The following shift and the health of Joan Bedloe had taken a turn for the worse. She'd been a little psychotic again, and Julia had her sedated - for her own good.

It was the dead of night when Joan started to come round. Felix sat her up, and gave her the drink of water she requested. On his way out of the room she half whispered 'I know what you've been up to.'

'Really,' replied Felix, thinking she was referring to her missing humbugs.

'You think you're too clever to get caught don't you,' she croaked.

'Caught doing what?' asked Felix indignantly.

'Murderer,' she hissed.

The hairs on the back of his neck stood up.

'I'd gone to get Arthur a book from the reading room the night he died. I saw you come out of his room smiling to yourself.'

'Joan, that's ridiculous. He was fine when I left.'

'Liar. I went in, he was dead.'

Felix felt a warm red glow rush across his face.

'So you did do it,' she said triumphantly.

He couldn't even answer, such was the shock. He quickly closed the door on his way out. His mind was racing; she had to go before she spoke to anyone else - even a deluded old bat could be persuasive. He leant against the corridor wall, cold and nauseous. Five minutes later he was back in Joan's room.

'I knew you'd come back for me,' said Joan, with Felix standing over her, pillow in hand 'couldn't wait eh?'

With a smile she went to press the buzzer held tightly under her blanket, but Felix had disconnected it from the outside, and his grin replaced hers. The first murder had been methodical, premeditated; this was expedient, but nonetheless thrilling.

Only a side light from the bathroom illuminated his silhouette, and Joan looked closely into his eyes as death came for her; her bony fingers trapped under the green floral duvet. She'd never noticed her age, or vulnerability, in the mirror.

Felix was still catching his breath when he heard Ivy approaching, opening the doors in the corridor one by one, checking the residents. He reached for his mobile, and rang the office phone. The door knob rattled just before Ivy turned around; it could be her suspicious boyfriend, spying. Everything was either love or death.

A week later and Joan, and Arthur, had been forgotten. Felix's correspondence was bearing fruit, and the delectable Dela Eden was looking forward to meeting him. Next to the theatre tickets, in his jacket pocket, was his resignation; things had started to get a little hot.

Chapter Two

London

'Go and wait upstairs Snowflake, I won't be long,' said Kofi, her pimp.

Snowflake silently obeyed, dispirited, and went to sit on the edge of the bed. She murmured a little prayer, whilst Kofi drew up the syringe in the kitchen. He wanted another zombie treading the streets, hooked on drugs, and soulless.

Snowflake was turning heads, but not enough cash. She wasn't trained for the more unusual requests. Kofi intended to change that, especially after two of his best girls had turned runaway. Besides, having smuggled her into the UK, she owed him a return on his investment.

She heard his heavy footsteps pounding on the stairs, and took one last deep breath as the door swung open. She was an African albino, white with brown eyes, and a beguiling pout. The name Snowflake was more of a taunt than a term of affection. Her real name was Tendai, though the punters called her many things. Kofi was as black as his name suggested, but no sugar; there was nothing sweet about him.

Kofi stood filling the doorway, whistling. He was stocky and muscular, not tall, with a neck like a bull's. In his right hand he held a syringe, and a tourniquet hung from his belt.

'Are you ready Snowflake?' he asked.

'Sure baby,' she replied.

'You're gonna fly high tonight Snowflake,' he said.

'I know,' she said, sitting on her hands.

'I said chill baby, not freeze,' said Kofi, as he went to close the window.

There was a golden striped cat balanced on the deep window ledge, watching him. He tried to shoo it away, but it remained defiant, staring.

Kofi sighed, reminded of the family cat back home. A shack, but nonetheless full of joy, until his father's death; Kofi was eleven. Then he became a worthless dog in the eyes of his stepfather. His mother's soothing tones never healed the sores. Later he washed up on these shores.

Snowflake crept up from behind, nervous, but there was no turning back. Swiftly she plunged a dagger into Kofi's neck; his shriek pierced the air, before he turned it blue. He staggered around to face her, each as shocked as the other. The knife slipped from her hand, hitting the frayed dusty carpet.

Kofi stumbled, his steps twisted in a drunken tango; an artery had been hit. An old commando, make that customer, had taught Snowflake the art of revenge. A perfect ten, and Kofi bowed out, crashing forwards.

Blood was dyeing Kofi's designer shirt, as he lay motionless on the floor. Snowflake saw the letter K shaved into the back of his head; this time it stood for kill. 'Snowflake' was the last word on his lips, before it melted away forever.

Tendai looked at the body in disgust, like so many times before, and considered the perversions she'd engaged to survive. Suddenly, uncontrollably, her stiletto stabbed into his face, repeatedly, until she stood there sobbing, alone. This time Kofi had been violated, and his wounds were splattered across her shiny blue shoes. She wiped away his fluids on the grubby soiled bed sheet.

Only one thing remained; to grab his cash and flee, before any of the girls arrived. She cleaned the blood from the knife, on back of the curtains. After prising open a speaker case, before the encroaching pool of blood gurgled at her feet, she grabbed a holdall, and threw in the bundles of grubby fifty pound notes. The other speaker was full too, but cocaine wasn't her game.

Dashing down the stairs Tendai fled into the night. Her prints were everywhere, but so were another dozen girls', and they were all untraceable illegals. The murder weapon was heading for the bottom of the Thames.

The streets were still mean, but not as cold. She no longer needed to display her wares, and her jacket was zipped up to the neck; although one hopeful driver slowed his car.

'Sorry love,' said Tendai with a nervous smile as the car door opened 'I've retired.'

Tendai recognised his silhouette, and a shiver ran down her spine. She knew he was the last person to have seen Lilu alive, and who knows maybe Sarah too.

Back at the bedsit Tendai was soon on her mobile to Mozambique, and her younger sister Eudy. On the bed lay a fortune in hard sweated cash; enough to take Eudy to a place of safety, and away from the muti gangs that dealt in albino flesh.

'I did it Eudy,' said Tendai euphorically.

There was a sigh of relief on the other end of the phone, followed by a note of caution.

'Don't worry, I don't even exist,' replied Tendai.

He checked the driver's mirror. The van behind was too close, and hurrying him along. He pulled into the bus stop and, waiting for it to pass, took a swig from the half empty flask of absinthe. He returned the flask underneath his seat, searching the streets once more. The trick was to keep the speed just right; too slow and he'd arouse suspicion, too fast and he'd miss what he was looking for on the mean streets.

Eventually he found her. She was in more of a hurry than usual, her jacket was zipped up to the neck, and there was a holdall slung over her shoulder. But her gait was ever captivating, and he crawled slowly to the kerb. The girls called him 'the Librarian'; he liked it quiet, and tattooed on his right forearm were the Libran scales of justice. His gloved hand opened the door in anticipation.

'Sorry love, I've retired,' said the hooker into the eerie shadows.

His heart sank into his stomach, and he felt cheated as he sped off, but she was too close to the bus stop, and the late night passengers, for him to grab her. He'd wanted to kill her tonight, just like the others, and he punched the dashboard in frustration. He decided to see Kofi instead, and demand an explanation.

The front door was open, and he let himself in. The television was on downstairs, but there was no reply from Kofi. He crept up the stairs and, from the landing, saw Kofi's hand lying on the carpet. On closer inspection he was dead, and it wasn't pretty, even with Kofi's gold and diamond teeth on display.

He saw two overturned speakers on the floor, and one was packed with coke. He rushed to the boot of his car, and emptied the blue canvas bag of the hammer, rope and foldaway shovel. He almost took the pliers, but he was no dentist. Feverishly filled the blood stained bag with his future.

He paused, took one last look around the room, and relieved Kofi of his gold chain and medallion. The talisman was engraved with a goat horned dog, and the cat on the ledge outside hissed as he placed it in his pocket. Then like spectres they were both gone.

Chapter Three

South Africa

The smoke was choking, his lungs burning, bursting. He pulled the door handle, and fell to the ground; rolling down the hill before the flames took hold. In the distance a shadow disappeared, one of the carjackers. The other he'd shot in the head during the struggle that had caused the crash. Then, as always, he heard the screams of his wife and daughter from inside the burning wreck; haunting, chilling. Their suffering branded onto his soul as the car exploded.

Shivering, he reached for the bedside bowl he'd learnt to keep at hand, and vomited. The nightmare was always the same, and his chest felt heavy, and tight. Gasping, he lifted up the window to get some fresh air. The rain had stopped, but there was only darkness to greet him; never any peace, just pieces.

A solitary jackal wailed, drawn out, then intermittent yelps; chequered with splashing from the Eastern Cape seaboard. Tall, violent waves crashed onto the beach at Southbroom, a short distance from the rented bungalow; the scattered ashes of his love trying to find their way home.

He surveyed the bedroom. Near the window, on top of a small rattan cabinet, was a photo of a much happier man with his family; ghosts. He heard a noise outside, a scampering; he slammed the window shut, and quickly grabbed his gun from underneath the bed. An hour passed before he finally put the weapon down.

Joost van Houten wore a beaten brow, and his smile was half-hearted. A year ago he had made a fatal mistake, stopping at the roadside to help at a staged accident. He'd struggled with the carjackers, condemning the ones he loved. His tears often wrote a prayer to take their place. He'd burn in Hell for eternity to bring them back.

Joost stared at the brass alarm clock on the bedside table; the ticking grew louder. It was 4 a.m., and in nine hours he would catch his flight - if he could hold out. The ropes of depression were binding him in knots, and his new medication hadn't yet kicked in. The gun was back in his hand, and he sat on the edge of the bed, forever alone. The barrel of the pistol pointed at his temple, yet there was no tremor in his arm, as he pulled the trigger.

He checked the half empty barrel, and grinned. He was one chamber out from joining his family. They'd just have to wait, but he couldn't stay in South Africa any longer; he needed to hide from himself.

Joost ran his fingers through his short dark hair, and then closed the photo album, returning it to the suitcase. He turned on all the lights, and took one final walk around the house; no more energy left to punch the walls.

Most of the memories he was leaving behind, favourite ornaments, his daughter's collection of theatre tickets, and the African masks his wife loved to collect; though there was one he couldn't bear to abandon, a long crocodile face mask he and Stella had chosen together in Johannesburg. Now it was heading to London with him, which with every passing moment seemed the most unlikely of new beginnings.

He grabbed the whisky bottle, and TV remote. A grisly new discovery waiting.

'Police are led to another mutilated corpse, in Oribi Gorge national park,' said the presenter.

The witchdoctor was handcuffed, looking nervously at the ground, flanked by cops. He'd determined his fate, unlike his albino victims, organs stolen for magic.

A haunting mist began to envelop the ground. It covered everything as it crept irretrievably towards Joost's front door. He heard the noise again, then a hissing, and this time outside his daughter's room. He ran in, and lifted up the window, nearly bowled over by the swirling wind.

A school essay, proudly signed Hildegard van Houten, was lifted like a paper aeroplane to the porch outside, before the window fell shut. Joost couldn't see through the fog bank, but a wild cat with stripes scavenged it between jagged teeth, and ran into the grasslands. Later, when Joost's flight touched down, it was dropped in Oribi Gorge, onto a simple stake in the ground. Nearby there was a wooden effigy, known by some locals as Dankoly - the voodoo god of revenge.

Chapter Four

Two Years Later

Felix was plying his trade in possibly London's dingiest nursing home. The corridors were narrow, and the air was stale. The lighting was gloomy, and the dark brown walls appeared glued together like subterranean insect chambers.

'I hear Molly passed away last night,' said Agatha, joining Felix in the office.

'Yes, a real shame,' he replied, invoking no sincerity in his voice.

Agatha glanced in the sink at the tablets.

'I found them on the floor in the TV room,' he lied.

Not all of the patients were compliant, and often the struggle wasn't worth it.

Agatha smiled, knowing the only tablets Felix never threw away were the sleepers. She was the nurse upstairs, burnt out, but quite fit in the dark blue uniform she wore to work. She could still turn a head or two, but her beauty was fading, and it scared her. She was divorced, liked a drink or more, and was occasionally inebriated on duty.

It was the start of the night shift, and Felix was stocking up the drugs trolley. Tablets he knew wouldn't be taken were already waiting to be washed away, along with others he didn't want to give, though he signed otherwise - naturally. Agatha was missing some omeprazole, and took a spare box from the cupboard.

'Try and stay away from the chocolates,' she teased Felix on her way out.

With his sweet tooth, and Dela's big meals, Felix had piled on the pounds since their wedding day. Whilst his East African wife remained eternally slim. He wondered if she'd ever swallowed a tape worm.

Felix pulled down the long sleeves on his tunic, hoping to hide the rope burns. Dela had lived up to her promises, but instead of a slave he'd found a mistress, and for the last fourteen months his suffering had been her delight - although often his.

Felix hadn't killed a patient since leaving Greenpastures, but he was inexplicably drawn to Ernest Downing, a hunched man with Huntington's disease. Perhaps it was the bleating in his voice, or the gentleness in his eyes, that marked him out, reminding Felix of his own weakness. Dela knew of Felix's past, and the two patients he had killed, but they shared a lot of dark secrets.

'Hi Ernest,' said Felix jauntily, bringing in his medication.

Ernest just nodded, and blindly tilted his head back for the capsules, before sipping some water from the other medicine tot. He wasn't fooled.

Felix joined Agatha upstairs. She was sitting in the resident's lounge with her feet outstretched, rubbing moisturizer into her hands. But Felix only rubbed his lower back, wondering how much longer he could keep going.

It was no use; his back was playing up again, and he couldn't sleep. He went downstairs and, instead of waking the carers, checked the patients. He lingered a little longer in Ernest's room, looking at the two African statues on the dresser, before almost lifting a pillow to finish him off.

'Another tiring night baby?' asked Dela, massaging his back, as he lay on the bed between mountains of pillows.

'As always,' sighed Felix, adding 'just a little lower.'

'Let me get some lotion,' said Dela, going to the bathroom next door.

She soon returned on top of him, wearing nothing but a scarlet silk dressing gown.

'Oh yes,' purred Felix.

He glanced at the clock, knowing Dela never gave him more than ten minutes of heaven; but there was plenty of hell.

'Only one night to go,' said Felix, and then he was off for four nights.

'Felix I'm doing a reading this afternoon. So sorry honey, but you'll have to ....'

'I know, stay out of the way.'

Voodoo high priestess Dela Eden Obi had all kinds of things going on in their high rise council flat in the heart of the city; fortune readings, talismans, and potions to contact the Spirits. But she didn't stop just there; she cured HIV, purportedly, and cast spells - occasionally using human body parts. And all with a soft gentle face.

'Can you manage that?' asked Dela smiling 'or have I got to tie you up again?'

Felix was caught in two minds, as he looked at her painted and curled lips.

'Don't worry I'll leave you alone today, besides you probably need time to wrap my birthday present,' said Dela smiling.

Felix gulped. It was Dela's birthday tomorrow, and he hadn't bought a thing. But he was worn out, and decided to get some rest first.

He could feel Dela rolling him in the bed. He'd overslept, and was running late for work. He quickly got dressed. As Felix tightened his belt, Dela searched her wardrobe for a colourful kanga dress, and one of the headscarves she loved so much.

Din, Dela's elder brother, arrived just as Felix was buttoning up his duffel coat. Din was always smiling, tall and thickset, but his relaxed demeanour could quickly turn. He bade Felix's farewell, before joining Dela in the lounge. She was kneeling in front of her Dankoly shrine, pouring gin over the fetish, whilst wishing the undoing of her best customer's competitor. Businessman Gasper Owido had prospered over the years, with Dela's blessings, but now he, and some others, were pushing for more powerful spells. Naturally these came at a higher price - for everyone concerned.

Din was also seeking his sister's powers. An old friend, Vankoni, was arriving from South Africa tomorrow, and he sought a charm to help him pass through immigration. Din had his own racket dealing drugs, and had a job waiting for him.

Felix went upstairs to see Agatha in the office, and drool temporarily over her uniform.

'Hi I'm Bheki,' said the agency nurse, holding the communication book.

'Where's Agatha?' asked Felix, momentarily disappointed.

'Who's Agatha?'

'She's the regular nurse.'

'I don't know, but the agency rang me this afternoon to cover.'

'Well pleased to meet you Bheki. I'm Felix.'

He'd never seen a live African albino before, only the head at the bottom of Dela's freezer last year. According to Dela the spells cast from those ears alone had paid for their last holiday. He gave Bheki a long hard stare. She was used to that, but Felix wasn't undressing her with passion, he was seeing pound signs.

Tendai Mathebula, the hooker from Mozambique, had become Bheki Ncube registered nurse. Fifty thousand pounds had helped the real Bheki retire early in Harare, in exchange for a red passport, and a nurse's PIN. The rest of Kofi's money had gone on her north London apartment, and smuggling Eudy into the UK.

Felix was still racking his brains on what to buy Dela in the morning, when he found himself in Ernest's room; he was fast asleep. The statues would make an ideal gift, and Ernest was too absent minded to notice them missing. He dropped the first one silently into the empty pillowcase, but in the mirror his eyes met Ernest's.

Ernest threw the bed sheets back, vainly searching for his walking stick. But a carer had moved it near the door, before tucking him in bed. Felix smiled.

'It's only because I care about those who suffer,' Felix lamented, picking up a soft fluffy cushion; white, and shaped as a lamb.

Ernest, grimaced as Felix approached, the latter's eyes shining. Ernest's heart couldn't take the strain, and he felt a crushing weight pressing on his chest. Feebly he reached towards the bedside table, and the medication on top, but Felix moved it just out of his reach.

Ernest's thin lips were now blue, pursed in agony, and he was struggling for breath.

'Tut tut,' said Felix, watching life ebb away, amused on the edge of the bed.

Felix checked for a pulse, but the silent killer had struck. Omitting Ernest's beta-blockers had been worth it, and Felix wasn't the one left red faced.

Felix quickly threw the booty into his car, before joining Bheki to soothe his nerves. She slipped the diary, crammed with notes, back in her Louis Vuitton bag.

Naturally Ernest was a little unresponsive in the morning, but it was just a paper exercise, and Felix didn't even have to stay behind.

Dela looked at them one last time. They were about twenty inches tall, one male the other female. It was always difficult to tell what she was thinking, but finally she released her verdict.

'Fakes,' she said 'good ones, but copies none the less.'

Felix sighed.

'Oh don't worry,' said Dela 'it's not your fault, and they do make a lovely present.'

He tried to raise a smile.

'Anyway, sit here, beside me, and give me a birthday kiss,' she said.

She patted the sofa, and Felix obliged, obediently.

'The gods have promised me a fortune, but perhaps not this way,' said Dela.

'I did meet this rather interesting nurse last night,' said Felix, trying to make amends.

'Go on,' said Dela not really listening, and placing the statues on the coffee table.

She wouldn't tell Felix about the underside 'Made in China' stamp. But neither would he tell her about Ernest. It felt like he'd bought something in the sales, only to discover it was cheaper the previous month.

'Yes, she's from Zimbabwe.'

'Oh,' said Dela, still deciding on the best position; though they were destined for the smallest room.

'And she's an albino.'

'Really,' said Dela.

Intrigued, she turned around to face him. Her eyes were glowing.

'Yes, and she has a sister too, who lives with her.'

'Now that is interesting.'

Felix could breathe again; god how he ached to please her.

'Perhaps this is what we've been waiting for. A little bloodshed perhaps, but you're not averse to that are you my dear husband.'

Felix grinned. Dela knew his strong points; he felt appreciated, loved.

Their body parts were worth far less in Africa, though equally valued. In Europe, exotic smuggled birds were expensive; extremely. Dela had customers flung far and wide, as well as her inner circle; she would have no shortage of buyers.

'Anyway,' said Dela 'it's my birthday today, and I think I deserve a little playtime.'

Playtime for Dela meant something altogether different for Felix, but still he was off for four nights, and wheals didn't last forever.

Their body language always gave the game away, and it was obvious, to anyone that knew them, Dela carried the whip hand in their marriage. But there was even more beneath the surface. The spare room was both a voodoo temple and a dungeon, and Felix was about to get his comeuppance.

Upon instruction he removed all of his clothes, his demeanour more humble than usual. His wrists cuffed tightly in front, he was pushed into a room where only candles lit the walls. The dungeon was decorated with tasselled whips, paddles both leather and wooden, various gags some ball, and all manner of unusual and wicked restraints. Images of vengeful voodoo gods, and their victims, screamed at him from the walls. There was a large serpent looking down from the ceiling, and in the middle of the room a pole, where the Spirits would communicate with Dela.

Mistress was head to toe in black leather. Evil personified, with the face of an angel. Her slave knelt as she rolled a mask over his face. His eyes peered through the slits, a metal zip undone across his mouth, but there was no safe word to save his torment - Dela just liked to hear his squeals.

Dela circled menacingly whilst berating her stooge. She held a cane, tapping it against the palm of her hand threateningly. And she wasn't shy in giving him a taste, scoffing at his excitement.

Ordered to stand completely still, welts were drawn across his behind with brushstrokes of the bamboo. The more he tottered forwards, the harder came the next strike. Obedience had to be instilled, but eventually satisfied a lesson had been learnt, Dela rested the cane, before giving her submissive chapter and verse on his incompetence. Felix stared forlornly at the floor.

His wrists were now chained to the wall above his head, causing him to stretch, whilst his ankles were forced apart with a pole. Dela's curses turned the air blue, as she clipped clothes pegs upon him. Eventually the hurt and frustration shot out of him, and he hung like a deflated vinyl toy.

Whilst chastising her charge for lack of control, Dela withdrew the devices, before handing him a cloth, and a bucket of warm soapy water. Once the dungeon was cleansed he followed her into the bedroom, head bowed in humiliation. Dela was awaiting her reward, and like any good pilgrim he kneeled before his goddess. Sex without humiliation was like murder minus the risk - routine; and both of his transgressions helped to turn his two dimensional existence into 3D.

With Dela napping Felix went to the laundry basket, and his tunic. He removed a sheet of paper from the top pocket. It was a photocopy of Bheki's timesheet. In the top right corner it read 'Caring Hands Nursing Agency'. He'd give them a call later today; he could do with the extra income.

Chapter Five

A cloud of anticipation hung over the roulette table, and gaming chips covered the numbered green baize, waiting patiently as the ball spun around the rim of the wheel.

'No more bets. No more bets, thank you,' shouted the croupier, as the ball hung loosely in the wheel, about to drop.

Din thumped the table next door, catching the pretty inspector's eye one more time. She sat perched on a high chair between both games.

'Seventeen black,' announced the croupier.

He placed the dolly on top of several coloured gaming chips, and cleared the table of all losing bets. Studious gamblers watched for any hint of a mistake - and any chance to cheat.

Odd had been empty until the very last second, but someone had slipped a hundred pounds onto it, just as the ball was dropping. It should have been removed, but the croupier chose to ignore it.

'One hundred pounds,' he said, pressing four £25 chips into the stack on odd.

Long red fingernails, curved like claws, swooped onto the two stacks.

'Thank you,' said Dela Eden Obi.

'You were lucky,' whispered Joost in her ear.

Joost van Houten also played the tables at The Four Horsemen, and he and Dela often bumped into one another; although they never asked each other's name. Casinos were for the anonymous.

'Luck favours the brave,' said Dela smiling.

In fact the croupier was the son of her neighbour, who just happened to owe a hundred pounds for the illegal skin lightening cream she sold.

Joost was having no such luck, and in the morning would be glad he'd left his credits cards at home. Self-destruction was his burden for leaving South Africa alive.

The croupier quickly paid out all other winners, pulled the wheel towards him to increase its momentum, and shouted 'place your bets please.'

He flicked the small white ball away from him, and it rocketed around the wheel under the brim. He was dealing a busy game, and hands were everywhere over the table. Another odd number was hit, and this time Joost chanced his arm.

'Late bet,' said the croupier with exaggerated disdain, and he slammed the chips back down on the table, in front of Joost.

Dela looked at him, and shrugged her shoulders. The inspector smiled. This time there was no Din, no distraction.

There were no windows, no clocks; time and season had been forgotten. Some sailed a pirate ship, others the Titanic. Walls were an international tapestry but hooked into a game, or a player.

Din wandered back from the bar, and joined his sister's side. The casino was a great place to sell his gear, and John Lacey, his runner, was with him. John had a permanent frown, and looked like something the cat had dragged in. He didn't walk between the tables; he hovered like a black cloud about to rain. He approached Joost, who promised to buy some smack later in the week. He'd long stopped taking the antidepressants, preferring to wallow in a high.

Joost only knew it was late, when he played his last chips on blackjack. John Lacey was in the crowd looking over his shoulder, and Din muscled in to remind him about his debt.

John looked a little worried; he'd already blown the money on his own habit, and Din was becoming impatient.

Joost was eyeing up one of the hookers that hung around the place, but they were too expensive. He'd pick up some street meat in his car instead.

Joost tumbled into his flat. He'd blown his brains at the casino, and then got wasted with a two bit hooker and a bottle of gin - only one thing remained. On the wall he swung the crocodile mask along, exposing the back in a recess. He delved his hand into the hollow, like a bear scooping honey from a tree, pulling out the last packet of heroin, and his kit.

Joost spilled a line of brown powder onto the creased tin foil, and gently heated it underneath with the gold lighter. As the smoke began to rise he sucked it through a thin glass tube, chasing the dragon.

The opiate was now jumping across his blood-brain barrier, like tiny soldiers racing into enemy territory. He slid into his chair and they raised the flag of victory - his demons were temporarily defeated.

Chapter Six

They recognised each other immediately; old friends from a distant life, and still bonded. Vankoni had slipped through immigration, and he and Din hugged one another.

'Good to see you old friend,' said Din.

'Looks like you've come a long way since the village,' said Vankoni smiling widely, and looking at Din's gold watch.

Din was also wearing one of his smart Savile Row suits.

'Wait until you see the car,' said Din.

Din lifted one of Vankoni's battered suitcases, and they made their way to the airport car park.

'How was Jo'burg?' asked Din.

'Hard work for us outsiders.'

Vankoni and Din had grown up together in Tanzania. But after a robbery gone sour Din had fled to the UK, whilst Vankoni limped to South Africa. He'd done some bad things to survive, forever watching his back. After six years he was making another fresh start; he'd send money home to his wife and kids.

Din wasn't married; he had girlfriends all over London, and played them off one against the other. He liked to unload, but they rarely got the chance to polish their claws in his den. That's why there was a spare room, and bed, waiting for Vankoni at Din's house.

Vankoni was suitably impressed with Din's sports car, and they headed for something to eat. Tomorrow he'd get some new clothes - after all they were blood brothers.

'Dela's looking forward to seeing you again,' said Din.

Vankoni smiled.

'But hands off this time my friend, she's married.'

'I knew Dela wouldn't remain single for long,' said Vankoni.

Dela had been married before, back home, though she had never told Felix.

'She's married to an English guy this time.'

'OK.'

'He's a nurse but don't let that fool you. Dela tells me he doesn't value life as much as some people would like to think.'

'I must thank Dela for this,' said Vankoni pulling a piece of paper from his pocket.

He had received it by fax at the airport, just before his flight. It was a sketch of a plane with the word Agwe underneath; the watchful Spirit of journeys.

'There's a ceremony tomorrow,' said Din smiling 'just like the old days. Feel free to come.'

'Chicken or goat?'

'Dog actually.'

'In my honour?' Vankoni wondered.

'I'm afraid not my old friend. Dela has quite a few followers over here as well. They want a gift to the Spirits.'

'Alright, it will be nice to see Dela again.'

'Just remember hands off this time, the husband's a friend of mine,' and they both laughed.

Chapter Seven

The heavy iron-gate slammed shut behind him, the latch falling swiftly into place like a guillotine. He made his way up the stone path, towards the church, and surveying the tombstones as he went. This was St Agnes, and his pallbearers stride suddenly halted. His searching hazel eyes pierced the skyline until he found him - the gargoyle.

'You look captivated,' said Eve, the new church curate, ghosting in by his side.

'He does have a certain charm,' replied Reverend James Middlemass.

James turned to face her, and a smile began to warm his cold face. The weather, like James' heart, seemed stuck in the freezer, but maybe a thaw was on the way.

'It's quite a building,' said Eve.

'Have you seen the gargoyle, I mean close up?' asked James.

'Never.'

'Well let's get you inside then. I think we just have enough time,' he said, checking his watch.

Eve marched briskly up the path, with James closing in the rear. She had long auburn hair that shined whenever the light passed by, and a faint hint of eau de toilette to set his pulse racing. James was fifty, twenty years her senior, but he was in tip top condition, and had something new to capture her heart.

They stepped under the stone arch, and into the church. There was a font decorated with cherubs to their right, and at the front, beyond the rows of freshly polished pews, boasted the octagonal pulpit, most of its gilded stencil rubbed off by the passage of time. They headed for the tower.

The steps snaked their way to the top, Eve went first. The thick cassock she delighted in wearing wrapped itself around her hourglass figure with every turn. They passed three stained glass windows, and James pushed gently against her to open the blackened oak door. He could feel her breath against his face.

On the roof there was a stiff breeze. They could see the tree tops swaying in the old village below, and hear the sea roar. Bishopsfield was on the coast, a short commute outside of London.

'Eve, meet St Agnes' very own resident gargoyle,' said James.

The church had been built in 1440, and the five foot monster was incorporated high above the entrance, to frighten away the Devil, and protect the congregation inside. The gargoyle was perfectly chiselled; his talons were carved into the church stone.

Eve delved into the pocket secreted in her cassock.

'Do you mind?' she asked, withdrawing a small silver case.

'No, not at all,' he replied as she lit a cigarette.

In fact he quite liked it; the way she held the cigarette, and puckered her lips to draw out the nicotine. There was something almost quite forbidden in it, and it suited her attire perfectly.

The wind was picking up a pace; the weathervane clattering above their heads. Eve stamped out the cigarette on the floor, and they made their way back down.

James hung his new woollen coat on the back of the office door, and sat on one of the hard wooden chairs, his long legs stretched forwards. Eve positioned herself near the old cast iron radiator, its pipes almost burning to the touch. Her thick black cassock was buttoned all the way up to the neck. It was tailored in at the waist, and stopped short just above her ankles, wrapped in dark blue nylons. Her shoes were flat, black, and heavily scuffed on the toes.

'The kettles boiled,' said Eve without turning to face him 'I'll have tea with milk, and no sugar.'

She already knew he was wrapped around her finger, and found it quite amusing; the way he tried not to stare, the awkwardness in his voice when she stood too close. But he was no means unattractive, and she knew half of the congregation swooned over him - albeit the older ones.

James made them both a drink. Certain she wasn't watching he poured a clear tasteless concoction into hers; a love potion.

Bought from Dela Eden Obi, to bring them as close as he dared imagine.

'Shall we get ready?' asked Eve.

'Of course,' replied James, awoken from his daydream 'for what?'

'James you're so forgetful. The church committee of course. What else could I mean?'

He smiled, he had a few suggestions, but now wasn't the time. They could here footsteps approaching. Someone had been kneeling in the pews, praying; she strained her neck around the office door.

'I'll go and get Lucy,' said Gladys the church warden.

'Thanks Gladys,' replied James, still looking at Eve's shoes. How could he forget?

A careless driver had put an end to his daughter's English studies at Oxford. Now she stuttered and spluttered her syllables, confined to a wheelchair.

James had lost his heart to voodoo years ago, whilst a missionary in Burundi, when healed of his own cancerous predilections. Then years later he met Dela Eden Obi, whilst in search of his daughter's cure; and now it had his soul.

Lucy entered the room. There was sadness in her eyes, because she knew what she used to be; the best catch in the village. But she was still the apple of her father's eye.

Her parents slept in separate bedrooms at their rambling vicarage, living on the memories of what they used to be, but Christine wouldn't fault him if her husband looked elsewhere. Lucy's accident had nearly destroyed him, and she understood his rebellion.

Lucy had been written off. The prayers said at her bedside were well intentioned but ineffectual; unlike the utterings of Dela Eden Obi. The vicar and his wife like, Rasputin's Czar and Czarina, were completely mesmerised.

'Hello James,' said Mr Pandalay, sitting next to Lucy's wheelchair.

Mr Pandalay, who ran a not too distant antiques shop, was looking dapper in his pin striped suit. He smiled at Lucy. Charles Carney, the vet, followed hot on his heels.

'I hope I'm not late,' said Mavis, who always wore her mousy hair in a bun.

'Well if you're late that goes for me too' said Gasper Owido, who was both officious and flamboyant. He wore a checked suit, and tweed flat cap.

Gasper was new to the village and nouveau riche. Bishopsfield wasn't stuck in the dark ages, but being the only African for miles around meant he was the talk of the town.

Last to arrive were Bill and Barbara who ran the village pub. Bill was in his mid-sixties with a ruddy complexion. His skin had the consistency of a potato, and his thick eyebrows were knitted together. Barbara had squeezed herself into a tight pair of jeans, but didn't have the figure for it. Her hair was long, and dyed blonde. She wore rectangular rose tinted glasses to hide the age in her eyes. The rouge lipstick was an attempt to make her lips look fuller, but had given up at the last minute.

The meeting began with a short prayer in aid of Lucy's progress. Then their important discussion began - items for the church bazaar. Only Eve and Mavis were blind to the knowledge that bound the rest of the group together. All secret societies had their code, and like snakes slithering in a basket they were intertwined.

The morning after he had offered a stuffed otter for the bazaar, Charles Carney checked his diary for the first appointment of the day. Mrs James was bringing in her Alsatian, Mr Troubadour, to be neutered, which gave him an hour.

He was already wearing his green surgeon's gown, as he lifted up his bag of instruments. There was a glint in his eye as he grabbed the key to the cellar. His hair was thin, and he wore round spectacles with gold frames. Charles was single, and lived alone. The practice adjoined his house, laying just on the edge of old Bishopsfield.

Charles flicked on the light switch, humming as he descended the stairs. Three caged dogs greeted him, and a ceramic table. Charles hadn't euthanized an animal in years, he simply knocked them out. Vivisection had always been his favourite part of the veterinary course, but those animals were dead, and it kind of spoiled his fun.

Charles looked at the cages for a fitting specimen, reminding himself the best would have to wait for Dela's ceremony.

'Patience my beauty,' he cooed to one excited mutt, as he patted her head through the wire.

For another he injected a muscle relaxant before sliding the bolt open. The dog vainly tried to lick his face.

'My you are a friendly one,' said Charles carrying the beast to the slaughter.

With his scalpels gleaming he covered up the other cages with sack cloth; he wasn't heartless.

Chapter Eight

Sure he was tormented, but that didn't stop his tongue hitting the floor. He'd never paid her any attention, not the attention she deserved. But now Bheki Ncube was standing before him, in her tightest red dress. It was all he could do to stay behind the desk. She'd had a day's beauty sleep since her last shift; and boy could he tell.

'Hi Bheki it's good to see you again. How did it go?' asked Joost van Houten, trying to stay calm.

'Good,' she replied.

'Here's my timesheet,' she said, handing him a slip of paper nonchalantly.

He looked at her, differently, intently, and she knew why; she could cause a pile-up.

'Thanks, payday's Friday,' he stammered.

'I know,' she replied coolly, and indifferent to his palpitations.

Joost ran a small nursing agency in north London. He had a partner who'd invested the capital, but he stayed away from the office; although today he might just have wished he hadn't.

'Take a seat,' said Joost 'please.'

'Oh dear am I in trouble?' asked Bheki, with mock concern.

Wearing that dress was no accident. They'd met a couple of times, but he'd always appeared dismissive, arrogant perhaps. She was curious.

In spite of his woes Joost was flattered by his advancing years. There was more character in his face, experience in his eyes, and an irresistible brooding look.

Joost was more interested in Bheki's curves, than what she had to say, and he wanted to rip her dress off. But he'd doubted he was her type; until now. The way she was playing with the pen on his desk hinted at a little more than boredom.

'I saw a friend of yours this morning,' said Joost.

'Oh really,' said Bheki, trying with all her might to look beyond Joost at the calendar on the wall, in which she had no real interest.

'Well a work colleague at least. Felix Gale, the nurse you worked with at Atoll nursing home. He came in to register.'

It was called Atoll, but in the office was known as At Hell. Joost always had trouble finding nurses to cover; the patients were bothersome, the care assistants unhelpful.

'What did you make of the place?' asked Joost.

'Difficult, I'd prefer something closer.'

'For you, no problem,' said Joost glancing at her knees, and the silk nylons; struggling to hide his feelings.

'Would you like a drink? he asked.

'Tea please.'

'Two sugars right,' said Joost smiling.

'I don't take sugar.'

Damn, thought Joost.

'Of course, you're sweet enough,' he said.

Bheki looked uncomfortable, she wanted him to squirm; at least for a moment.

Double damn; he wished he hadn't said that.

'Two teas Irena please,' he shouted into the office next door 'and no sugars.'

Bheki was warming to his approach, even if it did feel a little awkward. He wasn't smooth tongued, but perhaps that was a good thing; for now.

'There is a psyche unit near your part of town,' said Joost. 'And the pay is much better.'

He didn't want to lose her.

'How much better?'

'An extra fiver an hour.'

'When's the first shift?'

'Monday if you like.'

Actually there were shifts going tonight, but he had something else in mind.

'Two teas,' said Irena placing them on the desk, and looking Bheki up and down.

Now Irena was a beauty too, and Joost, not unnaturally, had a thing for stunners. But he was also drawn to the desperate hooker look, and, maybe unknowingly to both of them, Bheki's past had left its mark. Whether it was immaculate clothes and makeup, or dressed like a tramp with misapplied lipstick, and the darkest of eyeliner, he could be hooked.

'This hospital, what's it called?' asked Bheki, after giving Joost's eyes more time to disappear into her thighs.

He'd decided to let her know how irresistible she was, even if she already knew it. After all she was a traffic stopper - cut and dried.

'Blackfriars,' he replied, after putting his tongue back in his mouth.

'And have you an address?' she asked, wondering when Joost would make his move; unless he was a voyeur.

She needn't have worried.

'I have,' he said, shuffling to the edge of his chair 'but it's a little tricky to find.'

'I got lost the first time,' he added, trying to sound concerned.

He needn't have bothered with Bheki. She liked to despise her lovers.

Now was the moment to check his timing.

'If you're not doing anything this evening, perhaps I could show you where it is.'

He tried to stay humble, as if he wouldn't take her affirmation for granted.

Bheki waited, delaying her reply to perfection. Joost tried unsuccessfully to hide his consternation. His pulse was racing, and he couldn't bear to let her slip away. He untightened the knot in his tie.

'Maybe I could even take you out for a bite to eat?' he asked, throwing in his hand.

It was time to stop playing games, and at least Joost had laid his cards on the table.

'Sure, why not,' she said, still trying her best to look ambivalent.

'Eight O'clock?' asked Joost, reeling her in.

'Perfect.'

'Brilliant,' said Joost smiling.

And then just before an awkward silence could ruin the moment, the phone rang.

Bheki waved goodbye over her shoulder, certain he was watching her ass swing out of the office, hypnotised.

'Hi Felix,' said Joost 'I've got a shift for you tonight at Blackfriars.'

On the street outside Bheki smiled to herself. It had been easier than she'd imagined. She straightened her hem line, as a car screeched to a halt.

Chapter Nine

There was a boy's voice imprisoned inside John Lacey's head. He would whisper his spite, whilst John tried to escape the malice in a drug fuelled haze. John had never forgiven the boy, and the boy would never absolve him, for John was the boy and vice-versa. Abused as a child; despair, fear, and anxiety were some of the levers the boy pulled. John heard other voices too, but had never reached out for help, until he met Dela Eden Obi; he mistrusted authority figures, thanks to the priest.

The last voice John heard, before Dela came to his aid, was Sergeant Cooper. The Sergeant was a bully, and 'one mean son of a bitch' to use his own words. He was brutish and threatening, and wanted every 'wise ass filleted like a kipper'. John had been on the verge of snapping like a pencil, when Dela gave him the potion. The voodoo Spirits it invoked chased the ghoul away.

John had often seen Din around the casino, and even bought some gear. Eventually he became Din's runner. That was two years ago, but he'd now become a heavy user, and a liability. Some of the profit had gone into John's veins, and not Din's pockets; so much that he now owed five thousand pounds.

'Is that it?' asked Vankoni.

'Yes,' replied Din.

They were sitting in the car outside John Lacey's council flat, and it was time to collect his payment in full, one way or another.

On the greasy kitchen table in front of John were packets of cocaine, neatly parcelled, and some pretty LSD tabs. There was also a pile of heroin waiting to be cut, and sold to Joost van Houten. John checked the cupboards, but there was nothing he could use. He'd go to the shops, and get some milk powder. But looking through the net curtains, to see if it was still raining, he saw Din's car outside, and there was someone else with him. This wouldn't be a social visit.

John noticed the slim glass bottle on the sideboard. Inside there was some of Dela's powder. He mixed it with the heroin, then swept the drugs into his satchel. Tentatively he went outside.

'There he is,' said Din, and they both stepped out of the car.

The flats were like a warren, and John was down the ramp on the other side of the street before they could get near him.

'Don't worry,' said Din turning to Vankoni 'he'll be back.'

Din handed Vankoni a twenty pound note.

'Get us some food from the shops. We'll wait in here,' and he used a spare key to open John's front door.

'He had a break-in last year,' said Din 'and I bought him new locks.'

'Hello is that Mr van Houten?' asked John on his mobile from the back of the bus.

'Yes.'

'Joost it's me, John. I've got your delivery.'

'That's great, be at my place at seven, and don't be late, I'm going out tonight.'

John had already sold the coke, and it just gave him enough time to visit Mr Pandalay. He was sure the cash would placate Din.

Pandalay Arts and Antiquities read the sign in gilt edged lettering on the frosted glass entrance door. The shop itself was in a quaint arcade, surrounded by other suitable upmarket establishments. It was situated in Wellford, half-way between London and Mr Pandalay's cottage in Bishopsfield. It was on the tourist trail, and the rain tapped on the arched glass roof above their heads like a cash register.

To his friends Mr Pandalay was known as Pandy. John, however, was never invited to be informal.

'I have your blotters Mr Pandalay,' said John.

'Good boy.'

Mr Pandalay was 64, reasonably in good shape, apart from his asthma, and still looked debonair, cutting quite a dash in his silk suits. He was seated at the back of the shop, behind his large walnut bureau, which was respectfully cluttered.

John placed the rainbow LSD blotters next to the phone. Pandalay was old school, brought up on flower power, and loyal to his digressions. He pushed an envelope across the desk, and John checked the money.

'Oh Din was on the phone earlier, looking for you,' said Mr Pandalay.

'What did he say?'

'Not to worry, and things would sort themselves out.'

The moose's head on the wall was looking down at John, disdainfully. Below was a full set of knight's armour, and John wished he could wear it.

'Mind the step,' said Mr Pandalay, as John made his way out.

Too late, and he tumbled sideways into the angry stuffed bear in the window.

'Are you alright John?'

'Fine, thanks.'

He had a small cut on his left hand, it was bleeding.

'Well have a good day,' said Pandalay.

He didn't say see you next time.

Pandy picked up the phone.

'Hi Din he's just left. I told him what you said, not to worry.'

'Thanks Pandy.'

'He still looked a little worried though. I hope you're not going to do anything silly Din.'

'Of course not, you know me - peace man.'

Pandy smiled. He liked Din, though he wouldn't want to cross him, or his sister come to think of it; high priestess Dela Eden Obi.

John pressed the buzzer. He'd been caught in the rain, and looked more bedraggled than usual.

'Hello.'

'Hi Joost it's me, John.'

'Excellent, I'll come down.'

Joost appeared at the foyer. He was clean shaven, wearing his favourite crisp white shirt, with a thin black tie. His aftershave was citrus and cedar, with a subtle hint of mint. He really looked the business, and was reminded of his favourite English expression - the dog's bollocks.

John handed Joost seven bags of smack. He quickly buried them in his blazer pockets.

'Hope it's as good as the last stuff John.'

'Always quality Mr van Houten.'

'In that case it's worth the extra you charge. Here...'

He peeled some notes off of his silver money clip, handing them to John, who was already looking forward to passing them onto Din.

'Enjoy,' said John, and he was gone before you could say remember me.

The lift was out of order again, but Joost vaulted his way to the third and top floor. He put the bags inside the crocodile mask. The heroin was a beautiful beige-brown, ideal for smoking. He checked his watch, then the mirror; it was time to meet the delectable Bheki Ncube.

He switched on the lounge light, and nearly died a fright.

'Hi John,' said Din, sitting on the dilapidated sofa.

He'd take his suit for dry cleaning tomorrow.

'This is my friend; he's been dying to meet you.'

'Din look sorry about the money, but I've done pretty good today,' said John.

John emptied his satchel of the notes, and passed them to Din. Din shook his head.

'It's not nearly enough John, you know that.'

'So what's going to happen then?' asked John, nervously looking over his shoulder. But Vankoni was blocking the door.

'We've known each other a long time John, and Dela likes you. But in this business, reputation is everything. If my other pushers hear I've gone soft then I have a problem, and believe me I don't like problems.'

Vankoni nodded.

'I won't say a word Din, honest,' bleated John.

Din stroked his chin. There was stubble, and he was in two minds whether to grow a goatee or not.

'I know I can get the rest back soon,' pleaded John.

He was sweating profusely. Both men knew he'd promised before.

'I tell you what, let's go and see Dela, maybe she has a solution,' said Din.

He unfolded his arms, and his tone was lighter, less threatening.

'Why not,' said John, hoping Dela's fondness would save him from a beating.

'And John please don't make a run for it this time, or it really will be curtains,' said Din, whilst flicking back John's grubby nets from the window, and checking it was clear outside.

They walked to the back of the flats, and down a side street to Din's car, with John sandwiched in between.

Sergeant Cooper was whistling a requiem in John's ear, and perhaps Dela would give him some more of the powder. But at least Din and Vankoni were beginning to sound light hearted, even if he couldn't understand a word.

'Hi John,' said Dela as he was bundled into her flat.

Felix was doing a night shift at Blackfriars.

'Hi,' said John, trying to raise a smile.

'Din tells me you've got yourself into a bit of a mess.'

'Yes, but I just need a little more time Dela.'

'Of course you do. By the way how are the voices?' she asked.

Din and Vankoni were sitting side by side on the sofa, and Din had poured them both a scotch.

'Knocking at the door,' replied John.

He was thin, skinny even. And pale to the point of anaemic.

'Perhaps this will help,' and she handed him a tumbler.

'Relax John, we're all old friends here,' said Din. 'Here take it with a spot of malt.'

Din poured a drop of whisky into the glass tumbler. John looked around the room, everyone was smiling. There seemed no other choice.

John slouched back in the leather chair. The voices sounded muffled, everything was blurred. Worse, he couldn't move.

'Think you can manage it?' Din asked Vankoni.

'No problem,' he replied.

'Be careful,' said Dela as they dragged John to the bathroom 'Felix has just retiled in there.'

With John in the bath, Din and Vankoni went to work with the machetes. It wasn't long before he was at the bottom of Dela's freezer, and his parts would fetch a pretty penny in charms. Shame they couldn't let him scream though; that really would have increased the muti's power. Unfortunately John still felt every chop.

Chapter Ten

He was almost frightened to phone her number, in case it was switched off. All he could think about was that dress; the fabric, the cut, and most importantly - the contours.

'It's Joost. Where are you?'

'Right behind you,' replied Bheki.

She'd been watching him for a while, hiding in the shadows, letting his frustration build.

Joost gave her a kiss on the cheek. It caught Bheki by surprise, but she didn't admonish him. In fact her designs couldn't be any clearer. She wore a see through plastic coat, with a two-piece emerald suit underneath. Her make-up had been lifted from a porn review, and her shoes were pointed and the heels were high.

The bell bottom trousers were tight around her thighs, and with her long brown wig she stood just under Joost's chin. He was tongue tied.

'Shall we make a move?' asked Bheki, smiling.

'Sure. Hungry?'

'I haven't eaten all day.'

They took the short walk to 'The Blue Samurai', although why he was blue no one was quite sure, even the owner. Still they did the most fantastic sashimi and sushi.

The cloakroom staff took Bheki's coat; Joost preferred to hang his blazer on the back of a chair. He made sure his mobile was switched off, and the waiter took them to their table.

It was a small restaurant, where the prices more than made up for the numbers. There were live piranha in the fish tanks, but they weren't the only predators in tonight.

'Good to see you again Mr van Houten,' said the waiter, placing the crocodile bound menus in front of them.

'Thank you. It's good to be back.'

Bheki wondered how many women he'd brought here, but she wasn't celibate.

They were sitting at Joost's favourite table, looking out over the river. Bheki tried not to stare at him. Joost's jaw was square, and the symmetry in his face timelessly handsome.

'First time?' enquired Joost, as Bheki looked at the menu puzzled.

'Yes.'

'Then you can trust me to order?'

'Do I have a choice?' she asked.

'But let me warn you, I can take a lot of pleasing,' she said.

No doubt thought Joost. But then again, he had a lot of pleasure to give.

He was tempted to order the bento box for Bheki, which gave a little taste of everything, but he wanted them to share the moment. After seeing Bheki recoil from the squid, he plumped for wagyu beef nigiri with truffle salsa, and ponzu jelly. It was presented with rice, miso soup, with a side dish of sweet raw shrimps.

Joost had a couple of bottles of lager, whilst Bheki delicately sipped green tea. She'd resisted the wine list, wanting to feel every moment should Joost take the hint, and unburden himself of his manners.

The meal was a success, with cutlery and fingers, but they both knew what was really on the menu; their palates unsated. The waiter brought them each a bowl of red bean ice cream.

'So you don't hate the Boer?' asked Joost out of the blue.

'Why should I?' she replied, dabbing the ice cream from her lips.

Joost wanted to raise the temperature a little, and he sensed Bheki did too. The top two buttons on her blouse were now undone, and her foot was touching his underneath the table.

'Well you're African, allegedly from Zimbabwe,' he said.

'Meaning?'

'Just that I know a lot of Zim's, and you don't quite fit the mould.'

'Really,' she said, not in the slightest offended.

In fact the pretence was always a burden. She hated hiding her upbringing, but it had been the surest way to bury her past.

'You're right, I'm originally from Mozambique.'

'Now I've shown you mine, you show me yours,' she said.

Joost smiled. She did like to play.

'Two years ago I met this guy. He had all this cash to launder, and helped me set up the agency.'

'Lucky you.'

So he wasn't as clean cut as his appearance.

Bheki twisted the warm moist towel around her fingers, slowly removing the sticky paste.

'I'm going to freshen up,' she said.

Joost looked at his watch; there was still no sign of Bheki. Leaping up the steps to the washrooms, he caught Bheki as she was coming out; her sparkling purple lipstick newly coated. Joost held both of her arms, turning her around, and pushing her back inside.

Joost was on his knees, comforting Bheki, who gasped in delight. She was finished when Joost bent her over to proclaim his desire. Bheki held the washbasin tight, grateful her makeup was unsullied.

Joost returned to the table a little after Bheki. He could tell from the glow in her eyes they had some mileage ahead.

'You know Joost, I'm not really sure if I like you.'

She poked the tip of her tongue between her lips.

'Same goes for me,' he replied leaning forwards.

'Well I guess that's good news for both of us,' she said, smiling broadly.

It seemed harsh to part, upon leaving the restaurant. Instead they went for a stroll along the riverbank, not quite holding hands.

'It's called mosaicism,' explained Bheki about her features.

'It doesn't do it justice,' said Joost, still staring.

Bheki had African features, with a porcelain wrapper. Her brown eyes kind of read your mind in a filthy way. And under the wig lay a head of cropped blonde hair, ready for some role play.

'Thanks. But in Africa we have to be careful. It's not just the sun that can kill us.'

'I know it's the witchcraft too. There were quite a few albino killings before I left South Africa,' said Joost, his accent becoming more pronounced with thoughts of home.

'Why did you leave?' asked Bheki.

This was a tricky one for Joost. As much as he wouldn't relinquish the past, he didn't want to sound heartbroken tonight, even if he was.

'The crime,' he replied.

'Not man enough Joost?' she enquired, then bit his ear, hard.

'Bitch.'

'And for that I deserve ..?' she teased.

He quickly looked around, and led her down the embankment. Under the bridge, she was pinned to a wall. Their lips locked, and hands fumbled in the darkness.

Finally, her mouth slipped free.

'Let me make it easy for you,' she said, pushing him away, and hurriedly undoing her trouser buttons.

It wasn't too late for a pleasure cruise.

'My you really are an animal. And don't worry, I'm on the pill,' said Bheki afterwards.

Joost waved her off in a black cab. She'd almost changed her mind on sleeping at his flat. Instead she left saying 'don't worry I'll phone.'

As for Joost, he just had to see her again - with every living breath.

Chapter Eleven

Nightfall had sneaked into the village, and the good citizens of Bishopsfield were tucked into their beds. Though there were those with more esoteric tastes. Charles Carney was playing host, and Bill and Barbara were last to arrive; even if their pub was a stone's throw away.

Bishopsfield's resident vet was talking with Vankoni, and bestowing upon him all the hospitality a friend of Din's deserved. Charles was softly spoken, and when speaking, moved his hands in a demonstrative and languid fashion. He was agonisingly thin, and one had the feeling that senility would look little different on Charles than middle age.

What struck Vankoni most about the house were the real fur rugs, stretched across the wooden floors. Perhaps they gave his host strength, vitality.

'Excuse me,' said Charles 'I must check the kitchen.'

There were two enormous orange sofas in the lounge, calf leather, and either side of a marble table. On one sofa sat Dela, Felix, and Din. Across from them were James Middlemass, Gladys the church warden, and Gasper Owido. They weren't discussing the weather.

Christine Middlemass stood by the window alone, looking out at the night sky. Vankoni went to join her, at the far end of the room.

Mr Pandalay and his Mistress came down the stairs giggling, and raising an eyebrow or two. Pandy had an acquired taste for shemales, and Susie Chang, his long term Malaysian partner, had an even more alarming taste for short skirts.

Talking to Lucy was Dilwood Benson the businessman; often known as Dull Wood due to his staid conversation.

Circumstances had thrown together the oddest of bedfellows, but they had all, in one way or another, come to believe in Dela

Eden Obi, and her Petro voodoo magic. Petro because, as Dela so often put it, 'only evil gets things done.'

Gasper, Pandy, and Dilwood had all seen their wealth increase seven fold, or more. Felix and Din had stayed out of jail, and Charles was somewhere in the middle. Gladys at forty-nine was pregnant, although the father's identity was a secret. And after the doctors had given up, Lucy was no longer paraplegic. As for Bill and Barbara, they were still hoping for a windfall, but then again, they always did like to be last.

James was praying for a rather sinful blessing from the Spirits; to attract a new lover in the rather delightful shape of his virgin curate Eve. Fortunately Dela kept her patron's aspirations secret; at least from their betrothed.

'She's a little under dressed don't you think?' said Vankoni, nodding towards Susie Chang.

'Well don't worry, it's not a swingers party,' replied Christine.

Vankoni smiled.

'Besides my dear,' she continued 'she is a he. And stop staring, it's not polite.'

Vankoni laughed.

'Christine Middlemass,' she said, offering her hand 'pleased to meet you.'

'Vankoni,' he said, holding her warm smooth hand perhaps a little too long.

Christine had long blonde hair, and a devil may care look in her eyes. She was younger than her husband, with an hour glass figure. She could look both pompous, and raunchy. The stable lads that rode around the village often dreamed of her.

'I'm ...'

'I know,' interrupted Christine 'Din's friend.'

'And what is special about you Mr Vankoni?' she asked, before taking another sip from her cocktail. 'After all, we are a rather select group.'

Christine looked out at the night sky. It was clear, and for once you could see the heavens.

Vankoni was tongue tied, unsure how to reply. He could be vulgar, but was uncertain of the etiquette.

'Well don't be shy, I'm not a blabbermouth,' Christine goaded.

'My stamina,' he finally replied.

'I see. Then can you pursue what others avoid?' she asked, circling the rim of her glass with an olive.

'If my heart is in it.'

'And what does that require?'

'Excitement.'

'Damn,' she said facing the wall 'these suspenders are killing me.'

She was wearing a little black number, and hitched it up to straighten a suspender. There was a bulge in Vankoni's eyes, and elsewhere.

'I see,' said Christine smiling 'that's what you mean. It appears your mind is in my gutter.'

'Sorry,' said Vankoni.

'Now don't go soft on me,' she said.

'My circulation is fine.'

'In that case, perhaps you could escort me to an exhibition this weekend. James finds pleasing me such a chore, bless him.'

She slipped a card into Vankoni's jacket pocket, and he smelled her Chanel No. 5 one more time.

'Cosmology; I have a PhD. The odd lecture helps to buy life's little luxuries. Who knows maybe I can show you a thing or two?'

Vankoni swung around to see where James was sitting.

'Oh don't worry about him. He prefers tranny's too,' said Christine lying.

Vankoni quickly knocked back his double vodka.

Dela rang a small china bell, inducing instant silence. One by one they put down their glasses, and followed her down the steps, into Charles' cellar. James carried his daughter, and placed her gently on the one provided seat - an old cushioned rocking chair.

Rows of steel cages, covered with sack cloth, greeted them, whimpering mutts audible. Though Meadow, the golden retriever was wagging her tail as Charles approached; her lead tied to the iron legs of sink.

'Good girl,' said Charles stroking the top of her muzzled head, ready to set her free.

Dela wore a long red toga, and white head band. The beads around her neck rippled there applause, as she held a knife above her head.

'Ancestors, we dedicate this beast to you, and pray that the Spirits continue to bless us,' she said.

Charles held back the neck, open to incision, whilst Dela slit the throat. The blood was drained into St Agnes' chalice; kindly held by Gladys. Din and Vankoni kept the animal still, until it flopped in their hands, lifeless.

Dela placed the knife on Lucy's lap, upon a pre-arranged napkin. Thirstily, the priestess drank from the cup, before whirling around the room, entranced. Everyone stayed well back, praying, screaming; Gasper shouted the loudest, his fists clenched. They passed the chalice amongst them, each taking a sip of blood.

The timer on Charles's steel cooker buzzed. Fortunately lamb was on the menu, not dog.

'So what did you wish for Mr Vankoni?' asked Christine at the dinner table.

'Security and prosperity. And you?'

'Just a little excitement; life can be so tiresome.'

James looked up from his radish. He knew she was gorgeous, and no doubt many a trouser pocket was ruffled in her lectures. But even curators get bored with seeing the Mona Lisa every day.

Chapter Twelve

The wheel was spinning in front of him, with the croupier holding the ball. Joost flicked the gaming chips back and forth between his fingers, but he wasn't concentrating on roulette; Bheki Ncube was on his mind. But as always the guilt he felt for loving tarnished his joy.

Joost followed the ball as it whizzed around the rim; the brass spokes hypnotic. He saw a revolving car tyre on a burning wreck, in faraway South Africa.

Someone had placed a late bet, and the croupier quickly removed it.

'Too late,' he said.

The aggrieved gambler kicked the table leg. Joost heard a car door slam, and the words 'too late' echoed in his mind. He felt confused, was losing focus, and rubbed his eyes. Then he saw him, the carjacker that got away.

Their eyes locked. Vankoni more startled because he didn't relive the scene every night. Joost did a double take; he'd wrongly seen the face many times before. But it was really him, already edging away from the table. Joost got up to follow.

Vankoni strode to the lobby, opening the door into the cold night. He broke into a run, with Joost hot on his heels.

Both men were sprinting, when Vankoni jumped the barrier. He glimpsed Joost over his shoulder, pursuing him down the escalator. At the dark lip of a tunnel Vankoni heard a train approaching. Darting up the platform, he dodged the late night drunks, and jumped in.

Joost was doubled over, hands on his knees, and breathing heavily. The doors closed feeling his collar; he'd made it in the nick of time. He quickly removed his belt as a garrotte. But on the platform he could see his quarry waving him goodbye. Joost sat down before he was sick.

Vankoni phoned Din at the casino to explain his hasty departure, and why it was best, for now at least, to avoid the gambling den. Din couldn't stop laughing. Vankoni read the poster across the tracks, 'Do you have enough life insurance?'

He made it home, exhausted, like a punch drunk boxer at the final bell. Joost showered the sweat away; the remorse would take longer to go. He changed into loose denim jeans with bare feet, standing six foot tall. He wore no top, and was lean and muscular.

Joost checked the mirror one more time, before shaving his head. A short jagged scar scowled above his right ear; an unwanted souvenir from South Africa.

Joost lived in a converted warehouse, and the windows ran along one side; blue steel, and thick glass. There were few internal walls, and the floor was covered in soft rubber sheets. Thick pipes concertinaed around the flat, and blasted heat like a furnace. He pushed a DVD into the deck, and collapsed into his recliner, before pressing play on the remote. He drank brandy from the bottle.

'Wave Hildy,' shouted a woman's voice, and a hand was held out obligingly, rolling its wrist like a Queen passing by in a horse drawn carriage.

'How does it feel to be twelve?' asked the girl's mother, Stella van Houten.

'I wish to tell my subjects it is most excellent,' came a very regal reply.

Hildegard delighted in being theatrical, and wished with all her might to be a future star of stage and screen. Joost was holding the camcorder and zoomed in.

'Make sure you get my good side dad,' said the girl playfully.

Stella held her daughter's wrist and birthday bracelet as they both gripped the croquet mallet. They aimed at the hoop, then swung and smashed the ball together, but it skewed into the mulberry bush. The sun had gone in, and dark clouds were on the horizon. The first few drops of rain began to fall.

'We'd better get inside. Any last message your Majesty?' Joost asked his daughter.

'Yes. I love you mum. I love you dad.'

The camcorder switched itself off, its battery dead, and leaving a blank screen, an empty space.

A tear welled up in the corner of his eye before slowly rolling down his cheek. Then he began to sob uncontrollably, his head shaking, and held in his hands. If only he could see them both one last time, just to say how much he missed them, and sorry. For the guilt he felt was ever present and crushing.

He looked at the long crocodile mask on the wall. It was three foot long, and its snout pointed to the ground. The seller was from Burkina Faso, where masks mediated between the living and the dead. There was a chequered pattern carved into its body, and behind its eyes lay Joost's escape. Strangely there was a third eye in the forehead.

Ten minutes had elapsed, and the rush was taking him high above his worries. The warm solitary detachment would normally last a few hours, but tonight Joost had a visitor. He was cushioned from alarm, but nonetheless amazed as the crocodile scurried down the wall towards him.

'I said it was good stuff,' said the familiar voice.

'John?' asked Joost.

'That's right. Pretty amazing isn't it.'

Joost smiled. This was the strongest hallucination he'd had.

'I guess you think this is a hallucination,' said John Lacey.

'Of course.'

'Well I hate to spoil your high, but this is actually me.'

Joost laughed, but the claw on his foot felt pretty real, and those teeth looked mighty sharp.

'How is that possible?' asked Joost.

'Dela's powder, I mixed it with the heroin.'

'Dela who?' asked Joost.

John explained as best he could; the voodoo priestess, her brother Din, and Vankoni.

The medicine Dela had sold to ward off Sergeant Cooper had just gone up in smoke; well some of it. The only Spirit it now summoned was John, who lay on the floor in the guise of a crocodile. Joost played along, expecting to leave his mirage anytime soon.

Joost never let anyone close, for he was afraid of losing them again. So perhaps the crocodile was tapping into his subconscious, when he warned that Bheki Ncube was in danger.

'How do you know?' asked Joost.

'I've heard them talking. They want her for muti.'

Joost's tranquillity was definitely coming to an end.

'And Joost.'

'Yes,' he replied wearily.

'The other carjacker, the one you chased tonight, he's called Vankoni.'

'How do I know any of this is real?' asked Joost.

'Ask Felix Gale about his wife. He's coming to the office tomorrow morning, at ten,' said John.

It was news to Joost.

'Anyway times up,' said John. 'And Joost, if you want my help I only ask one favour in return.'

'What's that?'

'You get what's left of me out of Dela's reach. It's bloody cold in this freezer.'

Then the little crocodile scurried back up the wall, turned on the hook, and froze.

It was a couple of hours before Joost awoke, but the first thing he did was check the crocodile mask. It was the same as always, but underneath there were scratch marks clawed into the wall. Could it really be he wondered? He checked the drugs; there were six packets left.

Chapter Thirteen

Felix Gale's file was open on his desk, as Joost looked at the clock one more time. It was ten in the morning. Sure enough Felix's wife was called Dela Eden Obi, just as John had said. But he'd seen the file before, and it was easily a memory. There was a knock at the door.

'Come on in,' said Joost.

'Hi,' said Felix 'I've brought in my timesheet.'

'Please, take a seat.'

Joost looked at him. Felix was sitting cross legged with one hand on his knee. He wore navy blue slacks with a crimson sweater.

'Tea, coffee?' asked Joost.

'No thanks, I've just had one.'

Felix was cautious when it came to accepting drinks.

'What did you think of Blackfriars?' asked Joost.

'Interesting.'

'And the permanent staff?'

'Actually, very friendly.'

This wasn't always the case when you were an agency nurse.

'Funnily enough I was just checking your file,' said Joost. 'And the references. I must have known you were coming.'

Felix tried not to, but gulped.

'Oh they're OK. In fact the one from Atoll is very flattering,' said Joost.

Felix smiled. In truth they were desperate to offload him.

'You know your wife's name seems familiar. Is she a nurse?'

'No, but she does heal people - with traditional medicine. She's from Tanzania.'

'Really. I once knew a girl from Zanzibar who had a great remedy for insomnia.'

She did, but it wasn't the kind you'd find in a packet.

'Did you keep in touch?' asked Felix.

'I'm afraid not.'

She never got used to his nightmares.

'Well Dela makes all kind of potions, maybe she can help.'

'I might take you up on that, I still have sleepless nights.'

Joost casually flicked through Felix's file.

'Why the change from dementia care?' he asked.

'I was beginning to feel dead tired.'

'Well I've got another five nights to cover at Blackfriars. If you're interested.'

'Which wards?' asked Felix.

'Brent and Surrey.'

'I'll take them.'

Both wards were rehab, and the patient's had been sedated for years.

Joost wrote the shifts down for Felix, who'd already decided to go off sick, and leave Atoll nursing home for good. His back felt better already.

'Well thanks for dropping by Felix, and if there's any changes I'll give you a call.'

Felix got up, and straightened his tie.

'Just out of interest,' asked Joost 'does Dela do voodoo?'

Felix smiled.

'Of course, and business charms a speciality.'

'Let me think about that one.'

'No problem,' said Felix, and he left, leaving Joost to ponder if the crocodile mask had really spoken.

Late afternoon, and she saved him the dilemma of phoning.

'Hi handsome,' said Bheki.

'I was just thinking of you,' said Joost.

'And what were you doing?'

'Not what you would imagine.'

'Anyway, do you want to see me after work?'

'I'd love to.'

'OK I'll be waiting outside the offices. I've got somewhere I want to take you. But don't get too excited, it's your mind I'm after this evening,' and she put down the phone leaving Joost intrigued.

Bheki wasn't dolled up, but Joost's passion was still burning, and her tight boot cut jeans were romantic enough. Likewise she found his newly shaved head, scar and all, a bold erotic statement. It was late night opening in the British museum, and they were looking at an exhibition of West African art.

Joost tried to stay interested, but Bheki wasn't fooled, and it became pretty obvious he was more interested in her ass than the museum's assets. Although she'd checked her reflection several times in the glass cabinets, and was more than pleased with her own treasures.

Bheki hesitated at an Ngbaka statue from the Congo. It was 19 inches tall with a protruding stomach, and slightly bent knees. On its face was a string of scarification lines.

'You like this one?' asked Joost temporarily lifting his eyes above waist level.

'It reminds me of one I've seen before.'

She didn't want to say too much. Joost seemed decent enough, but men had a habit of disappointing her, and it was still early days.

They saw the rest of the exhibition, and as much as Joost tried to turn the conversation around, Bheki was determined to keep their discussion highbrow.

Joost was sitting across from Bheki, and stirring his coffee on the small round table in the cafeteria.

'Well don't look too disappointed,' she said 'you'll have plenty of time to undress me, and not just with your eyes.'

He smiled broadly.

'Just not tonight. Anyway I could do with some more work, and I hope sleeping with the boss gives me preference.'

'I've got plenty of work at Blackfriars.'

'Sure.'

'Which shifts?' he asked.

'Late's or night's will do.'

Bheki wasn't a morning person; at least not for work.

'Which wards?'

'I don't mind.'

'Brent tomorrow night?' asked Joost.

'Yeh, that's fine,' said Bheki.

Joost felt guilty throwing Bheki and Felix together, but if the mask was right then Bheki might help him flush out Vankoni.

'And now I've taken you out, where are you going to take me next?' she asked.

A backpack was standing on the floor at the table across from Joost. Amongst the embroidered flags was the tricolour.

'Paris,' he said.

Bheki was impressed, and gave him a peck on the cheek. He turned his mouth to hers, but was too late to catch her lips.

'You're good,' she said 'but don't get too cocky, not just yet.'

Across town there was a ripple of polite applause as Christine Middlemass finished her lecture. A throng of studious looking types gathered around her as she left the podium. She searched along the back wall, and beckoned Vankoni to join her. He did, but looked a little lost. Christine whispered in his ear, and he laughed. Soon they were pulling away in his new car.

Chapter Fourteen

The first snow of the season began to fall; only a light dusting but enough to remind Snowflake of Kofi, and how far she'd come. Bheki pressed the buzzer for Flat 6. She was deliberately ahead of time, and hoping to catch Joost off guard.

'Hello,' said Joost.

'Hi, it's me,' said Bheki.

'Come on up,' and the foyer door clicked open.

The lobby had black and white chequered tiling on the floor, and a couple of plastic aspidistras to welcome you. A colourful Persian rug lay at the entrance to the lift.

Bheki rode to the top. There were six flats in the block; two on each floor, and Joost was waiting for her on the landing. He was wearing black jeans, and a purple V-neck sweater with nothing underneath. He opened his arms to embrace her.

'You're early,' he said smiling.

'Guess I can't keep away. I hope you're not disappointed though.'

'Far from it.'

'Can I get you a drink?' asked Joost, as Bheki scanned his flat.

'Sure, rooibos if you have any.'

'On its way.'

Joost put the drinks on the small table in front of them, and gently nudged next to Bheki on the golden corduroy sofa.

'You really are gorgeous,' he said.

She wore no wig tonight, nor makeup, but her beauty couldn't hide, and hips never lied.

'Thanks Joost.'

He looked at his watch.

'You know we've still an hour before we leave,' he said.

Bheki knew what he was thinking, but she didn't want to get into a sweat before work.

'Wrong time I'm afraid,' she lied.

'That's fine,' he lied back.

'Mind if I take a look around?' asked Bheki.

'Be my guest.'

He sipped his rooibos tea as he watched her prowl around. She was wearing clothes to diminish the impact of her curves, but once you fell for Bheki Ncube you had trouble averting your eyes. She went to his bookcase.

Already Joost had a couple of brochures on Paris, from the Serpentine Travel Agency, and neatly tucked besides his historical biographies. Bheki turned away, and noticed the long crocodile mask hanging on the wall.

'Souvenir from a previous life,' he explained as she stroked the side.

She edged her way to the bedroom door.

'Go on, take a look inside,' said Joost, relieved Bheki hadn't examined the mask in more detail. 'After all, you'll be in there next time you visit.'

Bheki smiled, and was instantly reassured by what she saw. A double bed was fair enough, but there were no mirrors on the ceiling nor silk sheets on the bed. She opened his wardrobe. His clothes were out of fashion, but she'd have fun changing that. More importantly there was no women's attire; at least none he had forgot to hide.

'Satisfied?' asked Joost standing behind her.

Bheki nodded, and gave him a kiss, sliding her tongue into his mouth.

'I need the bathroom,' she said.

One final check in the medicine cabinet, and Joost was in the clear. He was either very methodical, or really was available.

They talked about Paris, and chose a hotel, but eventually time ran out.

'Are you sure you don't want picking up in the morning?' asked Joost, as Bheki opened the car door outside Blackfriars.

'No, I'll be fine.'

'Then phone me tomorrow, after you've had some sleep.'

'OK,' and she gave him a peck on the cheek, before waving goodbye.

'Hello, I'm working tonight on Brent ward,' said Bheki into the intercom.

The receptionist stared frostily back at her through the reinforced glass. How in hell's name had she got a man like that?

Before you could say psychopath, Bheki was sitting across from Felix Gale, and trying to concentrate on the handover. In her trouser pocket was a tie purloined from Joost's wardrobe. He'd worn it at the Blue Samurai, and she could kick herself for falling for him so quickly.

They were caring for seven male patients tonight. They all had a forensic history, and there were three murderer's present, not counting Felix.

The ward was in an L shape, with two locked doors at either end. Bheki and Felix did the drugs together, whilst the two care assistants sat in the common area with Lance, a patient. Clozapine was mainly on the menu, along with medication to reduce sex drive, and a few dolly mixtures for agitation.

Lance had been transferred to Blackfriars ten years ago after hearing voices in prison. He'd been serving time for double murder; his wife and her lover. Unfortunately he was also quite a big guy, and made the staff nervous, which meant a double helping of sedatives whenever he played up. Lance was a patient going nowhere, and he knew it.

'How did you get here?' asked Felix as they locked up the medicine cabinet in the office.

'Oh someone dropped me off,' replied Bheki nonchalantly.

Felix didn't say he'd seen her step out of Joost's car.

'I can give you a lift in the morning if you need one.'

'Thanks, I'll take you up on that.'

There was a tie sticking out of Bheki's pocket, and although Felix didn't want to let on he'd been staring at Bheki's assets, he had to say something. After all he was the nurse in charge.

'I'd put that tie somewhere else if I were you,' he said.

Bheki smiled uncomfortably, and placed it inside her Burberry plaid coat, hanging on the back of the door.

'Thanks,' she said, leaving Felix to ponder if it was Joost's tie, and who had undone the knot?

Lance wandered into the office to ask for a last cigarette, whilst Ethan and Zoe, the carers, camped out on the sofas for the night.

Felix went to get them all a drink, whilst Bheki followed Lance to the smoke room, and lit him up. Felix watched her, a beauty surrounded by so many beasts. He hit upon a mischievous idea, went to the office, and removed the tie from Bheki's coat.

Joost went back to his flat after dropping Bheki off, soaked in guilt. It didn't help that she'd taken his favourite tie as a keepsake; he was looking for a playmate, not a soul mate. He wondered what John would say?

Joost slumped on the sofa with his junkie's paraphernalia on the table, next to Bheki's cup. He was drifting in his halcyon, when out of the corner of his eye he saw the reptile scurrying along the floor.

'I guess you're feeling pretty bad about Bheki. She's a fine woman Joost, I just hope you know what you're doing,' said John.

'Me too,' replied Joost, and holding his head.

'Tell me John. Am I doing the right thing?'

'I can't answer that Joost. All I know is that when you get over here everything you did before fades in importance,' said John.

And he scampered full circle on the floor in relief, his tail brushing over Joost's feet. No more spiteful voices plagued him.

'Do you see other Spirits John?'

'A few,' and John knew where Joost was heading before he even asked.

'Do you think you could find Stella and Hildy for me?'

'I'll look Joost. That's all I can say.'

'I miss them so much.'

John changed the subject. He didn't do grief; he had enough of his own skeletons.

'I think you should buy Bheki a present tomorrow.'

'Sure. What would you suggest?' asked Joost, wiping the tears from his eyes.

'You could get the Paris tickets.'

John was no longer angry love had abandoned him. But he couldn't help wonder what man he would have been without the priest interfering.

'I've heard Dela talking with Felix. They're going to ask you over soon. Take them up but tread carefully,' said John.

'What about this guy Vankoni?' asked Joost.

'Don't worry; he's not going anywhere.'

'You will come back won't you?' asked Joost, suddenly panicked.

'I have no choice whilst you have some of the powder left. But once it's gone I can't help you anymore,' said John.

And then he was back on the wall, and Joost almost saw a twinkle in the crocodile's eye.

Felix never let on, and it was only in the morning he put Bheki out of her misery; they were in his car.

'I found it in Lance's room. God only know what he was going to do with it,' said Felix, and throwing Joost's tie on her lap.

Bheki wiped her brow with relief.

'Anyway you did the best thing keeping quiet. Owning up to mistakes only causes more problems in this game,' he said.

'Thanks Felix.'

'Perhaps you could do me one small favour in return?'

Bheki sighed. Did all guys want to get in her pants?

Felix saw her look.

'No not that,' and he laughed.

'Just tell Joost that Dela would love to meet him, and give him a business charm on the house.'

He paused.

'That's if I'm right, and you two are close.'

'I'll see what I can do,' said Bheki smiling.

For one thing she could smell Joost's aftershave on the tie again.

'Right then, let's get you home' said Felix.

Chapter Fifteen

Joost's melancholy had sneaked out, and he was on the landing waiting for the lift, when his neighbour opened the door. He had a bag of rubbish for the chute, and his wife was cowering behind him in the hallway. Though for now at least he had stopped beating her.

Joshua Templemead glanced at Joost, who raised his hand in cursive recognition. Like the police emissaries, Joost had tired of the domestic scenes, and mentioned a few home truths. Josh would never take the chance Joost was all talk, even if pound for pound they were an even match.

Joost was dying to phone Bheki, but tried to get her out of his mind. For her part Bheki was curled up in bed, with Joost's tie hanging from a wooden statue on her bedside table; a gift from her grandmother.

It wasn't off the peg from some swanky high street boutique, but seeing Dela's derriere in a white latex body suit could cause a riot. It was therefore a shame that Felix really couldn't see much at all. But that's what happened when you were lying flat on your back with a gas mask covering your face. He'd approached Joost to come visit, through Bheki, and earned his reward.

Whether it was age or the way his brain was wired, but the pain that Dela inflicted was exquisite. And perhaps it was the delirium brought about when she removed her devices that was so addictive. He couldn't be certain, but a restrictive upbringing had taught him sex had to be dirty, forced, and painful.

Dela sealed him to the table in a shrink wrap cocoon. Felix was up to his neck in it, and there was just one outlet in his mummification - the tip of his excitement. Dela grabbed a burning candle. Felix's gasps were muffled by the mask, and he was beginning to wish he'd never stolen a catheter from Atoll nursing home.

Dela applied a little lotion to soften the blow, and pushed down the medical device which went nicely with her shiny nurse's cap. Felix's bleating was amusing, but eventually she refrained and handed him his release. A frighteningly long knife cut Felix free. He kissed Dela's hand, and went to shower.

'It's her,' said Irena handing him the phone, and not bothering to disguise her chagrin.

'Hi Joost, it's me,' said Bheki.

'Hi gorgeous, had enough beauty sleep?'

'Yes thanks.'

'Good shift?' asked Joost.

'Fine.'

Joost looked at Irena who was lingering unnecessarily. Sure he'd hired her because she had great legs, but he'd never bedded her, and her jealousy was becoming tedious. Irena shuffled out on her highest heels.

'Do you know Felix Gale?' asked Bheki.

'Of course,' replied Joost raising a smile.

'Why?' he asked.

'His wife would love to meet you.'

'Let me guess, the voodoo charm he was telling me about.'

'Are you interested?'

'Why not. I'll give him a call.'

Joost's eyes lit up. John was for real.

'Anything else?' he asked.

'Not really. And you?'

'Maybe, but you know it's too late to play hard to get it,' said Joost.

'Likewise,' replied Bheki.

'OK, then let me spell it out, F-U-C-K, my place, tonight; if the timing's right?' he asked.

'Well why didn't you say? And yes the timing's perfect. Eight O'clock,' and Bheki put down the phone.

'Yes Irena?' asked Joost.

'Oh nothing, I just brought you a cup of tea.'

There was an extra button undone on her blouse. Shame really, right place, wrong time.

Joost contemplated recent events. The crocodile mask could help him bury the past, or rather Vankoni. And his infatuation for Bheki Ncube had also given his wallet a bulge, even if a few hookers were now struggling to pay the rent. And rather than doing his brains at The Four Horsemen, he just wanted to bang Bheki's brains out in his bed.

'Hi Felix,' said Joost on the phone.

'Hi Joost.'

'Hope I'm not disturbing anything.'

'No it's fine. I was a little tied up this morning but I'm OK now.'

'Bheki Ncube's reminded me of your wife's rather enticing offer.'

'That's kind of her. Well drop in anytime, Dela's got your sleeping powder ready.'

'Thanks.'

'When would you like to visit?'

'Is she in today?'

'All day.'

'Well no time like the present.'

'Alright, shall we say in ...'

'An hour,' cut in Joost. 'And don't worry I've got your address on file.'

Joost didn't want to give them any time to prepare a trap.

'Irena take my calls. I'm finishing early today.'

Irena sighed.

'Joost I really could do with some extra help in the office.'

'I'll sort it out,' he said.

'Soon,' she said.

'How about next week, is that soon enough?'

'That will be great.'

And he was gone, leaving Irena to ponder which hair style would make her irresistible.

'Pleased to meet you Dela,' said Joost as he stepped into the flat, and they recognised each other immediately.

'The Four Horsemen,' they said together.

'It's a small world,' said Joost

The hallway was painted a garish green and blood red, and certainly not to everyone's taste.

'Welcome to our humble abode,' said Dela extending a hand.

Joost wasn't sure if he was supposed to kiss it or shake it. He decided on the latter. Dela was wearing an enormous ring on her middle finger. He'd not seen it before; it was a golden serpent with emerald eyes, and was eating its own tail.

'Come and take a seat,' said Dela, ushering him into the lounge.

Joost passed the kitchen. The door was ajar, and he glimpsed the large chest freezer; poor John.

The spider was in the parlour, and Dela was eyeing him up. He was a handsome specimen of a man. Those strong arms were worth a fortune on their own, and the tongue, as Bheki well knew, was a real gem. They'd need a bigger freezer for Joost.

In the corner of the room was Dela's altar; a large black hexagonal table. There were eight, white, trident forks painted upon it, pointing outwards. Three lit red candles stood on top, each guarding an amber glass bottle, where inside floated viper's tongues in a thick gooey viscous. To the front was a small felt doll with two pins jabbed both into the stomach and the head. Joost didn't ask who it was; he just hoped it wasn't him.

'Drink?' asked Felix, as Dela began to wipe the inside of a tumbler with a cloth.

'Too early in the day for me,' lied Joost.

'Tea or coffee then?' asked Felix. 'Or hot chocolate even.'

'Sorry, but it plays havoc with the stomach acid,' he lied again.

'Anyway here's the sleeping powder,' said Dela unimpressed, and she handed Joost a small bottle from the window ledge. 'Just put one teaspoon in whatever you do drink, before bedtime, and you'll have no problem sleeping.'

'Thanks. How much do I owe you?' asked Joost, tucking the bottle neatly into his jacket pocket.

'Shall we say thirty pounds,' replied Dela, smiling an immaculate row of pearly whites. The front teeth jutted out, but this only served to enhance the thickness of her lips, which seemed to be wrapped around an invisible O.

'Great,' said Joost opening his wallet.

'And what would you say to a free fetish for fortune Mr van Houten?' said Dela with her tongue doing somersaults. No wonder Felix looked drained.

'That's very kind of you Dela, but please call me Joost.'

There was a beguiling fire lit in Dela's eyes which was becoming irresistible.

'What did you have in mind?' he asked.

Dela handed him a little wooden manikin.

'Place it near the entrance to your office, and new business will come knocking.'

'And if it does?'

'Then perhaps you can remember who gave it to you.'

'And that's all?'

'Of course.'

'Alright then, we have a bargain,' and Joost felt strangely drawn into touching her one more time.

Dela knew it, and would love to hear him scream. But not the way Joost would imagine. He looked at his watch.

'Well thanks for having me, but time waits for no man,' he said.

'Indeed not,' said Dela, and she placed her hand on his arm.

'I guess that's business' said Felix.

Joost indeed had business on his mind; the business of turning Bheki inside out with delight. Or was it Dela he wanted to please?

They watched him get into the lift, and Dela could sense something was amiss. The way Joost had stared at the freezer perturbed her, and his refusal to take a drink. Still he'd wanted her; she knew that much. But someone or something was protecting him; even the voodoo doll, with the label Felix had cut from Joost's tie pinned underneath, had no effect.

Outside Din and Vankoni waited in the car.

'He's on his way,' said Dela on the phone to Din 'he refused a drink.'

'It's the same guy alright,' said Vankoni to Din and rubbing his hands with glee.

Din kept his distance, but they managed to keep Joost in sight until he reached home.

'Got you,' said Vankoni 'looks like I'll get a chance to finish you off after all.'

Dela was alone in her temple, and all Felix could hear from the outside was her muttering. Eventually she flung herself out, drenched in sweat.

'He knows everything about us,' she said to Felix, who was sitting in the lounge with a chilled bottle of beer for company.

'John Lacey has told him.'

'He's dead,' said Felix.

'I know but his Spirit lives on, and in this flat,' said Dela.

'Isn't that so John,' said Dela, banging the top of the freezer.

'Don't look so worried Felix,' said Dela noticing his concern 'Baka will protect us; we just need a very special sacrifice.'

Felix raised his eyes, and almost wished he'd never killed anybody.

'But first things first, we need to move John out. I think a trip to the sea-side will do him good,' said Dela.

Bill and Barbara had a very big freezer, even if it was full of scampi and chips.

Felix would have preferred dropping John at the bottom of the sea, but Dela, who'd considered the option, couldn't bear to throw out such powerful muti. She'd just warn the publicans to show some discretion in the kitchen.

They didn't waste much time on small talk. What was the point? They were two wild beasts. Bheki's nails dug into Joost's back, but he wasn't the one screaming through the night. Poor Josh turned up the TV to drown out their passion; it was only his fists that could make a woman moan.

Chapter Sixteen

It was the evening after their bodies had realised they were inseparable, and with lust in the ascendancy. Bheki was working, and Joost had nipped out to the local off licence to buy some rum. He noticed Joshua Templemead pass by on his way home, and carrying a pizza box. He looked in a foul mood.

The lift was out of order, again, and Josh pounded the steps to the top floor. His wife had burnt the dinner, and his mood was still thundering. The light was dwindling as Josh approached.

'He's coming back,' whispered a voice.

The landing was pitched black as Josh fumbled for, and then dropped his keys. A dull thud was the only noise as the mallet dealt a heavy blow to the back of his head. Then like a falcon he was hooded.

'I'll get the car,' said Din to Vankoni 'wait here.'

They carried the body to the bottom of the stairs wrapped in a rug, and then, outside in a hail of sleet, threw him into the boot of the car. They'd be at Charles Carney's house in under an hour, and giving them plenty of time to freshen up.

Vankoni handed Din a slice of pizza behind the wheel.

'It's still warm,' he said.

'Pepperoni, my favourite,' said Din, and taking a huge bite.

Joost returned to his flat soaking wet, and in the darkness crushed a light bulb underfoot. After changing the bulb he noticed a set of keys on the landing. He pushed the keys through Joshua's letterbox, and swept up the broken glass.

It was way passed closing time when cars started pulling up at the village pub, The Crossed Heart. There was a special occasion, and some of the arrivals were even bringing their own carpet.

The drinking hole was close to the cliff edge, and the waves could be heard crashing into the chalk face. John Lacey was still trying to pinpoint his new surroundings, with little luck.

It was a clear night for stargazing, and Christine and Lucy Middlemass were the last to be warmed by the hearth, and the roaring flames. Bill was serving drinks from behind his bar, and Vankoni gave Christine a knowing smile.

There was a congenial atmosphere which belied the night's intentions. Dela had already prepared the cave, and her disciples were salivating over the prospect of new, more powerful, talismans.

An orderly queue formed towards the cellar, and then to the trapdoor underfoot. The Crossed Heart had been a smugglers den in days long gone, and well-worn steps were carved into the chalk beneath them.

'Don't worry,' whispered Christine into Vankoni's ear 'there's a handrail.'

Lucy was helped out of her wheelchair, and carried down between James and Din. The packaged entertainment was swung into the hole with less caution.

Candles lit their way, and after the first twenty or so steps the incline became less steep, eventually bottoming out into a huge moonlit chamber. The cave was halfway up the cliff, safe from trespassers and the tide, and they all looked out to sea. An old chiropodist's chair beckoned them forth, and there was a wicker chair for Lucy.

Some looked tentative, whilst others like Dilwood and Gasper Owido had a fire burning in their eyes. James too, the preacher man, was feverish with excitement; he'd been promised a very special part.

The rug was unfurled, and the unresponsive dummy tied into the chair. Din looked a little worried; he hoped he hadn't dealt a fatal blow, after all dead men couldn't scream, and that's where the real power of muti lay.

Felix removed the leather hood, one of Dela's first presents, and was dumbfounded. The captive was not Joost van Houten at all. Din and Vankoni looked at one another equally shocked, but Dela carried on as normal. Felix got the drift, and henceforth acted unsurprised. There was one good piece of news though; Joshua Templemead was starting to come round.

'Don't say a word,' wasn't the most reassuring wakeup call, and Josh knew he wasn't at a fancy dress party. For one thing the dagger held to his throat by Din was real.

Dela had trouble speaking up over the waves, but the screams from Josh, as Din and Gasper sliced him up, more than made up for it. It took half an hour before it was over, but they all had a piece of good fortune in their doggy bags. Only Gladys and Lucy looked a little sea sick.

Felix cleaned up for his mistress as the others started drinking upstairs. The bin-bagged leftovers would be thrown overboard, weighted down, on Bill's next fishing trip.

James Middlemass had Joshua's tongue in his pocket, to smooth a path to Eve's heart whilst the love potion still lingered. Christine didn't even ask why, after all Vankoni had his testicles in a neat little box to boost his virility; if he needed it.

Pandalay couldn't wait to bury the hand under his shop door to attract more customers, and their money. The screams had awoken the Spirits, and this really was powerful magic. Susie Chang looked dreamily over his shoulder.

Poor Josh went to his grave believing his wife had hired hit men, or really did have a lover, or both. Donations, and not commiserations, were gratefully paid to Dela.

Gasper handed the eyes back to Dela for a little concoction. He liked to play the stock market, and a little far sightedness wouldn't go amiss.

Joshua's spine had been the most difficult cut, but Lucy and her parents were hoping for a paste that would restore even more movement. Charles wanted the heart for courage; he could be such a ninny, and Dela would soon give him the recipe.

Back in London, in the early hours of the morning, the talk was all about Joost. Dela was concerned that perhaps the gods favoured him; Felix was worried the cat was out of the bag, whilst Din and Vankoni considered how to make amends.

Joost woke up with a pounding in his head. He'd really drunk too much the night before. The next pounding he heard was on his front door.

'Sorry to bother you,' said Rita Templemead 'but Josh didn't come home last night.'

Joost wasn't sure what to say.

'He put these through the letterbox,' said Rita, holding out her hand.

Joost kept quiet about the keys. It seemed strange, but who knows, maybe Rita could stop wearing the sunglasses to hide her bruises.

'I don't know what to say Rita, maybe he's left you. Besides you know what I think.'

'Nobody understands him,' said Rita.

'Sure, anyway ...'

'Of course, sorry to have bothered you Mr van Houten.'

Joost shut the door, and looked at the clock. Bloody hell it was eight a.m. already, he was supposed to meet Bheki at nine, and he hadn't even packed. They were off to Paris.

Chapter Seventeen

Joost tumbled out of the taxi, and ran to the platform.

'At last,' said Bheki.

She was too relieved to play it cool. Although she had contemplated slashing his car tyres should he jilt her.

'Sorry, I overslept with a sore head,' said Joost, before catching his breath.

'You want to cut back on the booze Joost. Still at least you haven't any other vices.'

Joost coughed.

'Anyway let's get on the train, we've only got ten minutes left,' said Bheki.

She was wearing a red suede cap, her favourite Dolce and Gabbana goatskin jacket, and hipster jeans. Her shiny leather boots, the ones with the steel buckles, ran just underneath her knees. Joost was unshaven, and had his clothes thrown on. Although ruggedly handsome came to Bheki's mind.

Joost threw their bags into the overhead compartment, before squeezing next to Bheki. He was gasping, but Bheki wondered whether he was still winded or infatuated.

Arriving at the Gare du Nord, Joost was forced to take his hand off Bheki's knee. After a ten minute ride to their hotel she helped him relax, and they were ready to explore.

'So how many partners have you had?' asked Bheki casually, as they sipped their coffees in the side street café.

'Real girlfriends as opposed to flings?' he queried.

'What do you constitute as a fling?'

'A casual sexual relationship lasting no longer than a month,' he replied, as though reading a dictionary definition.

'Let's count flings as well,' said Bheki.

'In that case I've had three relationships,' said Joost, counting them one by one on his fingers.

Not bad thought Bheki, considering his age and undeniable charm - if it was true.

'Is that three with me, or do I make four?' she asked.

Joost smiled. Her concern was endearing.

'You're the fourth,' he said.

Joost was too much of a gentleman to mention all the hookers he'd paid since arriving in the UK.

'And you?' he asked. 'Honestly,' he prompted, sensing her caution.

'Two,' she said.

'Good answer,' said Joost smiling.

Bheki too forgot to mention the punters who'd paid for her services, and half a dozen admiring suitors.

'So you were married once,' said Bheki, taking a stab in the dark.

After all, there had to be a reason for his abstinence. He wasn't a monk, and she already knew he had more vitamins than a health store.

'In South Africa.'

'What happened?'

'It's a long story.'

Bheki detected a sombre shift in tone, and knew she'd stumbled on dangerous ground.

'I've never been married,' she said, changing tack; they were on holiday.

'Why?'

'Guess I never found the right guy.'

An even better answer thought Joost.

'Any change on the Eiffel Tower?' he asked.

'Sorry Joost, it's too high for me.'

She had a good head, but not for heights.

'Alright let's visit the Montmartre instead,' he said.

'OK.'

Bheki was giggling over his shoulder, as the artist, sitting at his easel, finished the caricature. Joost's chin was drawn like an arrow, he had squinted eyes, and an anvil for a forehead. His scar appeared doubly menacing.

'We'll have to find you a bed at Blackfriars,' said Bheki, as Joost got up from the stool.

The artist nervously handed the drawing to Joost, who took it in the jovial manner it was given.

Bheki's cartoon was fundamentally sexual. Her lips were much thicker, and pouting. The eyes were thrown upwards with curled eyelashes, and if you could see the bottom half she was probably being screwed. Joost was delighted, and couldn't wait to hang it in his flat, above the bed; although he was hoping to see the real thing on a regular basis, at least for now.

After a dinner by the Seine, where Bheki drank too much wine, they headed back to the hotel. Bheki was unsteady on her feet, and it was just like old times for Joost. He could sense her vulnerability, and it excited him.

Bheki was lying on the bed almost unconscious, but could feel Joost unbutton, and then pull down her jeans. He bit her ear, before rolling her over, and pushing her head into the duvet.

She barely had the strength to move into position, as Joost hauled her up on all fours. The last thing she saw, before a pillowcase covered her head, was the money thrown in front.

Joost succeeded in making her feel like a cheap whore. And in between excesses he drank the mini bar dry, finally collapsing on the bed besides her.

A sudden splash of ice cold water on his face, and Joost awoke immediately.

'Did you enjoy yourself?' asked Bheki.

Joost's wrists and ankles were tied to the iron framed bed with curtain cords, whilst Bheki held a knife to his balls. He could feel the serrated edge press against his scrotum, but was hoping for some role play. He was about to be disappointed, this wasn't a game.

'Now, how about some real answers?' asked Bheki.

'Go ahead,' he said, his voice faltering.

'How many lovers?'

'I told you, five.'

'You said three, four including me.'

'That's what I meant,' he said 'three, I mean four.'

'OK Joost, don't blame me.'

The knife pressed even harder against him.

'One more time, and let me warn you, I'm not a patient person. How many women have you screwed?' asked Bheki, scowling.

'I don't know, hundreds I guess.'

'Oh my God,' she said 'you've lost count.'

'You wanted to know,' he said.

'And did you pay any of them?'

'Yes, all of them. Apart from four.'

'Make that three. Are you forgetting the notes you threw on the bed tonight.'

Bheki actually preferred to hear this; no romantic involvement. And she pretended for herself too; no tears when it was all over, as it inevitably would be - just like all the others.

'If you love hookers so much then what in god's name are you doing with me?'

Joost was scared, but he still had to smile.

'I'd answer carefully if I were you,' said Bheki.

'The truth?' asked Joost.

'Of course.'

'You look like a whore.'

He didn't mention John Lacey, Dela or Felix. They were far from his mind. Though it was true, he was screwing her senseless because she looked like a prostitute, a cheap filthy minded hooker. Not in her clothes, or the way she spoke, but in her eyes, her mouth.

Bheki laughed, leaving Joost confused.

'I don't get it,' he said.

Bheki had wanted to save the good news for later. She knew what men really wanted, but couldn't help herself anymore.

'I was a hooker once. Don't worry, way before you met me. And no I haven't got Aids.'

Despite the threat of castration Joost was becoming aroused.

'If it gets any bigger I just might cut it off,' warned Bheki smiling.

It helped. But it was going to be difficult for Joost, with Bheki's lurid past coming alive.

'I was a prostitute for three years. Anything went, almost, and mostly in grimy cars with dirty old men.'

Joost was almost salivating, and tried to think of something to dampen his ardour - Vankoni. It didn't work.

'Does that turn you on?' she asked, seeing the answer bobbing before her eyes.

'Of course,' replied Joost, as though it were as simple as liking vodka with lime.

Bheki kissed him on the forehead.

'You going to untie me now?' he asked.

'On one condition.'

'Go on.'

Joost had to repent by licking her lollipop ass all night, or until she fell asleep.

In the morning they faced each other across the breakfast table with tired eyes, and a knowing smile. At least they both knew who they were dealing with.

'Where did you get that knife?' asked Joost.

'It was a gift, from a friend. You would have liked her, she was a hooker too.'

'Do you still see her?' asked Joost.

Bheki knew what he was thinking, and playfully slapped his wrist.

'No, she vanished. No goodbye, nothing. She's dead.'

'How do you know?'

'Believe me Joost, I know.

He held her hand, gently.

'What was her name?'

'Lilu. She was a real beauty.'

Now it was Bheki's turn to look heart broken.

'I lost someone close too,' said Joost.

Though Bheki wasn't in the mood for heart ache.

'Come on,' she said, getting up from the table 'we're on holiday, and I want to take you somewhere.'

She suspected something terrible had happened to his wife, and was glad to have told Eudy where they were going. It looked like anything was possible with Joost.

They were standing in the sparsely populated Dapper Musee.

'I'm beginning to think you're a collector,' said Joost as they looked at another African statue through the museum glass.

'Only the one I told you about; a present from home.'

Actually there used to be two, but Bheki had leant its partner to Lilu to treasure for a while, and to look after her adopted sister. When she was spirited away, because she'd have never left without saying goodbye, the statue went with her.

'Look I know it's cold outside, but I'd really love to go up the Eiffel Tower,' said Joost.

'Well go on then.'

'Not on my own.'

'Oh I see. Now you want to frighten me.'

Joost laughed.

'I just want to share the fun.'

'Like last night I guess,' she said smiling.

'I tell you what, promise to tell me your biggest secret once we're at the top, and I'll come and hold your hand' said Bheki.

'OK I promise,' said Joost.

'Well what are we doing here then, let's go.'

The view was naturally spectacular, although Bheki wasn't looking.

'I'm waiting,' she said.

'This is really going to sound ridiculous, but you did ask.'

'Go ahead.'

'You remember that crocodile mask in my flat,' said Joost.

'The one that gave you palpitations when I touched it.'

'Yes.'

She had noticed after all.

'It comes alive.'

Bheki laughed so loud a group of tourists turned around to look.

'I knew you wouldn't believe me,' said Joost.

'But why would it do that?' asked Bheki.

'Well to cut a long story short it's helping me.'

'Alright, but I can think of someone else who could offer better help, like a psychiatrist perhaps.'

'No really, it sees things, Spirits. You know, voodoo and all that stuff.'

Bheki sure enough knew about voodoo, and the crazy things that could happen.

'Alright, here's what we'll do. When we're back in London ask your crocodile who gave me my statue,' said Bheki 'then I'll believe you.'

'That's it,' said Joost.

'Yep, simple isn't it,' she said.

She raised her eyes to the sky, and shook her head.

'If it knows that then perhaps you're not crazy after all. And don't worry Joost I won't tell anyone, I don't want you locked up just yet. Well not all of you.'

Bheki had time to take a few more snapshots of Joost, outside of Notre Dame Cathedral, for Eudy, before it was time to kiss Paris bon voyage. But boy had it been worth it!

Chapter Eighteen

Joost was looking down at the street below from his flat window. It was snowing again, lightly, but enough to let you know it was going to be a cold hard winter. His recliner was pushed towards the window, and he held a glass in his hand. Already the shop across the street had a Christmas tree in the front, and as he swirled his brandy Joost contemplated whether he would be giving Bheki a present, or kissing her goodbye under the mistletoe.

Having a knife to his balls was a sobering moment, although he was glad to have unloaded the truth about John. But what did she really want? What did she expect?

And what about him? He was certainly saving money, and she used to be a hooker; unless she was teasing him, but some of her recollections were too accurate. Paris was fun, but he'd have to find a way to keep her around without her getting too close; if that's what he wanted. But he wasn't sure. Would Stella forgive him if he fell in love again? Would he forgive himself?

If only he had a friend to ask, to trust. There was Dilwood his business partner, but they'd grown apart since his marriage; he no longer did drugs, or hookers.

He thought about Vankoni, and the threat posed from Dela. Involving the police could push Vankoni underground, and he couldn't afford that. On top of that, Dilwood had used dirty money to start the agency, and was still using it to clean a lot of his cash; where it came from Joost had stopped wondering long ago. He poured himself another stiff one, and looked at Bheki's cartoon.

'How did it go?' asked Eudy, as they finished getting ready for church.

Eudy was albino too, but had a lot more freckles than Bheki.

'Well he's a pretty unusual guy' replied Bheki, referring to Joost.

Eudy was living with Bheki, and heavily pregnant. The conditions were much less cramped than the bedsit she used to stay.

'Where's Themba?' asked Bheki.

'He's taking his mum to the airport. She goes home today.'

Themba was Eudy's husband. They were waiting for their own place, and hoping the baby would put them higher up the housing list. He stayed at the weekends, but in the week it was impractical; after all he was only human.

'What's he like in bed?'

'Adventurous,' replied Bheki smiling, pulling on her best white stockings.

'And?'

Eudy was applying the last of her makeup in the dressing mirror.

'A little deviant.'

'Aren't they all? But do you mean a little, or a lot?'

'A lot, actually.'

'Sounds like a perfect match then,' said Eudy laughing.

'Perhaps.'

'When do we get to meet him?'

'Pretty soon, but I don't want to scare him away.'

'I don't think there's much chance of that if he looks like this' said Eudy, pointing at the Parisian cartoon Bheki had pinned to her bedroom wall.

'Wait until you see the photos,' said Bheki, as Eudy zipped up her dress.

In the bin was Joost's tie cut to ribbons. Half of her loved him, whilst the other half hated him for making her feel out of control.

Themba joined them later, at Pastor Goodyear's Church of Loving Saints.

Gladys was sitting at the back of St Agnes, but the infant's cries still tore through her; bloodcurdling. She couldn't get the last poor wretch out of her mind, and how he had died; slaughtered worse than an animal. Somehow the victim had sensed her unease, and he kept watching her right up to his final moments. And yet here she was in church the following Sunday with some of the butchers.

She had to shut up the screams, and closed everything out. James was performing the christening, and as many doting eyes were upon him as they were the babe. She always leaned against Charles Carney amid these moments of crisis, but he was out of town for the weekend. She'd have to speak to James after the service, over a cup of tea and a slice of fruitcake she had made with Christine. Gladys had only pined for a child, although you couldn't tell she was nearly five months pregnant. She'd never bargained on murder when her pastor had first mentioned a less than Christian path.

Gladys stood up with the rest of the church to recite a eulogy in praise of Mr and Mrs Greene's newly arrived bundle of joy. Gasper Owido, who was no relation, nonetheless held up his camera for a few happy snaps for his soothsayer. Dela wanted an injection of cash, and was exploring possibilities. She'd also spotted her first wrinkle on her heavily coconut oiled skin.

'Full house Gladys, you should be proud; you've done a great job getting the church all spick and span.'

'Thanks James. I did have a little help though.'

'You shouldn't be too modest Gladys. You know your involvement is appreciated,' and he gave Gladys a knowing look.

He was trying to bolster her courage, but like a couple of the others suspected she was becoming a weak link. Christine had heard her throw up in the Ladies the other night at The Crossed Heart.

'Do you think we could have a word James, in private?'

He looked around, as though to say perhaps another time, but then Gladys' dejected demeanour helped to change his mind.

'Of course let me just tell Eve we're going for a stroll.'

He took Eve another cup of tea, before they braved the chill outside, and confidently whispered a little sweet talk now he had the tongue in his pocket. It was wrapped, naturally.

'Alright then Gladys I'm all yours.'

He nearly said I'm all ears, but with Gladys violently recoiling from the other night he thought better of it.

He listened, he sympathised. But eventually he had to say 'you knew what you were getting into Gladys.'

'It was stupid of me James. I was just so desperate to conceive.'

'And you have. What if you stay away from Dela and the rest of us for a while, would that help?'

'Sure, but I'm going out of my mind. I don't know what to do.'

'I hope you're not thinking of doing anything stupid Gladys. There's a lot at stake for all of us. And we're all just as guilty, remember that.'

'Of course.'

The worrying thing for James was that Gladys didn't look like she believed his last statement. And although she'd been present on many occasions she'd never truly stabbed, hacked, cut or sliced anyone or anything. It was perturbing, equally so since Lucy was improving, and Eve was beginning to melt to his charms.

Between two tombstones a frosted spider's net glistened in the sun. Gladys had to be spun a web too.

'Gladys look I'll sort things out for you, and in a short while you'll be free of us all with a beautiful bouncing baby on your knee.'

Gladys smiled.

'Just don't worry. I promise everything will be alright. Trust me I'm a vicar.'

'Let's see what you come up with James, but no more meetings for me, I've lost my appetite.'

'Alright, but just one last favour Gladys.'

'Go on,' she said wearily.

'Help Christine at the village bonfire next week, there isn't time to find anyone else.'

Gladys paused, but finally relinquished. After all what harm could it do?

'Why not,' she said smiling, and they both went indoors.

Meanwhile the fat spider gorged on another hapless mite.

Chapter Nineteen

Post Paris was an anti-climax, at least for Joost; Bheki was too busy working to notice. But her three nights at Blackfriars were coming to an end, and inevitably they would hook up. The break wouldn't do Bheki any harm; she needed a little time to think. Joost was a fine looking man, without a doubt, but could she trust him to stop crawling the streets? Then again she wasn't a saint, and at least she could hate him on a whim, if she needed.

The noise from next door was made all the more disconcerting by Bheki's absence. Mrs Jones it seemed had taken Josh's disappearance with good grace, and had taken a male friend for companionship. Whether this was the lover Josh would rant and rave about until the early hours of the morning he would never know. But it seemed an appropriate time to summon John.

'How was Paris?' asked John.

'I think we both had a good time,' replied Joost to the reptile looking up at his knees.

'And did you tell her about Dela?'

'Only about the manikin she gave me.'

Joost looked a little maudlin. He didn't really want to use Bheki at all, well not for that.

'It's a dangerous game Joost, but you don't need to play it anymore.'

'Why not?'

'Dela knows about you and me; they don't need any bait.'

'How's that possible?'

'After your visit she asked Eshu a few searching questions.'

'Who?'

'He's a messenger between the living and the dead.'

'It gets better all the time,' said Joost.

'Do you want to hear the worst of it?'

'Go on,' said Joost.

He took a deep breath, and readied himself.

'They've already tried to kill you once, but they grabbed Joshua Templemead by mistake.'

'So that's where the little devil went too,' said Joost with a grin.

'They won't stop now Joost.'

'Now why doesn't that surprise me? I guess I could always go to the police,' said Joost half-heartedly.

'Maybe. But what about the cash Dilwood launders through the agency?'

'You know about that?' asked Joost surprised; though he shouldn't have been.

'And more,' replied John ominously.

'And then there's your drug use, to say nothing of Bheki's false ID, and that's if they believe you. Do you really want them snooping around?' asked John, driving the final nail in the coffin.

There was another reason; a burden that weighed heavily on Joost's soul, especially considering his own misfortunes. It happened the night he first met Dilwood Benson. Joost suspected John knew about that too; after all didn't he know everything?

'OK then let's not be hasty,' said Joost.

'If I do see it through, I could get to Vankoni. But is that enough?' he asked aloud 'considering all the risks?'

'That's up to you. In the meantime why don't you take Bheki to see Dilwood and his wife,' said John.

'Why?' asked Joost surprised.

'I just think it might be a good idea.'

John was beginning to blur into the carpet, as the heroin high bade farewell.

'I'd better get going Joost. Just remember what I said.'

'Oh John before you go. Do you know who gave Bheki some kind of African statue?'

'Sure that's easy, her grandma, Akuaa Mathebula.'

'And John'

'Next time Joost, next time.'

Joost was bent over in the corridor, in front of a tall rubber plant.

'What on earth are you doing Joost?' asked Irena.

'Just checking the roots,' he replied.

'Why in heavens name would you do that?' asked Irena puzzled.

It was the only plant in the building, left by the previous occupants, and tended by the cleaner.

'Something I read,' he said.

Joost patted the earth one last time, and they entered the office together. He had buried the manikin Dela gave him.

'Tea?' asked Irena.

'Please.'

'Good weekend?' she asked.

'Different. And you?'

'Excellent.'

Irena had found a man of her own, and began to wonder what she had ever seen in Joost.

'Joost you haven't forgot about the help you promised me, have you?' she asked.

'Of course not. In fact I've got someone to start next week,' he lied.

'Well done. Then perhaps at last I can start looking for more customers. After all that's why you hired me isn't it?'

'Yes. And if you take a look on your desk there's a small present for getting us the Blackfriars contract.'

It was a set of French perfumes.

'Thanks Joost,' said Irena 'but a little commission would have been better.'

'Don't worry I'm working on it. I just need to run it past Dilwood.'

'Oh by the way he phoned last Friday. Wondered when you were coming over for dinner?'

'If he phones again when I'm out, tell him I'd love to see him, and I'll be bringing a friend.'

Irena knew it was Bheki but no longer cringed, she was more than happy with her new beau.

He'd been introduced by a boyfriend. That should have been old boyfriend, but he was determined to hang on.

'Aah Miss Ncube. Thank you for bringing him along, a truly fine specimen,' said the elderly African man with the thick spectacles.

The frames were tortoise shell and sat well with his grey hair. He looked like a UN peace ambassador; both authoritative and understanding.

Bheki was standing in Noah's upmarket pawn shop, but old Noah wasn't just a gold and gems kind of guy. He knew his African art. Shame he didn't see much of the real thing, until today that was.

'Naturally you would like to know the value. But first let me ask you, where is the other half?'

'I wish I knew,' said Bheki.

'Shame.'

Bheki looked dejected.

'Now don't look too sad, this is still an excellent piece, probably worth around 15K to the right collector.'

Bheki was pleased, although instantly knew the pair would have fetched a much higher sum.

'And the pair?' she asked.

'At least ten times as much, possibly even more.'

When she had recovered her breath she thanked Noah, and got ready to leave.

'By the way Jimmy's on his way. He asked me to call if you ever showed your face,' said Noah.

Jimmy was Noah's godson, and still believed he was Bheki's suitor. Which was kind of unfortunate since Joost was on the scene. Sure enough in the past she had kept one pot on the boil whilst cooking up another, but Jimmy had pushed dislike to nauseating. And now the only thing allowed to make her flesh crawl were horror movies.

'Sorry Noah but I've got to dash. Tell him to phone.'

'You going to take his call this time?'

'Sure.'

And she quickly joined the crowds outside. But she did hit upon a delectable plan. Why not let Jimmy and Joost slug it out? If Joost did the damage she could admire him, and if he lost then he was despicable. Either way she'd want to screw him. Eudy was right she was incomprehensible.

Chapter Twenty

'Everyone behave, he's outside,' said Bheki.

She was referring to Joost, and Eudy looked out of the window.

'He hasn't got two horns at all,' said Eudy mischievously.

'I just said he was a little eccentric, that's all,' said Bheki.

'Right,' replied Eudy.

'Hey you guys, shouldn't we invite him up?' asked Themba.

'I'm not ready,' said Bheki.

'Don't worry, I'll get him,' said Eudy 'can't have you not looking your best,' and she rolled her eyes.

'Themba take all those plates into the kitchen,' said Bheki looking out from the bedroom, where she was applying the last of her makeup.

Joost arrived hot on Eudy's heels.

'Drink?' she asked.

'As long as we won't be late,' said Joost.

He guessed all eyes would be upon him, and didn't want to stand out even more.

'We have plenty of time,' said Eudy 'and you can tell us all about yourself.'

'Eudy,' shouted Bheki from the bedroom 'just let the poor man relax.'

'OK Tendai,' said Eudy.

But then she put her hand to her mouth, realising what she had said.

'Don't worry,' said Bheki 'he knows. But try and stick to Bheki.'

Eudy looked relieved.

'Hi I'm Themba, Eudy's husband.'

'Pleased to meet you Themba,' said Joost as they shook hands.

Themba was wearing a suit, as was Joost, but Bheki had a surprise for him. The tie wasn't the only thing she'd taken from his wardrobe that evening, she'd also clocked his size, and had a brand new suit laid out for him on the bed. She really was making it difficult for him to run away, although after Paris it was the last thing on his mind.

Bheki joined them as Themba was flicking through his Bible. He underscored a verse with his finger, and then suddenly closed the book as though he had received a revelation.

'Thank you Lord for bringing Joost amongst us, and I'm sure this evening, with your guidance, will be a fruitful one,' said Themba.

Joost was wondering if he should say a few words of friendship and comfort, but Bheki ushered him into the bedroom just as he put down his tea.

'What do you think?' she said pointing to the suit sprawled on the bed.

He was more than a little surprised, not least because he knew Bheki didn't earn a fortune. Then again she obviously found the money to spend on her own upmarket wardrobe.

Part of Joost knew he was getting in deeper, and he was scared. But with the good grace in which it was offered he replied 'fantastic,' and gave her a peck on the cheek.

Joost quickly changed, smiled at his Parisian caricature on the wall, and joined the others. The suit was charcoal grey, woollen, single vented, and un-creased; unlike his faded and threadbare navy blue suit.

They drove in Themba's car to Pastor Goodyear's charismatic church. Now Joost had never been particularly religious, but there was obviously something out there; he just hoped it wasn't the gods that Dela worshipped.

The doors were open when they arrived at the hall, and something told Joost a lot more worshippers were expected. There were a few other white people present, and he wasn't the novelty he had expected. Although Bheki noticed he caught the roving eye of quite a few women. She hooked her arm underneath his.

Pastor Goodyear was treading the boards on the stage up front like an old pro. It had to be him, his face was pictured everywhere; on the booklets for sale as you walked in, on the huge banner that hung above the stage, and even on the bottles of miracle water they were selling on the table at the back.

The seats behind them, and in front, were quickly filling, and there was a hushed excitement. Joost hadn't been to church in years, but he'd never seen it like this - and this was a midweek evening. It was almost like a funfair; laughter, youth, and families.

The good pastor was short and stocky, a barrel of a man, who in his star spangled waistcoat could be mistaken from a distance for a clockwork penguin. But when he spoke the tone was hypnotic; lush with emotion and feeling. Soothing and searching at the same time. It was easy to see why the chairs were full.

Joost shuffled uneasily in his seat as the pastor's gaze fell upon him. There was a familiarity in his eye, as though he knew who Joost was. And then in a blink those same eyes seemed to bore right into his very soul. Someone handed Pastor Abel Goodyear the microphone.

'Heal us oh Lord, anoint us with your Holy Spirit, guide and protect us, and deliver us from sin,' said the good pastor to his flock.

Several of the congregation began to speak in tongues, and someone from the front row threw themselves to the ground wailing. They were gathered in a church hall previously abandoned, but now like most of the congregation it had been saved.

Those less moved were clasping their Bibles and praying. Some prayed for their own deliverance, others for a relative or a friend. Pastor Goodyear prayed for everyone.

Joost joined the singing that followed with a little evangelical spirit, and in spite of the overhead projector illuminating the words he could only bring himself to whisper. Bheki rubbed his arm both to offer support, and to acknowledge his efforts.

It was inevitable, at least to Joost, that the pastor would single him out for a brief talk. It therefore came as something of a shock when he was overlooked, as the pastor made his way through the milling throng for the intercession. Still at least Joost had the chance to whisper a few ribald suggestions in Bheki's ear. It was something along the lines of 'let us go forth and multiply'.

Someone called the 'singing preacher' took to the stage, and unsurprisingly sang, during which copies of his CD were offered for sale, as were booklets of the pastor's journey, philosophy, and revelations. The bottled blessed and cure all water did raise Joost's eyebrows a little, but it was all in a good cause, and he'd thrown his money away on much more sinful activities. Bheki was delighted when he queued all of fifteen minutes to get them some bottles. When he got back Themba was missing.

'He's been chosen to help the pastor,' said Eudy beaming with pride.

And when the pastor did return to his adoring fans Themba was five paces behind carrying his holy book. It was time for the sermon - after the offerings.

Pastor's voice was that soothing to Joost it was sending him to sleep. He disguised the matter, or so he hoped, by leaning forwards and pretending to pray.

Near the end everyone seemed to dash towards to the stage. The pastor was muttering in some archaic language, and touching people's heads. Some of them were falling backwards having been touched by a higher power. Joost, who was a tad sceptical, wanted to know what all the fuss was about.

Finally he was in the front row, and received his blessing. He felt nothing, although the guy next to him would have hit the ground like a rock, had he not been caught by two attendants.

Bheki was smiling when he returned to his seat beside her.

'Will you come again Joost?' asked Themba as they put on their coats.

'Let me think about it,' replied Joost.

There was a look of disappointment on Bheki's face.

Midnight and still no one wanted to leave Bheki's flat. Themba was discussing Africa's future with Joost, whilst Bheki and Eudy were going over the Bible passages from Pastor Goodyear's sermon.

'You haven't told me what you do,' said Joost.

'I'm an accounts assistant,' replied Themba.

Themba was too embarrassed to say he was unemployed, especially with Bheki making Joost look like some high powered businessman; which couldn't be further from the truth. In fact the whole operation was propped up by Dilwood's dirty cash.

Joost had never got to grips with the agency, with his head often in the clouds on drugs, or between some hookers legs.

'He's looking for a job,' said Eudy, more concerned with practicalities than pretensions.

'Well?' said Bheki looking at Joost.

Joost paused for a moment, losing himself in Bheki's beautiful lips.

'We do need a new office assistant, especially to process timesheets and invoices.'

'I could do that,' said Themba.

'Is Monday too early to start?' asked Joost.

'Not at all,' said Themba.

Good things really did come from Pastor Goodyear's church.

'What's the pay?' asked Eudy.

'Two hundred a week, cash in hand,' said Joost.

'Make it three hundred,' said Bheki.

'OK,' said Joost holding his hands up.

Themba and Eudy smiled.

'Bheki can I have a quick word,' said Joost.

'Of course,' and she ushered him into the bedroom expecting to be told off but Joost just looked at the statue.

'That's a great present from your grandma, Akuaa Mathebula.'

Bheki was dumbfounded. Not least because the pronunciation was correct.

'Well I never. Perhaps there's more to you than I thought Joost van Houten.'

She closed the door, and kneeling gave him what he'd prayed for.

Eventually Themba and Joost had to tear themselves away.

'See you Monday,' Joost shouted after Themba.

Back at his flat Joost went to pour a large scotch, but as he touched the bottle he could feel an energy surging through his head, and his body was shaking. He sat down with his knees knocking. Was it Pastor Goodyear he wondered?

Chapter Twenty One

He could see Barbara from his small fishing boat, above the chalk cliffs as he rowed further out to sea. She was hanging out the washing, and making everything clean.

For company he had the remains from the cave, neatly bagged and weighed down with bricks. He hauled them over the side without a prayer, but the victim would have plenty of company down below.

Bill had been a merchant seaman for most of his life. Whether or not he'd had a girl in every port Barbara never knew, but he'd always came back to her.

Retiring to The Crossed Heart their thoughts had turned to the afterlife. Barbara had never been a churchgoer whilst Bill had sailed the seven seas. Here he'd encountered the Liberian Augustus Jones, his voodoo teacher. Journeys to Brazil, Haiti, and the west coast of Africa furthered his beliefs; voodoo was a world church.

Lord Agwe had spared Bill's life in many a storm, and finally washed his soul upon the shores of Bishopsfield. He made an offering to his saviour, and gently dropped a piece of rock salt wrapped in blue paper into the sea.

'It's a real mouthful,' said Christine in her car with Vankoni. 'But if I shorten it to Vank it doesn't sound right.'

'Don't you have a middle name?' she asked.

'Chokwe,' he replied.

Christine looked bemused.

'But you can call me Koni if you like,' he said.

Christine smiled.

'Anyway where are you taking me? I hope it's not another lecture,' said Koni.

'Don't worry we're going shopping this time.'

Koni rubbed his forehead.

'It's all on James' card. And don't worry he's loaded.'

'Inheritance by any chance?'

'How did you know?' asked Christine.

'Dela told me.'

Christine elaborated just in case he'd missed some of the detail.

'His father Arthur passed away a few years ago, and left him a fortune. In fact that's where he first met Felix, at Greenpastures nursing home.'

'And then he fell in love with voodoo?' asked Koni.

Dela hadn't told him everything after all.

'James has always been interested, ever since his days in Africa. So it was natural for him to keep in touch with Felix and Dela. And then of course there was the accident,' said Christine with a hint of sadness, referring to Lucy.

'And you?' asked Koni, turning to face her.

She was plastered in make-up, with bright red lipstick, and her long blonde hair was in a ponytail. She wore black opaque tights with butterfly embroidering, and leather riding boots with buckles like stirrups. James hadn't batted an eyelid when she'd left the vicarage. Koni however was entranced, and couldn't help but pull her skirt a little higher.

'You haven't answered,' he said.

Christine's mind was elsewhere, in the gutter. It had been too long since she'd been a total tramp.

'It was quite simple really,' she said.

Simple at least for her, but she paused wondering how she could dumb it down.

'I majored in cosmology but minored in quantum theory,' she said.

Koni sighed.

'You did ask,' said Christine smiling.

'Go on,' he replied.

'Anyway to cut a long story short, you really can influence something over there by doing something over here, with nothing travelling in between.'

'Oh,' he said.

Christine was a little disappointed by his response, but it wasn't his mind she was after.

'It just vindicates voodoo, that's all,' she concluded.

Fortunately, before Koni started to think he was in class, they arrived at their destination - Wellford.

Christine parked tightly at the train station between a fence and a Japanese tour bus, although there were plenty of other spaces. Koni reached for the door handle.

'Don't be in such of a hurry, you haven't kissed me yet,' she said.

They locked lips in sight of the tourists, who were eating their packed lunch.

'They can see us,' said Koni.

'Really,' she replied 'well in that case we'd better not disappoint them.'

She undid her safety belt, and put her head on Koni's lap. When it was completed she checked all eyes were still upon them. and smiled for the cameras.

'Exhilarating isn't it,' she said to Koni, flicking back her ponytail.

He just mumbled.

With Christine safely out of the way James couldn't wait to woo Eve with his silver tongue.

'The parishioners love you,' he told her as they tidied up the altar.

'And what about you James?' she asked.

'I think you know. Well I think you're adorable.'

'Really,' she replied.

She wasn't sure what she was saying, or why she felt this way. Only that lately she was irresistibly drawn to him.

He touched her arm, just like in the dreams she'd been having, and with his hand holding the back of her neck pushed her mouth onto his. She couldn't resist, wanting him.

Eve backed onto the altar table, and, after lifting her cassock, James consummated their newest relationship. Dela could work miracles.

'I've wanted to give you this for a long time,' said James.

'I could tell,' said Eve, smiling.

'No not that, well that as well, but this,' and he produced a locket from inside his jacket.

Eve opened it, and saw the red pinkish leather inside.

'It represents my heart,' said James lying.

'James how sweet; I shall wear it always and it will be our secret, for now.'

James grinned; now she had no escape, and with the tongue around her neck would dangle on his every word.

Chapter Twenty Two

It was throwing it down with rain outside as Joost quickly got dressed. Bheki was, thus far, avoiding his flat and bedroom; she didn't want a hair out of place when they arrived. She was accompanying him to dinner at Dilwood's rather palatial residence, an old country mansion.

Time had flown since they had first met in Oxford. Joost had failed an interview for personnel manager, and the winter's night had quickly drawn in. On a tight country lane he and Dilwood collided. But they'd also hit someone on a push bike. After deliberating they'd agreed to leave the young woman to her fate.

Joost towed Dilwood's car to the nursing home he'd just bought, Greenpastures. Then, later that night, after they'd both drunk way too much, Joost was given an offer he couldn't refuse; the cash to start a nursing agency. They became partners in crime.

The phone rang.

'Are you still picking me up?' asked Bheki.

'I'll be there in half an hour.'

'And what if I don't like it?'

'Don't worry, we'll leave,' and he put down the phone; he wasn't in the mood to reassure her again.

Bheki rang him back, and slammed the phone down. Joost smiled.

Bheki was wearing a full length cream dress, and Joost, eager to please, wore the red and cream checked suit Bheki had bought him. He felt like a clown, but perhaps she wanted him to look as uncomfortable as she felt.

The electronic gates opened, and the driveway was as long as a street. In front of the house was a large drained ornamental fountain.

Dilwood greeted them at the door, and they were ushered into the lounge. Bheki looked familiar, but he couldn't quite place her, and she had never fully seen his face in the gloom.

Dilwood was well groomed. He had a goatee beard immaculately trimmed, but was going bald and combing his hair over to disguise the fact, or so he thought.

'Pleased to meet you,' said Dilwood's young Thai bride.

Dilwood was forty-nine, and Mai was at least twenty years his junior

There was an immediate empathy between Bheki and Mai, perhaps because they'd both been hookers.

The small talk helped break the ice, although Dilwood was a little staid, though Bheki sensed something was wrong.

'Would anyone like a drink before dinner?' asked Dilwood.

'Tea please,' answered Bheki.

Mai immediately went to prepare the silver tray.

'Are you still drinking the absinthe Dilwood?' asked Joost.

'What would life be without it,' he replied. 'I'll make us both one,' and he disappeared behind his bar.

No one made absinthe like Dilwood, and he loved the ritual. He took two crystal reservoir glasses down from the mirrored shelf, and filled the bubble with the emerald liquor. Then on each glass he sat a silver perforated spoon, and balanced a sugar cube. Pouring ice cold water over the glasses the drink turned into a milky opalescence - 'the louche'.

Everyone was on the sofas as a curious Dilwood looked at Bheki; he knew an albino once, but perhaps a little shorter, and certainly not as well turned out.

'So where did you two meet?' he asked.

'At the agency,' replied Bheki.

'You see I told you it was a good move,' said Dilwood to Joost.

Bheki was warming to him.

'And you two?' Bheki enquired.

'On holiday,' said Dilwood.

He was wearing one of his short sleeved silk Thai shirts tonight. Like the shirt, Dilwood was short and thin.

Bheki wasn't shocked by the large age gap, or at least didn't show it, and Mai who was initially nervous was appreciative.

When she went to prepare dinner Bheki followed her into the kitchen.

'Let's have some girls talk,' said Bheki.

Had she found a friend at last thought Mai, and tired of being stuck in an ivory tower; she hoped so, she desperately wanted to be herself.

Bheki helped Mai serve dinner, and it was no surprise to anyone that it was Thai cuisine.

A large crystal chandelier hung over the dining table, and along the back wall ran glass cabinets stuffed with artefacts; Meissen porcelain, oriental glassware, and some wooden carvings.

Eventually Bheki's eyes rested on the third cabinet from the window, and she nearly choked on her hot and sour soup.

'Are you alright?' asked Dilwood, genuinely concerned.

Her head was spinning, but on his right forearm she noticed the scar of a removed tattoo.

'Here drink this,' said Mai seated directly across the table, offering Bheki a small glass of water.

She downed it in one, but was still coughing.

'I need the bathroom,' spluttered Bheki, grabbing her bag.

'I'll show you the way,' said Mai.

At the top of the stairs Bheki was retching.

'Here use ours, its closer,' said Mai, opening a door at the top of the landing.

There were two sinks in the bathroom, his and hers, and next to each one a cabinet; on one were several bottles of aftershave, and a box of dark brown hair dye. Bheki drank more water from the tap, and splashed her face.

Reaching for a towel on a corner shelf she noticed a simple wooden box that looked lost amidst the opulence. On the lid the letters OSY were carved; the voodoo symbol for special protection. Bheki was intrigued, and looked inside. Amongst Dilwood's watches was a familiar gold medallion. She picked it up, and recognised the talisman immediately; a goat horned dog. The last time she'd seen it was around Kofi's neck.

'Are you alright?' asked Mai through the door, hearing Bheki spluttering once more.

'I'm fine thanks, I'll be down in a moment,' Bheki shouted back, and Mai traipsed down the stairs to re-join the men.

Bheki checked her clutch bag, the knife was still there, and composed her thoughts. She sent Eudy a text message, and calmly made her way back down.

'Feeling better my dear?' asked Dilwood.

'Yes thank you,' replied Bheki.

Halfway through the main course and right on time Eudy phoned on her mobile.

'Sorry,' said Bheki before taking the call.

'Not at all,' said Dilwood 'you're not a prisoner.'

Eventually Bheki put the phone away, and, knowing no one had understood a word, she did her utmost to look apologetic, before turning to Joost.

'It's Eudy. Themba's had a car accident, and she wants me at the hospital with her.'

She also kicked Joost's leg under the table for good measure. He got the message.

'Sorry Dilwood but we'll have to cut it short,' said Joost.

'What a shame,' said Dilwood 'we were just getting to know one another; and the pudding is sublime.'

'Another time,' said Joost.

'I'll take you up on that,' said Dilwood. 'I hope your friend is alright Bheki. I deplore traffic accidents.'

Mai looked the saddest of all, and already she could feel the crushing loneliness all around her, like the bottom of the deep blue sea.

'Nothing too serious I hope,' shouted Dilwood as they got in their car.

'What's really the matter?' asked Joost, as the high walls disappeared behind them.

Now was the time for Bheki to discover if she could trust Joost, although Pastor Goodyear had said he was a good man - at heart.

'He's got my other statue in his cabinet, the one I gave to Lilu.'

'So, he could have bought it from anywhere,' said Joost. 'If it is the one you lost.'

'He's also had a tattoo removed that I think were a pair of scales. That's all I know about the last man to have seen her alive,' said Bheki feeling sick, and opening the window for some air.

'That doesn't make him a killer Bheki.'

'Joost honey it doesn't matter if you don't believe me, but my pimp always wore a particular gold medallion, and it's upstairs in Dilwood's bathroom. He was killed too.'

Though she didn't say by whom, just as Joost didn't mention the real reason that brought him and Dilwood together.

Joost paused for a moment.

'When I first met Dilwood he had a zodiac tattoo, and you're right it was Libra.'

There was one man or Spirit thought Joost who would know the truth - John Lacey. It was time for Bheki to meet him.

Mai cleaned up, and then spent the next hour doing what she'd been bought for, and as happily as she could.

Just before he closed his eyes Dilwood remembered the way Bheki had stared at his third cabinet. He went downstairs to take a look at it. On the middle shelf was the African statue he'd taken from that whore's bedsit after killing her.

'Well I never,' he said under his breath 'Tendai Mathebula.'

Perhaps he should have listened to Din after all, and had them both killed on their visit, even if Joost was an old friend. Of course it would have been inconceivable for the slaughter to have gone unnoticed, but Mai's ungrateful bleating was becoming a trifle boring, and already he'd envisaged wrapping his gloved fingers around her neck.

But Din couldn't chastise him too much; it was Dilwood's drugs trail that was helping them enjoy a lifestyle to which they had become satisfactorily accustomed. Kofi's haul didn't last forever, and Dilwood was now a businessman who pursued more than one line of profit; Mai wasn't his only Thai import.

Chapter Twenty Three

Fortunately when he'd gone to collect Bheki, Joost had left his heating on full blast, and at least their shivers were quelled. But understandably there was a coldness that would not go away.

Joost poured them both a piping hot rooibos, he'd suddenly lost his taste for alcohol. Was Bheki right? And had Dilwood also recognised her? He must admit that even to him Dilwood looked creepier than usual. He could see the Caring Hands Nursing Agency slipping from his grip; for what it was worth.

Bheki didn't have time for Joost's procrastinations, and let him know it.

'Well let's see it,' she said, and for once she wasn't alluding to the bedroom.

He might have been in a quandary, after all he'd forgotten to mention his drug habit to Bheki, but events had overtaken them. He gently slid the crocodile mask on its hook along the wall, until most was suspended over an old chimney breast. Gingerly his free hand delved into the back, and he retrieved a brownish parcel wrapped in plastic, leaving just three behind.

'You're certainly not short of surprises,' said Bheki recognising the scene all too well.

'And I thought I had all your secrets,' she sighed.

'It's just an occasional habit,' said Joost.

'Of course,' said Bheki.

Joost ritualistically laid out his narcotic devices on the table.

'So no wonder the crocodile comes alive,' said Bheki sarcastically.

But that still didn't explain how Joost knew her grandmothers name. She'd give him a chance, besides she didn't fancy going back home in the pouring rain.

'I really hope we don't see a change in personality Joost,' she said, taking the knife out of her bag.

'You won't need that I promise,' he said 'not this time.'

But she felt fluttering in the pit of her stomach.

Joost began to inhale the smoke, and Bheki checked both the clock and the door; at least it wasn't bolted.

Joost took a few more puffs, and hoped he'd inhaled just enough to see his dragon without losing sight of Bheki.

There was no doubt Bheki Ncube had seen enough in her life to turn her hair white, but there was nothing like the sight of a pint sized crocodile looking up at you to shatter the calm; especially one that spoke.

'Don't worry,' said John 'I don't bite.'

Bheki said something in her mother tongue, and John laughed.

'We all speak the same language over here,' he explained.

Bheki laughed too, albeit a little worried.

'He is real,' said Bheki turning to Joost.

Joost stroked his chin and nodded, but John was becoming translucent. He clicked his lighter one more time, and smoked the rest of the powder. And he was mightily relieved; Bheki could see John too - he wasn't crazy after all.

When Joost finally joined them they were chatting like long lost friends catching up.

'Shall I tell him?' asked John.

'I think so, he might not believe me,' said Bheki.

'Dilwood murdered Lilu, and several other call girls. He's stopped for the moment because his sins are more organised - with Dela Eden Obi.'

That name again thought Joost, it was beginning to haunt him.

'And Joost, he recognised Bheki - eventually,' said John.

'So what do we do now?' asked Joost.

'You could run,' said John 'but you'll never be able to...'

'Hide' they all said together.

'You need to think about that,' said John 'but first let me save you both a lot of heartache.'

They looked at each other and half smiled, wondering what was coming next.

'Joost; Bheki killed her pimp Kofi, but I guess you could say it was self-defence,' said John. 'And Bheki when Joost met Dilwood ...'

'Oh no,' interrupted Joost 'not that,' feeling his own guilt rising.

He'd always hoped to look chivalrous to Bheki, and that night was far from gallant.

'At least the girl survived Joost,' said John.

Both Joost and Dilwood knew that from the local papers they religiously scanned days after the accident.

'And you never hit her,' said John, leaving time for the news to sink in before continuing.

'Dilwood had already run her over when you turned the corner. You just hit the bike thrown into the road.'

'And Dilwood knew this?' asked Joost rather naively.

John just grinned, and he had plenty of teeth to do so.

Joost smiled. One mill stone had been partially lifted from his soul. Only partly because he still wished he'd called for an ambulance, in spite of Dilwood's protestations.

'Can you think why he so desperately wanted to flee the scene Joost?' asked John teasingly.

Joost looked blank, but Bheki suspected.

'He'd killed someone else that night,' she said.

'Precisely,' said John 'and the poor girl's body was in his boot.'

Joost felt uncomfortable, but he'd been quickly reminded of another burden, and even with Bheki sitting next to him he couldn't help but wonder.

'Have you seen them?' he asked.

'Yes I have,' said John.

Joost nearly jumped out of his skin, and John answered his next question even before it was asked.

'They're fine.'

John didn't want to hear a long list of questions, in part because he thought it was impolite to Bheki, who he knew was smitten with Joost, so he got in ahead of him.

'They're staying with relatives. You remember Stella's aunt and uncle from Bloemfontaine?'

'Yes,' said Joost.

Life was full of heartache; Kobus and Tilly Jonker had been murdered on their homestead.

'They're having a ball,' said John.

Joost couldn't hold back.

'Can I see them?'

'That's not an easy one, although I will try. But Joost I suggest you tell Bheki about Stella and Hildy. It's a long time since you told anyone.'

Joost sighed. It was going to be a tearful night.

Outside the wind was blowing up a storm, and leaves could be heard rustling down the street.

'Look Joost I know this might be difficult for you, so in spite of what John said you don't have to tell me anything,' said Bheki.

But Joost began.

'We were driving to Stella's sister's house in the Western Cape. We were taking her a birthday present and Hildy was looking forwards to seeing her cousins again, two boys; they would always tease her.'

He paused and held a hand to his mouth for a moment, as though he was about to mention the unspeakable.

'It was my fault, I stopped at an accident, or at least I thought it was.'

Bheki could see the hurt in his eyes, and it was difficult to watch.

'We were carjacked. I killed one in the car causing a crash, and the other got away.'

'Is this the guy now in London?' asked Bheki.

'Yes,' answered Joost.

Joost had gone silent, so Bheki had to coax him.

'And your wife and daughter?' she asked.

Joost could barely speak.

'Both killed in the crash,' he said 'burnt alive.'

Bheki had never seen a man cry before, not like this; deep from within his soul. Tears rolled down his cheeks, and she wiped them with a tissue from her bag.

She wasn't quite certain what to say, as Joost went to a wooden trunk in the corner of the room and lifted up the lid. He removed a photo album and placed it on Bheki's knee; they flicked through the pages together.

Finally, after Joost tried to hide his grief, and another cup of rooibos, Bheki had to say it.

'I'm not Stella, and I never will be.'

'I don't want you to be,' he said.

'But I also don't want you to hate me for not being her.'

Joost gulped. Is that what he'd been doing? And not just with Bheki?

Bheki felt a little guilty for turning the focus onto her, but she couldn't help it.

'Can you really love anyone again?' asked Bheki.

'Don't get me wrong Joost I can just do sex, for now at least, but I want to know the bottom line,' she said.

'I'm not sure' said Joost 'can you give me some time on that one?'

'Why not, but don't take too long,' she said smiling gently.

Joost kissed her hand, and led her into the bedroom. There was no deviance to set the mood or perversion to heighten the thrill, just honesty and tenderness as their bodies entwined.

The alarm was sounding and Joost stretched out his hand, but Bheki was already in the kitchen whipping up some eggs. She was also wearing his old pyjama top which hung just above her hips and looked devilishly fetching.

'Let's see what the weather's like this morning,' said Joost in his dressing gown and throwing back the curtains.

'Strange,' said Joost 'I've never seen that before, not up here.'

'What?' asked Bheki.

'A cat on the balcony.'

'Let me see,' said Bheki, and she just caught sight of the feline before it turned away and jumped out of sight.

They had both seen its stripes before, but only Bheki had been party to the most peculiar set of green eyes.

'I guess he found a shelter from last night,' said Joost.

'How do you know it's a he?' asked Bheki.

'Because he's not afraid of heights,' answered Joost.

Bheki playfully bit his ear, which had an immediate arousing affect.

'Not after last night,' she said but Joost was back to his old self, and a little rough and tumble helped blow the cobwebs away from both of them.

'You know I've got to get my statue back,' said Bheki over breakfast.

Joost put more marmalade on his toast.

'You think you can manage it?' he asked.

'Well actually when I say me, I mean you and Themba,' she said, and as though she was just asking him to take out the rubbish.

Joost poured more tea for them both.

'It's worth a pretty penny when put with the other,' she said.

'Pairs always bring more pleasure when put together,' said Joost, and licking his lips for good measure.

She was just as beautiful first thing in the morning.

Joost was still contemplating the proposal, when Bheki decided to give him the bitter truth.

'You do know the agency is doomed don't you.'

Joost nodded.

First Vankoni, then Dilwood; both in Dela's murderous circle. It looked like they were in a fight for their lives, and the idea of involving the police was a non-starter.

'Don't look too worried,' said Bheki rubbing the top of his shaven head 'at least I know you're not mad.'

They made an early start with Joost all set for the office, but he had to drop Bheki off first. It was still raining, so he left her waiting in the foyer as he went round the side of the building to the garages.

'You do know she's mine don't you,' said a menacing voice from the shadows.

Before he could answer there were two thumbs pushing into his throat. Joost cupped his hands together, and struck a blow upwards to free himself. It worked, but he was choking and disorientated; an easy mark for the floor as he was bowled over.

It hardly seemed fair, so before the boot struck his head Joost buried his tactical fountain pen into it again and again. The attacker screamed and fled, hobbling from the scene.

Bheki who'd become impatient just had time to see Joost's assailant hot foot it.

'Are you OK?' asked Bheki helping Joost from the floor.

'I've been better,' he said 'then again I've been worse. But I'll have to change.'

He picked up his titanium plated fountain pen, screwed the cap back on, and they returned to his flat passing a singing Rita Templemead on their way up.

'I'm sorry Bheki but I should have said a long time ago. Dela and her cronies are after you for muti,' said Joost.

That alone didn't surprise Bheki, she just never thought it would happen in London.

'The world's getting smaller,' she eventually said.

What she didn't let on was that far from being Dela's henchman, Joost's assailant was her ex-boyfriend Jimmy. Still judging by the look on his face he wouldn't be back for his engagement ring anytime soon. She'd tell Joost at a more receptive moment - probably when he was screwing her.

Chapter Twenty Four

Twilight had let itself into Bishopsfield, and for one Bonfire's night at least the skies were clear, although there was a storm brewing on the horizon.

Inside St Agnes sat most of the church committee. Dela was with them, and with no outsiders present James abdicated his authority.

A few hundred yards away was a mountain of chopped wood waiting to be lit. Country folk had travelled from far and wide, and some townies too, to watch the display.

As tradition would have it James and Christine would wheel Guy Fawkes from St Agnes to meet his fate, showing the unity of church and state in condemnation of those who had sought to overthrow the monarchy.

'Where is she?' asked Felix.

Gasper Owido looked at his watch, whilst Mr Pandalay sitting next to him looked a little sleepy. Either that or Susie Chang had worn him out.

Finally the door creaked open, it was Gladys, and she looked frozen.

'Sorry I'm late everyone,' she said.

'Not at all,' said James 'here let me get you a drink to warm you up.'

'I'll get it,' said Dela. 'Glady's take my seat, it's near the radiator; you look like you need defrosting.'

'Thanks Dela,' said Gladys, and trying to stay calm.

'Where's Charles?' she asked.

'At a farm. Apparently it's an emergency,' said Christine.

Vankoni was sitting next to her, and James was oblivious to their body language, or chose to ignore it.

'And Lucy?'

Lucy was fond of Gladys, and likewise.

'She's with my curate Eve on the common. They can't wait for the fireworks,' answered James.

'Slice of cake anyone?' asked Dilwood.

Christine had baked the most delicious marble cake.

Well everyone seemed alright thought Gladys.

'I thought you needed a hand?' she asked Christine.

'Indeed,' said James for her 'but let's finish our cake first.'

Little Gladys looked almost mouse like as she nibbled on her sponge, and as she drank her tea she felt eyes upon her.

'You'd better be off,' said Dela to James 'and take the traitor with you.'

Bill and Barbara had arrived late, and weren't quite sure why James ignored the straw Guy on the floor. Instead he went to Gladys.

The look in Gladys' eye was one of deep sadness. She knew she'd been tricked, but couldn't even protest, or beg for mercy; Dela had slipped a little something into her tea, and she was paralysed.

'This isn't just any ordinary club Gladys, you should have known that,' said Dela, spitting out the words. 'You can't just up and leave when you want.'

Dela was now swinging a cake knife menacingly.

'Your sorry tongue could have got us all locked up for life, and because of that I'm going to end yours. But not before I take this.'

Dela forced Gladys' mouth open, and cut out her tongue expertly with one slash; she placed it on the table.

'Now James, and Christine, if you would please take out the trash,' said Dela.

They were about to lift her straight into the barrow before Din whispered in James' ear and they changed her first. She was like a rag doll; just like the Guy.

Dela relaxed back in her chair, and glanced at the others. It seemed from the look in their eyes everyone had learnt the lesson.

'Aah that's where you've been hiding,' said Dela to the purring feline with the green eyes underneath the table.

The striped moggy jumped on her knee, and Dela clapped her hands to get everyone's attention.

'Lord Baka has graced us with an appearance. In future let's not disappoint him,' she said.

The sharped toothed cat pawed the tongue on the table top before suddenly running off with it out the back door.

'Well don't be surprised anyone,' she said, before looking at a rather timid Felix.

'What's the matter dear husband, cat got your tongue?'

Charles Carney was slamming the boot on his 4 x 4 when he felt a chill sweep through him.

'Gladys,' he shouted, before he quickly jumped behind the wheel, spinning off from the muddied farmland.

There was a loud cheer on the common as James and Christine arrived with the effigy. Eve felt pangs of jealous seeing Christine at James' side.

James hauled Gladys all the way to the top of the bonfire, as Christine held the ladders. Gladys was pushed into a wicker throne, and James couldn't bear to look at her. He quickly shimmied back down, and with Gasper's help they placed the ladder out of harm's way.

'Here, you do the honours,' said James to Eve, as he pushed the matches into her hands.

She smiled.

The crackle of flames could soon be heard taking hold of the wooden pyre, and the crowd roared their delight. No one could see the tears streaming down the cheeks of the Guy.

Charles Carney was flushed in the face as he joined Christine and Lucy.

'Where's Gladys?' he asked.

Christine just nodded to the top of the bonfire, and Charles understood immediately. He held onto his inner pain, but looked at Dela murderously across the common. Not only had she killed Gladys, but his unborn child too.

Suddenly there was a loud whoosh, like a rocket pipe, and then more like an invasion. Explosions in the sky lit up the night with speckled gunpowder.

In the morning, when the embers had died down, Bill would help clean up the mess and spirit away Gladys' bones. As for now, he and Barbara forwent the bonfire; there was too much custom in town.

They didn't all just rush off, that would have been impolite, and besides they had plenty of business to discuss. So eventually nearly all found themselves in a quiet corner of The Crossed Heart. Charles was feeling sick, and had gone home.

There was a major problem in the offing, but they had no need to worry; after all the gods were on their side, or so said Dela.

Dilwood was knocking back the absinthe, specially selected for him by Bill. Mai was at the other end of the bar chatting with Susie Chang; there was no need for them to know everything. Lucy was also with them; she could be a little over sensitive at times.

Gasper Owido was wearing his corduroys and riding boots, and sitting crossed legged with a pint of real ale in front of him.

'So it appears Mr van Houten knows all about us,' he said.

'And his girlfriend too,' said Felix 'the albino.'

'A challenge indeed,' said Gasper.

'So remind me why the police aren't involved?' asked Gasper.

'The girl's a murderer, and Joost has been laundering money for dear old Dilwood,' said Felix.

'And he wants the chance to kill me,' interceded Vankoni.

'Oh yes the unfortunate incident in South Africa,' said Gasper yawning.

All eyes naturally fell on Dela.

'I have a plan,' she said 'starting with the girl.'

'Unfortunately Mr van Houten has proved a little resilient, but once we have the girl he will be like a fish to the bait,' said Din.

'And how do you expect to bring the girl here?' asked Christine.

'I don't,' replied Dela.

'So you're going to kill her elsewhere, but then what about the muti?' asked Gasper.

'She's going to come right to us,' said Dela smiling, and she placed a little bottle of powder on the table in front of them.

'I think you can manage that Felix, don't you?' said Dela.

As the night wore on Christine and James finally got to bend Dela's ear on Lucy. The paste made from Joshua Templemead's spinal cord had showed results. For one thing Lucy now had feeling in her right leg, but they were both of a mind something stronger was needed to complete her recovery.

'Lucy's now ready,' said Dela 'to walk again.'

James and Christine both smiled, and hugged one another. It was almost like old times; they were both in love again, just not with each other.

'But are you ready?' asked Dela ominously.

'Whatever it takes Dela, I've always said that,' said James.

'Then we must prepare a very special birthday cake for Lucy,' said Dela.

Lucy was twenty-two in ten days' time.

James and Christine both knew what that meant, though they weren't prepared for the detail. But that wasn't the worst of it; the cost would clear out the last of James' inheritance.

'Well James?' asked Christine with Dela's eyes upon him.

'Of course,' he finally said 'what's a father supposed to do?'

Chapter Twenty Five

It was surprising how little you actually needed to know, and how forgiving those around you could be if you knew even less.

Bheki was back on Brent ward, and the regular nurse Tony, who'd taken an instant shine to her, was making all the excuses for her shortcomings.

'They just don't teach the nuts and bolts on the course anymore,' he said as Bheki struggled to draw up the syringe.

'I know,' said Bheki 'I mean what's the point of all those essays on social inequality and disease?' And she raised her eyes to the ceiling.

Tony was standing well back; he didn't like the look of Bheki waving the syringe in the air. And he'd had a needle stick injury only the other day, when another agency nurse was on duty - Felix Gale.

'I'm ready,' said Bheki.

'Not quite,' said Tony 'aren't you forgetting something?'

Bheki looked none the wiser and smiled. She'd checked the barrel for air bubbles.

Tony sighed and put the syringe in a kidney dish to carry to Carlos' room. He threw in a small sticking plaster.

'Are you sure you're happy to do it?' he asked.

'Of course,' she answered.

There'd be no better chance to learn than tonight she thought.

'I'll get him ready,' said Tony adding 'right side,' just in case Bheki hadn't checked his notes.

When Bheki entered the room Carlos was bent forwards over a table, and with his pants down around his ankles.

Now where should she give it? Upper left or bottom right quadrant? Oh well here goes she thought. Fortunately Tony had gone to the office to answer the phone. When he came back Carlos was fastening up his trousers.

'Best jab I ever had,' he said 'never felt a thing.'

Bheki smiled at Tony.

'And I was beginning to wonder if you'd ever trained as a nurse,' he said.

Not too far away in the gloom, Dela sat in a car with a small felt doll. Behind its midriff was a small sticking plaster, covered in the owner's blood and carelessly discarded in a bin. In the doll's stomach she twisted a pin, whilst Felix waited for a call.

An hour into the shift and Tony was doubled up on the floor. There were worst places to have an appendix nearly burst, and the duty Doc had him rushed to A and E. His replacement would be there in half an hour.

Bheki looked shocked; Joost had promised to keep them apart. Unfortunately the hospital's deputy manager had phoned him direct.

'Hi Bheki, how's things going?' asked Felix.

'So so,' she replied.

They went into the office so Bheki could give a quick handover. Zack the carer knocked on the door.

'I've made everyone a drink and brought in some cakes; it's my last shift tonight,' he said.

Now who could refuse that, and a smiling Felix held the door open for Bheki.

'Cream horn?' Felix asked Bheki after looking at the goodies on offer.

'No thank you, an iced tart for me,' she said, helping herself.

'Let me get the sugar,' said Felix.

On his return from the kitchen he was smiling to himself.

'Shall I be mother?' he asked before adding 'two spoons Bheki?'

She nodded, just before they heard shouting.

Carlos had just taken it in the ass, but his simmering feud with Lance was in danger of boiling over. Felix and Zack went to investigate.

'Sorry I'm late,' said Jan the other carer and finally arriving on duty.

'What's it like?' she asked Bheki whilst taking a seat. 'Mmm cakes,' she added.

'So so,' answered Bheki.

Zack, who knew the patient's better than anyone, thought it best to split them up, and Lance joined them in the common area, whilst Felix calmed down Carlos.

'Help yourself Lance,' said Zack.

Lance washed the doughnut down with the cup of tea Bheki passed him; she didn't want sweetening up tonight.

It was the middle of the night, and although Felix was watching Bheki like a hawk it was Lance who felt incredibly restless. He just knew he had to escape, and there was a place he needed to be - a small village by the sea.

It was 7 a.m. and a bleary eyed Felix checked the patient's rooms.

'Has anyone seen Lance?' he asked the others, who were now seated in the office, filling in the patient notes.

They shook their heads.

'I'll help you look,' said Zack.

At this moment there was no real panic, but after they checked the bathroom, the kitchen, and all the other patient's rooms, it was evident he was missing.

'In here,' shouted Jan from Lance's room.

She held his curtain wide open. Just outside the window a metal bar was bent forwards, and from it, trailing to the ground, were knotted bed sheets.

Bheki looked over Felix's shoulder, at the mangled bar.

'Oh my,' she said 'he must be possessed.'

Felix just grimaced, as Zack beat him to the punch, and sounded the alarm. But at least he remembered to sign the hourly observations whilst no one looked.

Felix had to stay behind, and explain Lance's absence, whilst Bheki made her get away with the others. Felix hoped she was in a rush to be somewhere, and she was, but not where he would have liked.

Meanwhile at the train station, a man with his head down slammed the carriage door shut.

Chapter Twenty Six

He should have been elated he was out, and under normal circumstances he would have been; after all he'd been dreaming of this moment for years. But he wasn't quite certain how he'd managed to escape, or more importantly where he was going. Although there was something guiding him, an unexplained compass in his head that was pointing him to Bishopsfield. Lance opened the newspaper, and tried his best to look inconspicuous.

There was a heavy knock at the door, and Charles went to answer.

'Come on in my dear,' he said.

'Thanks,' said Lance 'I don't know why, but I just had to be here.'

Charles looked confused; this was definitely not Bheki Ncube.

'I was hoping you could explain,' said Lance forlornly.

They were still in the hallway when the phone rang.

'Wait here a moment,' said Charles, and he dashed into the lounge.

'Yes, but it's not her, it can't be - it's a man,' said Charles.

'Very tall, yes, quite powerful looking,' Charles continued to explain.

There was a long pause on the other end of the phone, whilst Charles nervously looked at the door.

'That's brilliant,' said Charles sarcastically 'and what do I do with him in the meantime?'

'I'll do my best, but make sure they hurry up,' said Charles before hanging up.

'Let me get your coat,' said Charles to Lance 'and come and take a seat.'

'I'm confused,' said Lance as he followed Charles into the lounge.

If Charles had seen his file he wouldn't have turned his back quite so quickly on Lance.

'Don't worry,' said Charles 'soon it will all make perfect sense - to both of us,' and he looked at the clock.

'You see my dear fellow I'm not sure why you're here either, but someone is coming to explain,' said Charles.

Bill and James arrived within half an hour, and helped settle poor Charles' nerves, but not Lance's, who was immediately suspicious of the newcomers.

'I'm not going back,' said Lance sensing the unease in the room.

And he didn't care how many there were; at least no one could inject him here.

'Back where?' asked James hoping to throw him off guard.

Didn't they know thought Lance? In that case how much should he reveal? But if no one knew where he'd come from, then where was he supposed to go?

'What do we tell him?' asked Felix in the car.

'Well I don't think we can let him see you Felix,' said Din from the backseat.

'Or any of us for that matter,' said Dela.

'Then what do we do?' asked Vankoni sitting next to Din.

'You still know how to use this Din?' asked Dela taking a wooden pipe from her bag.

Din laughed.

'Well it's been a long time, but I guess so.'

'And the dart?' asked Din.

'Here,' she said handing it over.

Felix looked terrified.

'Don't worry Felix, I'm not that upset with you,' she said 'not yet.'

'So what's it all about?' Lance asked the others, becoming increasingly agitated.

'That's what we're hoping to find out,' said James.

'Maybe you have amnesia,' said Bill following James' line, and trying to throw Lance off the scent.

Lance scratched his head.

'Don't worry, Dela will be here soon, and she'll explain everything,' said Charles.

Lance wasn't looking too impressed.

'Has anyone got a ciggie?' he asked.

'No,' answered Bill knowing no one else smoked, but James reached into his jacket pocket.

He opened a silver cigarette case, and offered one to Lance.

'Eve forgot them at St Agnes,' he explained to a suspicious Bill.

I wonder if he knows about Christine and Vankoni thought Bill, who'd seen them standing awfully close at The Crossed Heart.

'A light?' asked Lance.

'Sorry,' said James.

Lance looked around the room for weapons, and decided to smash James on the head with the large glass vase, and then tackle Bill with the poker, if he had too. Charles he would take out last, and more slowly.

'Let me look in the kitchen for some matches,' said Charles quickly leaving the room.

The evil eye from Lance had sent a shiver down his spine.

'At last,' said Din to himself in the undergrowth, and he tapped on the window.

Charles got the message, and gently unlocked the back door for Din.

With Din now crouched in the hallway Charles shouted Lance to join him, and get a light from the cooker. At the bottom of the stairs the dart hit Lance in the neck. Immediately he screamed and went to pull out the needle, but the poison knocked him to the ground; Lance had been injected - again.

For once Dela looked apologetic, although it wasn't really her fault, and at least she still had her magic touch.

'Alright gentleman I know it's not Bheki Ncube, but let's not look a gift horse in the mouth,' she said.

She saw the opportunity for both a sacrifice to the Spirits, and some extra muti for the freezer.

'But we'll have to be quick,' she said.

117

Din and Vankoni carried Lance up to the bathroom, whilst Charles got some plastic sheets from the cellar. Dela was already on the phone to the others, and offering her services for free. Everyone wanted to improve something; be it Gasper's golf swing, or Charles' horticultural skills. Well now was the chance, and it wasn't costing an arm and a leg.

Lance was still stunned, and even more confused as they all queued up; Dela prayed for them on the landing. First in was Gasper who landed a swing with his nine-iron at the back of Lance's head. Then Bill let him have an uppercut with the knuckledusters he'd brought along; he would love to have the fighting prowess of his younger days.

Charles did a little nip and tuck with his secateurs, which wasn't a pretty sight, but at least there was a shower above the bath. James was taking forever to decide but in all fairness he had little with him. In the end he borrowed Charles' iron; he'd always been useless around the house.

Vankoni was denying his infatuation for Christine, despite their passion, but he ached to be her equal out of bed as well as in it. He used the silver fountain pen she'd bought him, and hoping to increase his knowledge. He crossed the t's and dotted the eyes.

Felix was just too maudlin to take part, and as Dela's husband none of the others questioned him.

Din was last, and finally decided to use Charles' broom handle as a makeshift barbell. He just hoped he bulked up even more, and didn't become obsessively tidy.

'Din, Vankoni, you can bag him up now,' said Dela, and with everyone else downstairs they prepared Lance for the short trip to Bill's freezer.

'Well at least the poison dart put him out of his agony,' said Charles to Dela.

'Charles you're so sweet,' said Dela 'wrong but sweet'

Din winked at Charles. He'd only hit Lance with a mild tranquiliser, just enough to keep him paralysed as the real fun began.

Dela decided to keep an eye on Charles. Gladys had been a rotten apple, but Charles had been nestling in the same barrel.

Chapter Twenty Seven

Joost stared at the phone on his desk, and letting it ring. He didn't recognise the number and was frightened to answer.

'Shall I answer it?' asked Themba.

'No it's alright,' said Joost biting a fingernail, and looking forlorn.

Ever since Dela's manikin had appeared on his front door, nursing homes were falling over themselves to book staff. Ordinarily this would have been great, only the truth was sinking in; it was do or die. And shortly there would be no Caring Hands, whatever happened.

'She's late again,' said Themba, referring to Irena.

It wasn't that she resented Themba's appearance in the office. God no, she'd been asking for another body for ever. She'd just learnt there was more to life than end of life care.

Joost put the phone on silent, and logged onto the business account. Dilwood had withdrawn 10K last night, which was unusual. He decided to pay Themba a month in advance and take 5K for himself, whilst it was still there.

'Hi guys sorry I'm late,' shouted Irena into Joost's office, leaving her umbrella up, and putting it next to the radiator to dry.

She wasn't just wet from the rain, and had bags under eyes. Her hair was ruffled, and the zip on her skirt was slightly undone below the top button. She couldn't have made it any more clearer why she was late.

'It must be love,' joked Joost as she walked by to the kitchen.

'He's just a nice guy,' said Irena smiling 'I'll bring him in to meet you one day.'

Irena didn't say he was always asking about Joost; but he was.

Joost was just glad Irena wasn't fawning over him anymore, and she actually looked pleased whenever Bheki phoned.

Irena transferred the calls to her office, and was soon busy booking shifts for the rest of the day. Maybe she could start up her own agency with the remnants of Caring Hands thought Joost. But he was dreading telling her it was all over; she'd been his rock.

'Ouch,' came the shout, quickly followed by 'bloody hell it's freezing.'

'Hello,' said a voice 'I'm John.'

There was a pause. He'd met a lot of new people lately - and they'd killed him.

Eventually he said 'Lance, pleased to meet you,' and his head was a lot clearer, even if it was separated from the rest of his body.

He hadn't felt like this in years. He was back to his old self, sharp as a pin.

When the rest of Lance had joined him in the freezer, Bill slammed it shut. John was glad of the company, and it didn't take long for Lance to enlighten him in their tomb full of scampi.

The chips flipped between his fingers, and he looked through the crowds at the door. But still he didn't come. He'd vanished into thin air, never even returning for his coat. Vankoni wasn't the only one to give The Four Horsemen a wide berth; Dela and Din were also absent punters.

At the end of the table, a big ass in a tight dress was looking even more like cake on a plate, as it pressed into the rim of the table. Joost could even make out the outline of a suspender belt, but despite feeling horny he refused to be hooked. The last of his three grand, unlike Joost, was blown.

'Hi Joost,' said the dress 'remember me?'

'Sure, Monica, right.'

'You got any sugar left for me?' she purred in his ear.

'Sorry honey,' he replied.

'Never mind, you can have it on credit,' she said 'I know you're good for it.'

That wasn't the only thing Joost was good for, as half the hookers in town knew.

'No can do babe, I'm trying to be good.'

'Don't worry,' she whispered in his ear 'I'll be bad for both of us.'

Joost was tempted, and her voice was hypnotic.

'I've got a date,' he stammered.

'Well why didn't you say,' said Monica 'I love a party. Why don't I come along?'

Now he was hooked; line and sinker. But he wasn't sure how Bheki would take the news.

'I'd love to Monica, but I can't ask her that.'

Monica raised her eyebrows.

'You surprise me Joost. I guess it must be love then.'

'But don't worry,' she added 'you'll ask one day, men always do.'

With that Monica, like a bird of prey, moved on and sharpened her claws ready for the next titbit.

Joost left the club for Bheki's. She wasn't working any more, but doing a lot of praying.

Any motel would have done for Koni, but Christine insisted it had to be this one. Their room was overlooked by the back of a nursing home.

Agatha went to close the window, always at the same time like clockwork. A tight elastic belt with a silver buckle pinched into her dark blue nurse's uniform, and making her hips appear wider. She unscrewed a flask and poured herself a stiff one. Across the way someone opened the curtains.

'Shouldn't they be closed?' asked Vankoni.

'Not at all,' replied Christine as her dress fell to the floor.

She immediately had Koni's attention and mounted her bull as he lay on the bed. Koni really did have the stamina for a long hard night, and Agatha watched the two love birds at play.

During the games Christine caught Agatha's gaze whenever she could. It was even better than when she brought her toys.

Felix knew he was in for it; they were back at the flat, and Dela had her hands on her hips. She then pulled her naked 'manimal' along by his most prized possession, until he was facing the wall. His nose was pushed against a small drawn circle, and he remained obediently still.

'Stick it out,' screamed Dela, and his posterior lifted upwards.

Dela was sitting on the sofa holding a leather belt. As she slapped it into the palm of her hand she kept repeating 'Bheki not Lance.'

Felix was scared; he hadn't had the strap for a long time, and it came as keen as hell. He kept his nose in the circle, avoiding extra punishment.

'Ah well,' sighed Dela 'let the lesson begin.'

It was difficult keeping your ass in the air when you knew what was coming, but Felix was well trained.

Six of the best, then ten more; Felix felt ready to faint. Dela too was becoming light headed with the sight of the wheals, and the bruises were already turning purple as she counted fifteen.

'Steady,' she ordered as Felix waivered.

'All done,' she said on the stroke of twenty, and finally becoming overwhelmed by desire.

Chastisement was no longer required, but Dela did blame Felix for her actions. And she gently coaxed an admission of guilt out of him, whilst rubbing lotion onto his cherry red behind.

Because he'd made Dela feel guilty for hurting him, her pain doll had to sweeten her up. Felix lay with his head in a sling underneath the queening chair as Dela closed the bedroom door, and picked up a book; he was in for a long night.

Chapter Twenty Eight

Mrs Greene waved goodbye through the front bay window as her husband left for work. She was busy putting up the laundered net curtains, and standing on a stepladder. Adam their first born was asleep upstairs in his cot.

They had a new build house on the outskirts of Bishopsfield, and were very comfortable. Richard Greene was a diamond dealer. He didn't care where they came from, or whose blood was spilt on the way. His own life was sanitised.

Dela was with Christine at the vicarage as they donned their respective tunics. Dela was a nurse, and Christine a health visitor. Christine was petrified; this time she really was getting her hands dirty.

Vankoni picked them up in a stolen car, and kept his hands on the wheel. Although Dela already guessed what they'd been up to.

As Vankoni waited a little further down the street and out of sight, Dela briskly marched up the path with Christine dawdling behind. Dela rang the doorbell.

'Mrs Greene?' asked Dela.

'Yes.'

'Sorry we're a little late, but it's been a busy morning,' said Dela.

Mrs Greene looked them up and down a little suspiciously, but a uniform could work wonders. When Dela held up an ID badge, stolen by Felix on an agency shift, her guard dropped completely.

'I don't understand,' said Mrs Green.

'Just a quick call to check on Adam,' said Christine becoming conscious of her silence.

Mrs Greene still had the door only partly open, and was shielding herself behind it. The chain was on.

'No one told me about a visit,' she said.

'Has the hospital not written?' asked Dela with mock concern.

'No.'

Jane Greene was running her fingers through her short black hair.

'Typical,' said Dela turning to face Christine, placing her large bag on the floor.

'And I was looking forward to seeing him,' said Christine 'the hospital say he's as cute as a button.'

'Would you mind phoning them Mrs Greene?' asked Dela.

Jane Greene paused in thought.

'All right, but please come and wait inside, it's starting to rain.'

'I think we're in for a storm,' said Dela.

Jane had made a fatal mistake, and as she turned around to make the call Dela stabbed her in the back. Dela calmly went upstairs, whilst Christine nervously watched the door. What had scared her most was the smile on Dela's face as she had twisted in the blade repeatedly; she really was a psychopath.

It didn't take much to suffocate a baby, and Dela thought how much fun Felix must have had in the nursing homes. She stuffed the little corpse into her bag, and they both stepped over Mrs Greene on their way out. It would be a difficult day for Mr Greene; this wasn't the sort of thing that happened here. The dirt was always hidden, and his guilt would be magnified by the trip he'd made to see his mistress.

Before dumping the car on waste ground far away and torching it, Vankoni dropped his passengers off at the church hall. Christine was an excellent cook, and they were going to bake a cake. After all, it was Lucy's birthday tomorrow.

Chapter Twenty Nine

'Where did you get to the other night?' asked James Middlemass as he adjusted his dog collar in the long framed mirror.

'Oh just a little gazing,' replied Christine as she checked her emails at the desk.

'At the observatory I guess,' said James.

'Naturally, it was a great night for seeing stars,' said Christine with a mischievous smirk she kept hidden.

'I'm seeing the Bishop this morning. I think they're going to offer me a promotion,' said James.

'James, I couldn't bear to leave Bishopsfield.'

'Not even if they made me a Dean?'

'Really,' said Christine excitedly; she'd always been such a snob.

'Let's wait and see,' he said.

'Will you be back in time for the start of Lucy's party?'

'I'll make sure. After all its cost me £28,000.'

This was the sum Dela had requested to make Lucy walk again, and cure her once and for all.

James left Christine to finish her emails, and lovers prose, to Vankoni. What a fool she was if she didn't know he'd been reading her not so secret emails for years. But what did he care, he was smitten with Eve, and she was dancing to his tune.

Joost had arrived at Bheki's last night hoping to whisk her back to his flat, but Bible study was still in play, and he wasn't prepared to face the ordeal with a group of strangers, so he left early. Still Bheki was kind enough to answer his prayers in the back of his car before saying goodbye.

Joost looked at the crocodile mask on the floor. It had fallen off the nail, and the last three packets of John's gear were tempting him. Besides which, was John trying to get in touch? It was enough of an excuse, and he religiously laid out his kit on the table.

'At last,' said John.

Joost was becoming ever confidant with the little crocodile, and patted the deep rugged scales on his head.

'What is it my friend?' asked Joost.

'I know where I am, thanks to someone else joining me.'

'Go on,' said Joost.

'In Bishopsfield.'

'Is it far from here?' asked Joost.

'A little over an hour's drive.'

'You remember your promise Joost?' asked John.

'Of course, and I will get you out.'

'Can you make that two of us?'

What harm could a few more chops of frozen meat do thought Joost?

'Yes,' he said.

'I told you so,' said John.

'Told me what?' asked Joost.

'Not you,' said John 'Lance, he's in here with me.'

'Killed by Dela I presume,' said Joost.

'Yes, and in a botched plan to grab Bheki.'

Joost's heart sank, and as he learnt the grisly details he regretted Bheki's involvement even more. John could sense his despondency, as Joost stroked his shaven head.

'You must lie low until the time is right,' said John.

'How low?' asked Joost.

'Very, and without a trace.'

'You mean leave the flat?' asked Joost alarmed, but already thinking he had an excuse to move in with Bheki and Eudy.

John could read his mind.

'Bheki will have to move out too.'

'They know where she is?' asked Joost.

John just sighed. Felix may not have driven her all the way home after their night shift together, but Vankoni had followed her the remaining distance.

'ASAP Joost,' said John.

'I get the message,' and he looked around his flat.

There wasn't that much he needed to take.

'If I could make one last suggestion?' asked John.

'Go on.'

'Take a look around Bishopsfield, it should come in handy.'

'And Joost, there's only two packets left.'

'I know,' snapped Joost.

He wasn't angry at John, and they both knew it. But quite naturally he was feeling a little fraught.

John had time to hand over some names, and a few properties of interest in Bishopsfield, before he and Lance were left to get on like a house on fire.

'Hi Bheki,' said Joost down the phone.

'Missing me already?'

'What are you doing today?' he asked.

'Nothing much.'

'Fancy a drive?'

'Sure. Where to?' asked Bheki.

'Bishopsfield, it's a little coastal town not too far away.'

'I'll be ready in an hour.'

Dino, nicknamed Dino-saw, due to his slashing a memento onto his victims' foreheads, was taking his last walk along the landing.

'Time flies eh boss,' said Dino.

'Just try and behave Dino or you'll be coming back,' said the slightly built prison officer with the keys dangling, and jangling, from his waist.

'Not me boss. You'll be doing more years than me.' And Dino bellowed out his characteristic laugh, like a machine gun.

There were a couple of goodbye nods from fellow cons on the wing, but mainly there was disinterest. No one really wanted to think what was on the other side of the wall, until it was there time to get out.

Dino swaggered along in his prison blues, with the next bully ready to fill his shoes. Three years for extortion, had been a good exchange, and his younger brother Jimmy had kept the family loan sharking business going.

A long cardboard box was slid across the counter, and Dino went into a holding pen to change back into his civvies. The trousers were tight, thanks to all the duff and custard, although the prison gym had stopped him exploding.

Dino was escorted into the yard, and a little door in the gate opened to let him out. He wasn't holding a bag with his prison number written on the side; his radio and dominos could stay where they were.

Little brother hobbled forward to give him a hug.

'What's happened to your foot?' asked Dino.

'Some geezer stabbed it,' said Jimmy.

'You want me to sort him out?' asked Dino.

'Let's talk about it in the car.'

'How's Bheki?' asked Dino.

'We split up.'

'No bro, don't say that, she was a real honey.'

'I know.'

'You think you can get her back?'

'Maybe, but there's some dude in the way.'

'No problem bro, let's pay back the guy who mangled your foot, then we'll sort him out.'

'It's the same geezer.'

Dino laughed.

'Even better, two for one.'

'How's Marie?' asked Dino hoping the news wasn't as bad, although she'd always written, and visited, whenever she could.

'She's at mum's house, with the kids, waiting to see you.'

'Yeh man, that's what I want to hear. Party!'

Joost took one last look at the screen. Dilwood had put his cards on the table, clearing the account, and there were no invoices due until the end of next month.

No job, not much ready cash, and soon no home, although he could always sell it; if he survived. There was only one thing to do - go for broke. And why not, he'd felt suicidal for years.

Chapter Thirty

'Happy birthday to you,' they sang in unison.

Even Charles Carney joined in, although he was still spitting mad at Gladys' funeral pyre.

'Light the candles,' shouted Gasper.

'Make a wish,' said Christine before Lucy blew them out.

It was a monsters ball, with the murderous group capped in party hats at the vicarage.

As Christine cut the birthday cake into slices for everyone, Dela came from the kitchen with a second. This one had a special recipe, and was for Lucy, and Dela, alone. Unlike the wrapped presents this treat would put her back on her feet; it had been dedicated to Sakpata, the god whom rules disease.

Dela cut the cake into eight slices, leaving one portion for her. It wasn't to make the magic work, but rather the flesh of a new born would rejuvenate her looks. Not as if she needed it, but she was a narcissistic psychopath.

Gasper made a toast with a little pomp, and Pandy looked lovingly into the eyes of his TV lover. James and Felix were already knocking back the refreshments courtesy of The Crossed Heart.

James could hardly wait for Lucy to feast on Dela's slice, and was a little disappointed when she didn't leap out of her chair. Dela explained in his ear.

'Lucy must eat the remaining slices one a day for the next six days. Then she will no longer need her props - ever.'

James smiled and quickly passed the good news onto Christine. He stood close to the cake Dela had baked, guarding it. But soon this wasn't enough, and he took it upstairs into Lucy's room.

'Don't drink too much my dear,' whispered Dela to Felix.

He had to drive them back to London tonight. Din and Vankoni, had other business; there was a shipment due from Thailand, and Dilwood needed help to unpack it.

'Darling I forgot to ask, how did you get on this morning?' Christine asked James.

He sighed.

'Did they offer you a promotion?' she asked.

'I'm afraid not,' he finally said.

'Never mind, at least we get to stay in Bishopsfield, and everyone will be amazed with Lucy's recovery,' said Christine.

'Indeed, it will be a miracle,' said James raising a half smile.

There was something bothering him. Someone had complained about his relationship with Eve. Apparently he was too flirty; but how could he hide his joy? In stark contrast he and Christine often appeared cold and reserved together. He was ordered to sharpen up his act, and no more compromising positions.

They'd walked along the promenade hand in hand. Sure they were always one zipper away from ripping each other's clothes off, but it had become more than infatuation. It didn't have to be said because they were both afraid of rejection, but they were falling in love. You could see it in Bheki's eyes, and the way Joost moved around her. God how he'd hate to lose her, but they were on dangerous ground, literally - they were in Bishopsfield.

They hid amongst the stream of tourists for protection, like minnows in a shoal. They shared an ice-cream under the darkening skies, and fish and chips in the downpour, darting for cover under an old beach chair store. Joost wore a cap brought down over his eyes, whilst Bheki flattered a pair of shades. And whenever the opportunity presented up shot the umbrella. They were dying to see inside St Agnes, and Mavis who was on the door took their donation.

'No photos,' she said.

Eagle eyed Bheki was quick to scan the walls until she found what she was looking for - a picturesque tapestry.

'Let's take a closer look over there,' she said pointing.

She'd seen it many times before; voodoo symbols hidden in church. The old gods secretly worshipped in the heart of the colonists temples.

The scene was of Adam and Eve in the Garden of Eden, nothing peculiar there, but the serpent was rainbow coloured, and almost coiled in a circle.

'That's Dambala,' whispered Bheki to Joost 'god of the dead.'

Joost wasn't surprised, and examined the scene closely; studious like an art connoisseur.

The tapestry was eight foot long and half as high. It was framed by a glass screen, and screwed to the wall. It was a recent gift to the church, but it didn't say from whom.

'Notice the closeness of the serpents fangs to its tail' said Bheki 'almost as if he's about to eat it.'

Joost nodded.

'It's the circle of life,' said Bheki.

'Should we fear him?' asked Joost.

'Actually he's the protector of albino's,' said Bheki smiling and moving on.

'That's interesting,' said Bheki.

Someone had carved 'Our Saviour Yahweh' into the side of the pulpit. What caught her eye were the letters O, S, and Y, which were gouged much deeper into the panel. She ran her fingers along them.

'OSY. The word protects enemies from troubling you,' she explained to Joost, who was beginning to feel he was on a school trip, or at least a guided tour.

It was impossible to introduce a goat horned dog, unless you had a medieval painting of the damned hanging in church, but there was a mysterious wooden emblem hanging outside the vicar's office. No one paid it any attention, as it was simply a gilded sketch of a key and a door. It could have been the family crest of the local Earl, but it wasn't. It was one of the voodoo symbols for Eshu, the messenger between the living and the dead.

Mavis rang a small bell, and Joost and Bheki followed the other day trippers outside.

Mavis couldn't wait to join everyone else at the party, and wondered if the Bishop had read her anonymous letter about James and Eve? Frolicking in church like young lovers, and poor Christine!

Joost's heart was beating fast, partly because of what he'd seen but mainly because of where they were headed - The Crossed Heart.

'A scotch with ice, and an orange juice,' Joost ordered at the bar, whilst Bheki quickly sat at an empty table.

'Any meals with that?' asked Barbara.

'No thanks,' he replied.

'Scampi and chips is our speciality,' said Barbara after detecting a tourist's accent.

'I'll pass,' said Joost.

But he did watch Barbara disappear round the back when someone else ordered her special.

'So where should we go?' asked Bheki.

She'd seen the destruction voodoo wrought on albinos, and had decided to move out of her flat. Besides they would be moving in together, and it was kind of romantic.

'I was hoping you might know,' said Joost.

Bheki shook her head.

'What are you going to tell Irena?' Bheki asked.

'It's not an easy one. I can't tell her the truth, but I don't want her to feel abandoned.'

'So chivalrous,' said Bheki sarcastically.

She hadn't forgotten the jealousy in Irena's eyes when they'd first met.

'I'll think of something,' said Joost downing the last of his whisky.

'I'm just nipping to the Ladies,' said Bheki, and they were both reminded of the Blue Samurai. Unfortunately The Crossed Heart was too busy for such delights.

While she was gone Joost couldn't resist the chance to see John's tomb, and stepped through a side door marked 'staff only' in bold letters. At the back of the kitchen was a large chest freezer.

'Can I help you?' asked the voice.

The gnarled face looked like a mean and washed up prize fighter who feared no one. That and he had a rolling pin in his hand.

'Sorry, I'm after the toilets,' said Joost.

'Out the door and on your left,' said Bill visibly unimpressed.

Joost quickly made his way out.

Joost and Bheki left soon after, and before Bill could try staring under Joost's cap any more. They took one last drive by the village vet's, and onto the open road.

The rain was getting heavier, and Joost could hardly see. They were halfway home, on the outskirts of Wellford, when the windscreen wipers stopped keeping up with the downpour. There was a sign ahead, 'Hotel Mephisto.'

Joost tapped the bell on the desk, and a man with black greased hair came out to greet them.

'Good evening Sir, may I be of assistance?' asked Mr Wheatley.

'We need a room for the night,' said Joost.

'Of course you do Sir,' said Mr Wheatley looking Bheki up and down.

He could spot hookers a mile away.

'A double room Sir?'

'Yes please.'

'The only one free is number sixty-six on the top floor. It has two single beds - will that be a problem Sir.'

'We'll manage,' said Joost.

Mr Wheatley clapped his hands, and an even older gentleman, also wearing black trousers, white shirt, and a waistcoat, came out from the back. Neither wore a tie around their starched collars, and their name badges were in cherry red.

'Take them to their room Mr Crowley.'

'Would you like a morning call Sir?' asked Mr Wheatley from behind the desk, as Mr Crowley pressed the button to call the lift.

'Please, and make it six,' said Joost.

'You are an early bird Sir,' said Mr Crowley.

Mr Crowley was diminutive but with large eyes, and in the lift Joost had to stand in front of him to stop him staring at Bheki anymore.

'Have a good night Sir,' said Mr Crowley who hovered around forever but still received no tip.

'If you don't mind me saying Sir, she's a real beauty that one.'

Joost slammed the door shut and they both laughed. An hour later and they were still trying to keep the noise down. They just hoped Mr's Wheatley and Crowley weren't watching on a hidden camera.

Dela had been quite fascinated by Pandy's shemale lover at the party, and everyone knew she wore the finest lingerie. Perhaps it was time for Felix to mimic the third sex; she'd make a start on her sissy slave tonight.

Dela went into the lounge, and poured another gin over her fetish whilst Felix had a tepid bath; his ass was still sore but worse was to come.

'Did you enjoy the party darling?' Dela asked Felix as he dried himself in the bedroom.

Dela had that tone in her voice which meant there was something else on her mind.

'Yes,' he replied.

'And what did you buy the birthday girl?'

'A gift card.'

'How sweet,' said Dela 'not stockings and suspenders, or long knitted socks, you pervert?'

'Of course not Dela,' replied an indignant Felix.

'But you wish you had. Then you could fuck her in that chair.'

'Dela, honestly,' said Felix almost thinking she was joking - until she bit the end of his nose.

'Here you try it,' and she threw a pair of black stockings, with red seams and heels, onto the bed.

Felix knew better than to argue, and put them on before Dela fastened a high suspender belt around his chubby torso. She quickly fastened the eight suspender clips into place.

'Move bitch,' she said as she positioned him on the bed.

'You think it's fun having every other manimal trying to get inside you, do you?' she screamed.

She fastened the strap-on peg around her waist. Another little present of her own she'd been saving.

'Well you try it,' she said after applying a little lotion to the tip.

Felix let out a yell.

'Don't be such a cry baby,' said Dela 'this wasn't even the biggest one in the shop.'

For Felix this was the final act of submission; Dela had become the man.

Chapter Thirty One

Joost looked at Bheki across the table, as Mr Crowley brought them a fried breakfast dripping in lard. It was a bit slippery, but they needed fattening up after last night's exercise.

Sitting away from them were a couple of ladies who tried to be discreet, but couldn't help from staring at Joost. He was both annoyed and flattered, but did notice they had rather large hands, and both were wearing chiffon scarves around their necks.

'This place is a tip,' said Bheki looking around at the décor.

There were bunches of tattered artificial flowers on the tables, and the chairs were padded in tacky green velour. There was a stained red carpet covering most of the floor, but not in the corners where it gave up.

Joost poured them both a coffee.

'It's not the Hilton for sure but,' he hesitated 'the location couldn't be better.'

Bheki looked at him.

'Joost you can't be serious.'

'Well it is halfway between Bishopsfield and London, and Dilwood's is just on the other side of town.'

'No way Joost.'

She'd been in establishments a lot seedier than the Mephisto - just, but she didn't like the way Messieurs Wheatley and Crowley looked her up and down. The place was ghastly, and who on earth was Madam Fang Fong? There were posters of her everywhere, and she looked awful.

'Alright, but what if we stayed in another Hotel nearby.'

'Perhaps,' said Bheki.

She didn't really want to live out of a suitcase, but then again she did want to live.

'You're sure we have to leave London?' she asked.

'You know, as well as I do, what they're like. I wish I'd never got you involved,' he lamented.

'Joost darling, as soon as Felix Gale saw me I was involved.'

'You can't be the only albino in London,' said Joost.

'Of course not, but once they get you in their sights they never give up,' said Bheki, referring to the muti gangs.

'Unless they die first,' and she drew an index finger across her throat.

Bheki well understood the predicament they were in; she'd grown up with death forever one step behind.

Joost was polite enough to ignore his role in bringing Bheki and Felix together; she was still a porn star but no longer his pawn.

The roads were still wet as they drove out of Steeple's End but the storm had died down - for now.

Joost pulled the zipper all the way around, and flattened the bulge in the middle delicately, after all, the suitcase contained his most valuable possession - the crocodile mask.

Joost wasn't taking long moving out of his flat. With the awful deaths of Josh Templemead and Lance on his mind he couldn't stay put.

Bheki took one last look in the bedroom.

'I'm going to miss that bed,' she said with a smile.

'Well we could try it one last time,' said Joost.

Bheki tried her best to look reluctant, but Joost wasn't even watching her face. If he had, it would only have inflamed his passion.

In the evening they were sitting with Eudy. She was younger than Bheki, and didn't have that dejected hooker look around the eyes that Joost found so irresistible. And her baby bump was getting bigger.

'I can manage at Themba's for a while,' said Eudy.

Themba rented a room from a distant relative, and sharing the bathroom would be a problem, but Eudy was more concerned for Bheki. The doorbell rang.

'That will be Themba,' said Eudy 'and thanks for paying him yesterday Joost.'

'No problem. I just wish I could do more, but you know ...'

'The business has to close,' said Eudy.

She tried to hide her feelings from both of them. But moving out of Bheki's flat, and Themba unemployed again, was a bitter disappointment.

Joost and Themba shook hands, and Bheki brought in a pot of rooibos tea.

'Can you help?' asked Bheki, referring to her missing statue.

'Sure,' replied Themba.

There would be no charge, this was family business.

'It won't be easy,' said Joost.

'Nothing ever is,' said Themba smiling.

And then they prayed; all of them.

Joost had a long day ahead of him, and he wasn't sure which would make give him the most anxiety; giving Irena the bad news, or breaking in to Dilwood's mansion? And what if Dela and her cronies were there? Then the lamb would have come to the slaughter. Anyway first things first, and he boldly stepped out into the snow.

'Joost, where have you been? I was worried,' said Irena as Joost entered the office, shaking the snowflakes from his coat.

She was no longer infatuated, but was genuinely concerned for him. After all they'd had a rapport long before their respective lover's arrived.

'A little down in the dumps,' said Joost, and he looked it.

He might be doing his best to look self-assured in front of Bheki, but his troubles were mounting up. He just had to remain focussed, and think of Vankoni.

'I'm afraid I have some rather bad news Irena. You might want to sit down,' he said.

'It's alright Joost. I already know, the agency is closing,' said Irena.

Joost's jaw dropped open.

'How did you know?' he asked.

'Dilwood phoned the office yesterday and told me.'

'Did he say anything else?' asked Joost.

'Only that he'd be seeing you soon, and straightening things out,' said Irena.

'I must say though,' she continued 'I'm a little surprised. We've been inundated with new customers recently.'

'Have you told the staff?' asked Joost.

'Not yet, I was waiting for you. After all you're the boss.'

They both smiled, then hugged one another. A while ago it might have led to sex, but now they were just friends saying goodbye.

'I'll miss this place,' said Irena with a tear in her eye.

'Me too,' said Joost.

'But don't worry Irena you can have everything from here; the staff, the customers, the whole shebang.'

'That's kind of you Joost,' she said, perking up.

'And if you can get a van this week you can even take the furniture,' he said.

Irena was now thinking of keeping the office, but Joost didn't want to tell her the rent; without Dilwood's drug money propping them up it was unaffordable.

'Hey you know what, I haven't even asked about your boyfriend,' said Joost 'what does he do?'

'He's a businessman like you,' replied Irena.

'That's good, and what's his business?'

'Entertainment,' she said with a look of that's all you get.

'And I almost forgot,' said Joost 'you'll have to take the lucky charm.'

He went outside the office into the corridor, leaving Irena scratching her head.

'Not you as well,' said Irena as he presented her with Dela's manikin.

'What do you mean?' asked Joost.

'Oh nothing, it doesn't matter.'

'So what's the future hold Joost?' she asked whilst closing her laptop.

'For me or for you?' he asked.

'For you of course. I know where my future lies,' she said smiling.

'Who knows,' he replied 'for now I think I'll just take stock.'

'Back to South Africa?' she asked.

'Maybe.'

Irena knew all about Stella and Hildy, and the pain in Joost's heart. At one time she'd hope to heal it, before she'd been swept off her feet.

'But Joost, why are you closing the office - really? Dilwood was terribly vague, and you're not much help either.'

Joost sighed.

'Let's just say me and Dilwood are going our separate ways.'

They turned off the lights for the last time, and Joost pressed his office keys into Irena's hand.

'Here you might as well keep my set as well. I won't be back,' he said.

Outside it was still snowing.

'Well I guess this is it Joost, good luck.'

Irena was wearing a thick coat with a fake fur collar to keep her warm. She wore black boots up to her knees with patterned woolly tights and just for a moment, as she smiled at him, he regretted not having screwed her in the office. He tried to give her a peck on the cheek, but she turned away smiling, and waved the engagement ring he hadn't noticed.

'We're getting married next month,' she said 'I guess you could call it a whirlwind romance.'

Chapter Thirty Two

Themba was sitting on Joost shoulders, looking over the wall. They'd just seen Dilwood leave in a hurry, with their own car parked off road behind a barn.

'All clear,' said Themba, and he scrambled onto the stone wall.

Joost threw a bag of tools over; this was going to be a smash and grab.

The boundary was older than Dilwood's mansion. The first great Hall had been raised to the ground in 1790, and not rebuilt until the roaring twenties.

Joost reached for Themba's outstretched hand, and hauled himself onto the wall. But a gust of wind caught them unbalanced, and they fell into the thick snow on the other side. They dusted themselves down and laughed; nothing broken.

They could see the mansion in the distance, bathed in a green ghoulish light from the night lamps. The windows had a stone ledge underneath, and were equidistant from the entrance hall.

They used the trees for cover, but were conscious of the deep footprints they were leaving behind.

Soon they were on the edge of the fountain. There was a solitary bedroom light on upstairs, and Joost knew Mai would be at home.

'Let's go round the back,' whispered Joost.

They skirted around the country pile hopping from one bush to another.

'That's the dining room,' said Joost, pointing to the far end of the building, cloaked in darkness.

They slowly made their way across the snow, and examined the window. It was toughened glass, and there was no free edge to prise out the frame.

'Let's try another,' said Themba.

Next to the kitchen was a pantry with a small stained glass window. It was art deco, and the only pane Dilwood had not replaced. It was their only hope.

Joost wasn't a cat burglar, and felt fraudulent as he silently fumbled through his tool kit. Nonetheless he decided on using the old hand drill to chew into the wooden frame. He pushed the bent wire from a coat-hanger through the hole, and on the third attempt slid the latch across. He lifted up the window relieved, and Themba squeezed through the gap, but there was no space for Joost. For a moment they both stood still, but no alarm sounded to break the deadly silence.

'Themba,' whispered Joost, and again with no reply.

'Are you OK Themba?' he asked.

Finally Themba's arm twisted out of the window, and he pointed along the building back to the dining room.

'Got you,' said Joost and with the snow crunching painfully underfoot he made his way along the house.

The window was now unlocked, and Joost tumbled in head first.

The light switched on, and Themba was sitting down. He looked apologetic, and standing behind him was Mai, pointing a gun to his head.

'I saw you both on the CCTV as soon as you got over the wall,' said Mai 'I was surprised to see you though Joost.'

'Have you called the police?' was Joost's first thought.

'I think we both know Dilwood wouldn't want the police questioning you.'

'So what's the plan?' asked Joost 'wait for Dilwood to get back?'

'Don't be silly. I was hoping we could help each other,' said Mai.

'That's kind of awkward with a gun pointing at my friends head,' said Joost.

'Oh this,' said Mai 'it's just a toy,' and when she clicked the trigger a lighter flame shot out from the barrel.

Everyone smiled, although Themba was more relieved than most.

'Here let's all go and sit in the lounge,' said Mai 'I'll make us a drink.'

'Sorry Mai but not for us,' said Joost.

After what had happened to John he wasn't taking any chances.

'I understand,' said Mai 'Dela's been up to her tricks again, hasn't she.'

'You know?'

'Of course Joost. Don't you know Dilwood talks in his sleep?' said Mai. 'But then I guess you two aren't that close anymore.'

Joost glanced at the statue again.

'Be my guest,' said Mai.

Joost opened the glass door, and removed it.

'You said we could help you,' said Themba feeling a little left out.

'Could you?' she asked.

'If we can, but what would you want in return?' asked Joost.

'Only to get away from here,' said Mai.

'But you can walk out anytime,' said Joost.

'Not quite,' said Mai, and she lifted up her long dress.

There was a surveillance tag around her ankle.

'He'll know as soon as I leave the grounds or cut it free, and I've got nowhere else to go.'

'What about the police?' asked Themba.

'Where do you think he got the tag? His contacts would return me like a lost pet,' said Mai.

Joost was turning the statue in his hands.

'Is it the one?' asked Themba.

'Yes,' said Joost.

'If I'm still here when he gets back he'll kill me,' said Mai brushing away a tear.

'Don't worry you're coming with us,' said Joost.

Mai immediately hugged him.

'Let me pack a small bag,' she said.

'Quickly,' said Themba checking his watch.

They'd already spent too long, and no one knew for certain when Dilwood would be back.

With Mai upstairs, Joost walked along Dilwood's polished glass cabinets, before a silver chalice caught his eye. It had a shield on the front, but on its own it wasn't a trophy; it kept them. Joost curiously emptied the contents onto the dining table; a necklace, several pairs of ear-rings, a large thumb ring, a skull and crossbones brooch, and a souvenir he half recognised from Oxford; a bicycle reflector fashioned in the shape of a butterfly.

'I wonder how he would have remembered me?' asked Mai returning to the room.

'What do you know about this?' asked Joost picking up the bent bicycle reflector.

Mai smiled broadly.

'Lucy Middlemass. She's been here with her parents, and the others. Wonder what she'd think if she knew Dilwood had tried to kill her.'

'I wonder,' said Joost.

He took the butterfly, but left Dilwood's other souvenirs behind in the cabinet; now they really did have business between them.

At the edge of the wall, and with Bheki's statue in the bag, Joost cut Mai free. There was no sound, but they all knew wherever Dilwood was alarm bells were ringing. Mai hung tightly onto her little case; it was all she owned in the world.

Din was sitting in the car ahead of them, with a pretty brunette in the passenger seat, when the alarm sounded. Dilwood reached into the pocket of his beaver fur coat, and switched it off.

'What was that?' asked Vankoni.

'It's Mai,' replied Dilwood 'she's flown the coop. But don't worry she won't get far. Besides, it will be fun to see her brought back like a lost dog.'

Dilwood's misogyny was carefully veiled, although Mai knew long ago he hated women. In his mother's eyes he'd always been the reminder she wanted to forget, of the rapist that stole her innocence, and he had to take the punishment. In bed he was both selfish, and sadistic.

'Din, I still can't believe we found one another,' said the brunette.

'I know, it's incredible isn't it.'

'Have you fixed a date yet?' she asked.

'For?'

'The wedding silly. Don't tell me you've forgotten.'

'Of course not,' said Din 'that's why I've brought you here.'

They were on the edge of a forest covered in snow, and with a full moon hanging low in the sky before them.

'Din you're so romantic,' and she kissed him on the cheek.

'Where did Joost say he was going?' asked Din looking out of the car window.

Irena tried to hide her annoyance, but at times it seemed Din was more interested in her old boss than her, even though they'd never met.

'He wouldn't say Din.'

'What, nothing at all?'

Din was fuming with rage, and she had never seen him like this. He was always sweet as pie.

'No.'

'Surely he must have said something, or given you an idea?' His voice was booming.

'I'm sorry Din, but he wouldn't say anything. Can we please talk about the wedding instead.'

Din calmed down immediately, and for a second he valued her love.

'No I'm the one who's sorry Irena. I know you wouldn't lie to me, and you really are a lovely girl. But please understand, it's not in my hands anymore.'

Din looked terribly sad.

'What do you mean Din?' asked Irena, but he couldn't speak.

He just banged the car horn, and Vankoni and Dilwood drove up behind them.

'Din what's going on?' asked Irena, but he just stepped out of the car, leaving her all alone.

'Din you're scaring me,' she shouted as he walked away, but it was all too late.

Din walked into the woods to clear his head, whilst Vankoni and Dilwood dragged her out of the car.

Din had wanted to shout 'make it quick' to Vankoni, but he couldn't even do that after all the muti murders. It was the first time screams, anyone's screams, had pierced his heart. They chopped out her atlas bone for Dela, glad they'd donned plastic aprons.

They buried Irena in an unmarked grave, deep in the forest. And with it the last vestige of humanity that Din owned.

Chapter Thirty Three

Bheki and Eudy weren't at the flat when they returned, but they hadn't moved out just yet; it was midnight prayer at The Church of Loving Saints.

'You want me to stay here?' asked Mai.

The cramped conditions were a stark reminder of what she had left behind.

'Don't worry they're moving out tomorrow,' said Themba.

'In the morning,' said Joost, and he went into the bedroom, to place the statue he had next to Bheki's.

They made a pretty pair.

'Then where do I go?' Mai asked Themba.

'Are you the praying type?' he asked.

'Only in difficult times,' she replied.

'In that case let's go to church.'

There was someone on the door; the biggest guy in the flock. The church was neither a rehab nor drop in centre. But if you were serious about worship you were welcome. Joost, Themba, and Mai, were greeted with smiles and handshakes as they arrived.

Bheki had been nervously watching the entrance form the back of the church, and saw them arrive. She waved her hand in the air.

'Over there,' said Themba, and he rushed to Eudy's side, and the bump.

Bheki got up from her seat to hug Joost.

'Did you get it?' she whispered in his ear.

His broad smile gave her the answer.

Bheki held Mai's hands, and in the look that passed between them knew she had left Dilwood.

'Don't worry,' she said 'we'll take care of you.'

Mai had been in the country for years, but felt like a poor new arrival, lost and scavenging. She had to remind herself of Dilwood's threats.

Pastor Abel Goodyear held the microphone on stage, and was mumbling into it.

'Save them Lord, and lead them out of bondage,' he prayed.

If only he could lead Bheki into it, thought Joost.

'Let them not dress in borrowed robes dear Lord,' the pastor glanced at Joost 'but remain true to your divine guidance.'

'He wants to see you afterwards' said Bheki, looking proudly at Joost.

Themba gave him the thumbs up.

When the prayers had finished, in the early hours of the morning, Pastor Goodyear made a beeline for Joost; the two men faced one another.

'Come, we must talk,' said Abel.

The pastor saw the momentary concern in Joost's eyes.

'Don't worry they can come along too. The prophetess will look after them.'

The prophetess, also known as Miriam Goodyear, was the pastor's wife.

Joost was chauffeured to the pastor's West London residence, with the others following at the rear.

They sat in the back, making small talk on the way. Joost was convinced there was much more to the pastor than met the eye, and was struck by his two gold rings; they were thick enough to be knuckle dusters. Each was on a middle finger; the right bore a crucifix, the left OSY.

Joost and Abel were on the middle floor, in the study of the large house. The pastor picked up a cigar from the lacquered box, and offered one to Joost.

'No thanks,' said Joost.

'A glass of brandy then?' asked Abel.

Joost nodded, and Abel poured two very large glasses. They sat across from one another in the green leather chairs.

'It seems that you lead a very interesting life Joost.'

'You could say that,' said Joost.

'And what would you say?'

'Cursed,' but then he paused for a moment 'apart from Bheki that is.'

'She's quite a girl isn't she? And a nice big ass too.'

Abel winked. Ordinarily it wasn't what you'd expect from a man of the cloth, but Abel Goodyear wasn't an ordinary pastor.

'Tell me,' asked Abel 'what's she like in bed? As good as she looks?'

'Better,' said Joost grinning.

'So you do have some things to smile about. But I do know of the sadness in your heart,' said Abel.

'From Bheki?' asked Joost.

'A little, but not all. My wife contacts the Spirits on occasion.'

'Voodoo Spirits?' asked Joost.

'Yes but not Petro, Rada.'

'Is there a difference?' asked Joost.

'Dela Eden Obi is a Petro high priestess. Rada voodoo doesn't kill or injure, it nurtures, protects, loves.'

'Is that why you wear the OSY charm?' asked Joost.

'Of course.'

'But I thought you were a Christian,' said Joost.

'I am that too, but it's all the same. There is good, and then there is evil. It doesn't matter who builds the fence in the middle, only which side you are on.'

Joost got his point, and Abel was certainly prospering from his religious philosophy.

'But what about your congregation?' asked Joost.

'They also see no difference. Prayer offers the chance to connect with the divine.'

They both took another sip of brandy. A golden striped cat pushed the door open, and sauntered confidently into the room, looking at them both.

'A friend of yours?' asked Joost.

'Indeed, he comes and goes as he pleases. Sometimes we don't see him for months; he's probably come to see you.'

'Actually I think he's Baka,' added Abel, almost whispering.

'Baka?' asked Joost.

'A protective Spirit that takes the form of an animal. But be warned he's also evil, and can turn on his owner bringing misfortune.'

The cat jumped onto Abel's lap, and he stroked it gently.

'Perhaps he has brought you and Dela together to fight it out,' said Abel.

The cat purred, and Joost recognised its green eyes from the time outside his window.

'So you know about Dela,' said Joost.

'Naturally. She's famous in certain circles. But not everyone knows about the muti,' and he tapped the side of his nose.

'In fact,' said Abel 'she's my biggest competitor, which is why I have brought you here.'

Joost readied himself. Already he knew he couldn't disappoint Bheki, and that in turn meant he couldn't let Abel down.

'My church has been built on donations, and I wish to repay a debt of gratitude to three of my benefactors.'

'And you think I can help?' asked Joost.

'Yes, indirectly. But the real help would come from one John Lacey.'

'The crocodile mask,' said Joost.

The pastor smiled.

'Bheki has told you?' asked Joost.

'I am her pastor Joost, but please don't be angry with her.'

Joost cherished her too much to be cross, and in a way he was pleased that Abel believed too.'

'Please explain,' said Joost.

'The three individuals I have in mind have all lost precious ones.'

Joost knew how they felt.

'The Prophetess has tried in vain to contact them. But I feel Mr Lacey would have more success, as he's already on the other side.'

Joost saw the look of hope in Abel's eyes, and already he didn't want to disappoint him, but was it possible? After all John had never brought Stella and Hildy forth.

'I can try,' said Joost 'when did you have in mind?'

'Tomorrow night.'

'I'm still trying to find a place for Mai,' bargained Joost.

'The little Asian girl can stay here' said Abel.

'It's a deal,' said Joost.

'Bravo,' said Abel, pouring them both another large brandy. 'And by the way, my friends know all the right people. Bheki's statues are up for auction soon, are they not?'

There was just one small problem, Joost was running out of heroin; he'd just have to let John know on the night.

Joost finally joined the others downstairs. Bheki and Mai had rekindled their friendship, and the prophetess offered Mai temporary residence.

Daylight filtered through the kitchen blinds, as the cook made them breakfast. Bheki wondered if Joost was upset. He wasn't, though he intended to spank that ass that everyone seemed to admire.

Joost was still drawn to the hotel Mephisto; it looked seedy and desperate. And he now had a bargaining chip with Bheki, Pastor Goodyear's goodwill.

Chapter Thirty Four

James Middlemass was sitting across from Eve in The Crossed Heart bar. Eve might have expected James to be staring deeply into her eyes whenever she spoke, or at least be rubbing his foot against hers underneath the table; something he was quite fond of doing at church meetings. But far from it; James was staring at the student help, and glass washer, behind the bar.

'He's not rinsing them properly,' said James.

'For God's sake James does it matter,' said an exasperated Eve.

Of course it didn't matter, and before last week it wouldn't have mattered to James either. But when he helped to kill Lance with an iron he had, after all, wished to improve his domestic skills.

James looked at Eve's cassock, and at last she thought she had his attention. That crease needs ironing out he thought.

'I'd love to do your laundry,' said James.

Eve laughed loudly, and thinking it was just another one of his kinks that he kept surprising her with; still it was better than the anal sex she pretended to enjoy. And what was it about him anyway? She was undeniably drawn to him like a moth to a flame, but she couldn't understand why.

'James when are you going to leave her?' asked Eve, referring to Christine.

'I can't do it until the new year,' said James.

This wasn't a surprise to Eve. After all there was poor Lucy to consider, and then all the Christmas services; nativity plays, carol singing, raffles, and the rest. She wasn't a hard hearted bitch, but she had to have him, and all to herself.

'But you are going to leave her?' she asked.

'Of course,' he replied smiling.

Eve tried to hold his hand under the table, but there were other parishioners in the pub, and James still didn't know who'd reported him to the Bishop. Nonetheless Eve grabbed his reluctant hand.

James' ardour was cooling. The Bishop had fired a warning shot across his bows, Christine had a lover of her own, and now his only financial security lay in staying with the church. He needed to undo the spell he held over Eve, and to stop her from hanging on his every word.

Eve could tell something was amiss, and felt insecure. She held onto the locket that James had bought her, always worn around her neck. It contained a little part of his heart he had said, and inside was a piece of what looked like red leather.

'Do you still want me James?' she asked with thoughts of hanging herself in St Agnes at the back of her besotted mind.

'Yes my love,' he replied 'you are always uppermost in my thoughts.'

But in reality his mind was far away. The curtains needed ironing he thought, and tonight. He'd worked through everything else in the house; clothes, bed linen, and even the towels.

'Here let me take another look at the locket,' said James.

'Why?' asked Eve.

'I was thinking of having it inscribed, that's all.'

'James you're so thoughtful,' and she pecked him on the cheek.

'Eve please, we have to be careful,' and he looked across at the packed bar.

Bill was standing there, and he beckoned James towards him.

'I won't be a minute,' said James, and he took the locket with him.

'In the kitchen,' said Bill.

Bill entered from the back of the bar, and James joined him through the 'staff only' door.

'I hope you know what you're doing James,' said Bill.

James smiled uncomfortably.

'Look I'm not worried about you sleeping around, but don't tell the poor girl any of our secrets,' said Bill.

'Never,' said James 'scouts honour.'

Bill wasn't convinced, and quite liked Eve himself. He really didn't want her to end up as one of Dela's offerings.

James glanced down the kitchen at the freezer, which first held John, and now Lance too.

'Are we OK to speak?' asked James.

'Don't worry about them, they can't hear us from here,' said Bill.

'Anyway to be honest Bill I want shot of the woman. I thought she was what I needed, but look at me I'm an old man; we'd be a laughing stock together,' said James.

'It doesn't matter what other people think James, but you're right it wouldn't work,' then he paused 'without Dela's magic that is.'

They both smiled.

'Look James you've had your fun, but now get rid eh.'

James looked down at the locket in his hand. If he got rid of Josh Templemead's shrunken tongue from inside, then Eve would no longer swoon at his call. He took out the 'piece of his heart', and held it in his fist.

'Bill you know I've always wondered, but what is it that Dela does for you?' asked James.

James surmised some sordid sex goings on with the slightly effeminate Felix involved, and he wasn't the only one.

'I'm just waiting on a promise, that's all,' said Bill, and he remained tight lipped.

Bill and Barbara had a fear. It wasn't unnatural, but it loomed large in their lives, permeated everything they did. In spite of knowing there was a Spirit world, or perhaps because of it, they were terrified of death. Dela had promised to return them from the grave, once she had found the key.

Dela had been toying with Joost like a cat with a mouse, and the Spirits had foretold the crossing of their paths long ago, although not by name. She didn't know how, but Joost would lead her to that very key in which Bill had placed so much faith. Joost was also destined to help her decipher its power, somehow.

James stepped back into the crammed bar. Barbara rushed by with her hands full, bumping into him. His palm opened, and out flew the tongue. He couldn't be expected to grab it back, or even look for it on the plate for that matter, but he was a little taken aback when Barbara placed the scampi and chips in front of Susie Chang. Mr Pandalay threw James a wink; unlike the vicar he wasn't remiss to put his hand on his mistress' knee.

'I believe that's mine,' said Eve stretching out her hand.

Really James should have put it back around her neck, but they both understood their predicament.

James took another swig from his pint glass, before placing it on the beer mat.

'Honestly,' he said 'this table's filthy.'

'James if that's all you have to say I'm off,' and she looked at him in a different way.

His silky patter had gone, and she was no longer bewitched. In fact he made her feel uncomfortable, and all the things he'd made her do. But he hadn't made her, she'd wanted to explore his kinkiest fetishes, and he had plenty of them - but why? She no longer understood.

'James I really am going,' she said 'and don't worry you can stay here, I'll make my own way home.'

Eve looked over her shoulder. Thank goodness he hadn't followed her out. If he had groped her she'd have probably died of fright. And to think, she'd given it to him on a plate.

James watched her go and grinned. At last it was over, but he didn't like the way Susie Chang was staring at him.

John Lacey smiled ruefully to himself. James Middlemass, the priest who had stolen his childhood was one of Dela's followers. Now why had that surprised him?

John wanted to talk, but Lance had gone to see his wife again. Her jealous lover was smouldering, although not with passion. He'd killed Sharon and then himself with a knife covered in Lance's prints. Now she could return to Lance's arms whilst her killer languished in the dark place with the other tormented souls.

'Felix, thanks for coming, I'll be in touch later today,' said the matron.

With The Caring Hands Nursing Agency closed, Felix had picked himself another permanent job. It was elderly, but at least he'd been promised no lifting. Dela thought he was mad, but he hated asking her for hand outs, besides it was only three nights a week.

Felix scanned the residents in the lounge on his way out. Five of them were already dressed in pyjamas, sitting along the back wall like store room dummies, with two more arguing purposelessly in the middle of the floor; it looked like his kind of place.

Bheki placed the two statues in the scruffiest bag she could find. She was riding the tube to the auction house, and wanted them raising as little attention as possible. Pastor Goodyear had already pulled some strings, and they were going to be appraised this morning. If they were genuine they would make the revised catalogue, and the next auction. She said a little prayer for grandma Akuaa and Joost; one was her past, and the other she hoped would be her future - for this morning at least.

Chapter Thirty Five

Bheki threw her cases onto the bed, and almost fell on top of them. She quickly regained her balance knowing if she had fallen Joost would have pounced on top of her. Not as if she would have minded, but she just had to have some clean bed linen first. No one was picking up the phone, and Joost went to the lobby to arrange some.

Talking to Mr Wheatley behind the desk were the same two ladies who had taken such a shine to Joost at the breakfast table. When they finally turned to leave they were without their make-up or their scarves. Well I never, thought Joost - tranny's!

'No problem at all Sir. I shall get Mr Crowley to bring it up.'

'Oh and Sir,' said Mr Wheatley, as Joost readied to turn around 'Madam Fang Fong's here at the weekend. She's a real pro,' and he winked.

Neither Joost, nor any guest for that matter, could miss the horrendous posters of Madam Fang Fong that hung everywhere, leaving little escape.

'Not my cup of tea,' replied Joost.

'That's what they all say Sir, at the beginning,' said Mr Wheatley, as Joost headed to the bar for a quick drink.

Before Joost returned to their room Mr Crowley had delivered the new linen, and Bheki had made the bed. She was in the bathroom undressing as Joost placed a twenty pound note on the pillowcase; she was in for one hell of a pounding. And whether it was the décor or just the sentiment, but Bheki was feeling like a hooker again; the bed was clean, but the day would be dirty.

'Here, you've been good,' said Joost, and he slipped another twenty into Bheki's pants.

She could have remonstrated, but she was feeling too sleazy, and licked Joost's face.

'I guess we should rest now,' said Joost, lying back on the bed, finally worn out.

'Must we?' asked Bheki.

'For a little while.'

Bheki was borderline manic depressive, and when she flipped either side of the line it brought out her inner hooker. Joost preferred her depressed though, she was easier to control.

On the way to Pastor Abel's, Joost stopped the car at an ornate village post box surrounded with Ivy, and pushed in a little packet addressed to Lucy Middlemass. Inside was a bent bicycle reflector, and a message - 'Dilwood's still a bad driver.'

Pastor Abel was in the dining room.

'They'll be here in an hour. Anyone care for a bite to eat?' he asked.

'I don't think I could take anything else in,' said Bheki.

'What have you got?' asked Joost.

'Well Mai does some great Chinese food,' said Abel.

'It's Thai,' said Bheki 'she's from Thailand.'

'Really,' said Abel 'anyway the foods great; although I think Plackcedes is a little jealous.'

Plackcedes was their cook.

Abel went to the door, and shouted his wife who duly arrived

'Miriam, ask Mai to bring us in some bites, nice and hot.'

'Drinks anyone?' asked Miriam.

'Cola please,' said Joost.

'Make that two,' said Bheki 'I've been working up a thirst all day.'

'And something to cool your tongue dear,' said Miriam to Abel.

'Another cola,' he said with twinkle in his eye, and he carefully watched her ass leave the room.

'So how's this going to work Joost?' asked Abel.

'I was hoping you were going to tell me,' replied Joost

'You're the magician my boy. Just tell me what you need,' said Abel, as Mai brought in the food, and three colas with ice.

'Let me think,' said Joost.

Disguise and deceit were soon rejected as devices, leaving John to do his thing once Joost had beckoned him forth. The problem was there were only two packets of John's calling card left; Joost couldn't use them both so that left ten minutes for each visitor - period.

The mask was centre stage, in the middle of the dining table. Joost, Abel, two large African men, one slightly more portly than the other, and a sombre Englishman who gave his name as Frank Sleigh impersonator, sat around, and equally spaced. The order of service had already been designated, and all eyes fell upon Joost as he inhaled his snuff.

John Lacey was a little taken aback at the numbers, and felt like the freak at a travelling carnival.

'Sorry John I haven't got time to explain, but can you help my friends? asked Joost.

The 'friends' tried to hide their horror at the diminutive reptile, even though they'd been pre-warned.

'Are you sure their friends Joost?' asked John.

'Acquaintances then,' said Joost.

He didn't really have time for semantics.

John could sense Joost's urgency.

'Alright Joost let's have it,' said John.

'In a nutshell, three grieving gentleman with three dearly departed to contact,' said Joost.

John sighed, and was glad that Joost only had one packet remaining. Otherwise he would be touring the globe like Harry Houdini, who incidentally was a barrel of laughs.

'Let's get going,' said John.

Pastor Goodyear held a stopwatch in front of him.

'Ten minutes each gentleman,' he announced, and the séance conveyor belt began.

The first had lost a wife, the second contacted his dead mother, wanting to know where the will was hidden. But the most poignant reuniting was Frank's, who like Joost had lost a daughter; through leukaemia aged just 14. His was also the most tearful.

The widowed gentleman had a second wife to console him, although no more as he learned she'd poisoned his favourite wife. And the lost son discovered the will was hiding behind a painting of his step-sister, which wasn't a good sign.

'Thank you and farewell,' said John, who'd actually enjoyed his moment of fame.

'Be careful Joost,' was the last thing they all heard, as the little crocodile froze before their eyes.

If Joost wondered why John hadn't found Stella and Hildy so quickly, John was saved from saying they weren't ready for the heartache.

Frank was still rubbing his sore eyes as the pastor escorted the two African gentlemen to the front door. They shook his hand exuberantly.

'Now don't forget the auction,' said Abel referring to Bheki's statues.

'Do not worry Abel,' said the most portly 'it has been well and truly earned.'

'Is there the chance of another visit to see our dearest?' asked the other gentleman.

'I wish there were,' replied Abel 'but unfortunately the means to such an end ran out tonight.'

As much as he trusted the Pastor, which in truth wasn't as much as Bheki would have liked, Joost hadn't mentioned the solitary remaining packet; after all it could save their lives.

Frank Sleigh was dabbing away the eyeliner that had ran onto his cheeks. He was in his early fifties, and already divorced, when his daughter had died. He'd piled on the pounds recently, but wore a girdle to hold in his stomach. Joost looked at him, there was something familiar about the face but he couldn't quite place it.

Bheki came back to join them.

'Ready to eat my dear?' Abel asked her.

Bheki shook her head.

'We've got to go Abel,' said Joost 'some unfinished business.'

'It's alright Joost, and thanks for sharing John. What are you going to do with him now?' asked Abel.

'I guess I'll keep the mask as a souvenir, now all the powder has gone.'

Had the Pastor tried to catch him out thought Joost, and why was Frank staring at him so intensely?

'Yes, and thank you from me,' said Frank 'although it wasn't easy.'

'It's hard to let go of love,' said Joost.

'I know, but at least she's OK' said Frank.

A look was exchanged between them that could only be shared between two grieving father's.

Bheki was feeling miffed, but at least this time Joost didn't hold onto his melancholy. He was depressed sure enough, but Bheki had the antidote in her pants, and if he was feeling guilty then hell she had no objection to beating him black and blue. In the beginning she'd found it disconcerting with clients, but it hadn't taken her too long to enjoy it. And maybe she'd uncover the not so secret camera in their hotel room too, and let Wheatley and Crowley in on the show. Bheki smiled to herself, when the mood took her she could be a real bitch.

Chapter Thirty Six

Lucy buttered more toast, and with the plate balanced on her lap wheeled herself back to the breakfast table. As always, Christine had left today's newspaper, and any mail, on the table. There were two items of correspondence; one from an old university friend, she recognised the hand writing, and the other a small packet.

Damn she'd forgotten the jam, and without thinking stood up, and walked towards the fridge. She grabbed the jar, and just as she returned to the table her legs began to buckle. She fell into her cradle.

'Oh my God,' she said aloud, although there was no one to hear her; the house was vacuous.

She leant forwards on the edge of her chair, and pushed her legs to the ground. She couldn't stand again, but there were only two slices of Dela's cake left; soon she would have no need of her chair.

She ripped open the top of the packet, clawing inside like a bear for honey. Then it reappeared - a bicycle reflector fashioned in the shape of a butterfly, by a love struck beau, who'd faded into the background after the accident.

She'd never asked about the wreckage on the lane, and always assumed the police had mopped it up; so where had this come from? And who'd posted it? She looked down at the scribbled note on the table 'Dilwood's still a bad driver.'

Did it mean Dilwood Benson had run her over? After all there weren't that many Dilwood's around. But who would know of their association, and who in heaven's name had posted it? She twisted the butterfly in her hand, and a gentle smile sat upon her face. Maybe next year she would continue her studies, after all, she could say she'd been to Lourdes.

Felix sighed as he drove up the hill to The Cedars Care Home. He had mixed emotions. It was nice to be nursing, if you could avoid the hands on, and sleep through the night. However the patients could still be demanding, and more often than not he had a short fuse. He made his way to the staff room where matron was waiting.

'Hi Felix.'

'Caroline,' he acknowledged in return.

She was smart and courteous, had always dreamt of being a nurse. She genuinely cared for her patient's, and lived and breathed the nursing code. She was the antithesis of Felix.

'I'll get the carers,' she said.

Ten minutes later, Felix was facing his night staff; Janet, Tina, and Roy. They were all in their forties, spick and span, and talked about the residents as though they were old friends. It wasn't a good start, but perhaps they were trying to impress.

'Ready for bed Harold?' asked Janet in the TV room.

'Not yet,' he replied, and Janet went along the line.

Felix was disappointed, watching in horror as no one was frog marched to bed.

Felix continued giving out the meds from the trolley, and Roy helped him recognise the patients, whilst Janet and Tina made the teas.

Throughout the night hourly checks were completed. Those that needed turning were, and none of the buzzers were disabled. The staff slept, but only on their hour break; there were plenty of other jobs to do. Sort out the laundry, prepare the breakfast tables, and for Felix, check the care plans.

Felix hated it, and already it was making him ill. Even though he never lifted a patient his back was playing up. Psychosomatic, but nonetheless he wasn't coming back.

There was one chink of light, when he was forced to change a dressing on Gertrude Souza; a dear old lady in her eighties, racked with arthritis. She'd led an exemplary life, spending much of her fortune on the needy. But it wasn't pleasant having others clean your mess, and she felt embarrassed by the loss of dignity. She wanted a way out, and somehow sensed Felix could help.

'Kill me,' she whispered in his ear, as Tina stood at the end of the bed holding her new dressing.

Felix hated this; his work scrutinised by the carers.

'Are you alright Gertrude?' asked Tina.

'She's fine,' snapped Felix.

'Actually can you check on Alice for me,' he said 'she sounded a bit chesty earlier on.'

'Sure,' said Tina, marching off.

'What did you say dear?' asked Felix.

'Please, kill me,' wheezed Gertrude.

Felix wasn't sure if this was a good thing or bad. He'd never actually murdered anyone who'd asked for it; then again there was always a first time.

'Don't be silly dear,' he eventually said.

'I helped in the war you know,' said Gertrude.

'Good for you,' replied Felix.

This tittle tattle always got Felix's goat.

'I could see it in the soldier's eyes, those that had killed.'

Felix knew where Gertrude was going, so he helped her along.

'I'm a nurse dear, not a killer.'

'I can tell,' said Gertrude unperturbed 'the others won't do it, there too gentle, but you, you've killed before.'

'That's ridiculous,' said Felix.

'We'll see,' said Gertrude smiling.

Break time, and Gertrude's words were still going through Felix's head. Should he, dare he? He'd never killed anyone on his first day, but then again he wasn't coming back. In the end he decided to leave with a bang.

She didn't fight as the pillow blocked out the light. Felix mopped his brow, and went to join the others in the lounge.

'How did you get on with Gertrude?' asked Tina.

'Did she ask you to kill her as well?' asked Janet.

From the expression on Ralph's face they knew she had.

'Let me guess,' said Roy, and he mocked Gertrude's voice 'I could see it in the soldier's eyes, those that had killed. The others won't do it but you're a killer, I can tell.'

'Don't worry Felix, she says it to all the new staff. No one's killed her yet though,' said Janet.

As morning arrived Felix felt even more anxious, and insisted on checking the patients alone.

'Everyone's fine, no incidences to report, and I've updated Winifred's care plan,' he handed over.

Caroline was disappointed with his rush to escape, but it was only his first shift, and perhaps he was exhausted.

'See you tonight,' said Caroline, as Felix left.

Not a cat in hell's chance he thought, and nearly flew to his car.

When he got home Dela was holding up the phone 'it's Cedars,' she said.

'Hi Felix, its Caroline here, matron at Cedars.'

He could tell from her voice something was wrong.

'Hi Caroline,' said Felix.

'Bad news I'm afraid, we found Gertrude dead this morning. Can you come in this afternoon, and write a report.'

'Of course,' he replied, and before he could add 'what a shame' Caroline had put down the phone.

Felix looked terrified. Was his predilection about to catch up with him?

'Have you been a naughty boy again?' asked Dela.

Felix nodded.

'It's not your fault sweetie,' she said 'it's mine. I've just let you have too much freedom. Anyway don't worry, it'll be swept under the carpet like all the others, mark my words.'

Felix felt relieved; after all Dela was rarely wrong.

'But Felix, I must reign in your impulses.'

Felix felt a knot in his stomach.

'From now on you must wear this,' and she held up a clear plastic chastity cage - a CB6000s to be precise. The s stood for small.

'But Dela ...'

She held a finger to her mouth.

'No protestations Felix. Here I'll even help you put it on.'

Soon the tiny padlock was snapped shut, and Dela put the key on a chain around her neck.

'There, now no more squabbling, and if I think you've been a good boy I might even unlock you - now and again.'

Felix sighed. Torture with relief was one thing, but this was purgatory.

Dela was right, and, although Caroline was disappointed, there was no evidence of foul play. Felix was naturally saddened, and wondered aloud if he could have done anything better, but they were both relieved he wouldn't be coming back. As for the doctor, another death certificate helped pay for that golf club he was missing, and he needed something to catch up with Gasper Owido; his swing had improved tremendously recently.

Chapter Thirty Seven

'It's too short,' said Mr Pandalay, referring to Susie Chang's hem line.

'Pandy honestly,' she said exasperated 'it's either too short, too revealing or too flirty. I've got to wear something darling.'

'I wish you weren't going at all,' said a miserable looking Pandy.

'I know, but it's the one night of the year I get to go out on my own.'

'Look I know I'm being a real meanie, but do you have to go this year?' asked Pandy; just as he always did.

He was sitting on the edge of the bed, and next to a pile of clothes Susie had taken out of the wardrobe to try. There were plenty more inside.

'But Sin-derella must go to the ball,' said Susie. 'Anyway help me choose some heels, I think I like this dress the best.'

'Well at least take a coat,' said Pandy 'you might catch your death.'

'You're so concerned,' said Susie, and she kissed him on the forehead.

'And don't worry I'll phone to let you know I'm alright,' she said.

Susie was choosing her outfit for tonight's event in Steeple's End at the hotel Mephisto, and she couldn't wait.

Charles Carney was propped up against the sink, whist Lucy made them both a cup of tea.

'I can only stand for five minutes at a time,' she said 'but tomorrow I should be able to throw away that chair,' and she cast a cursory glance at her wheelchair.

'All thanks to Dela,' said Charles sombrely.

Charles had filled the void since Gladys' demise, and given Lucy another shoulder to lean on.

'Yes, Dela,' said Lucy, although there wasn't a tone of thanks in her voice either.

'Charles do you think the means always justify the end?' Lucy asked.

She didn't know all the grisly details of the cake, and she didn't want too, but she knew Dela well enough to know it wouldn't be pretty.

'I used to, but not any longer,' replied Charles, looking at the cacti on the window ledge.

He must get some more bonsai trees he thought. He was becoming a real devil with the secateurs.

Lucy sat back in her chair, and Charles joined her at the table on a pine stool. He rubbed his scalp.

'I miss Gladys you know,' he said.

'Me too,' said Lucy.

'Who knows maybe I'll be next?' he said.

After the bonfire this was a thought that had crossed everyone's mind, apart from Bill's and Barbara.

'Hey guess what, I got this in the post the other day,' said Lucy, changing the conversation.

She put the bicycle reflector on the table.

'It's from my accident,' she said.

Charles picked it up.

'So who's it from?' he asked a little intrigued.

'That's just it. I don't know. But there was a rather cryptic message in the same package.'

'Go on,' said Charles.

'Dilwood's still a bad driver.'

'Well I only know one Dilwood, and I suspect you do too' said Charles.

'Yes, Dilwood Benson.'

'Of course someone could be trying to stir up trouble, but come to think of it he does own a nursing home in Oxford,' said Charles.

He got up to rinse his cup in the sink.

'Well I can't ask him outright, can I?' asked Lucy.

'You could,' said Charles.

'But what if he freaks out?'

168

'Well then you know he's the one that hit you,' said Charles, looking out into the garden and all the wonderful shrubbery.

'And then what do I do?' she asked.

'That's entirely up to you. What am I supposed to do about Gladys?' he said.

Lucy lamented.

'We're all Dela's prisoners,' she said.

'Perhaps. It's that pesky cat again,' said Charles, and he opened the window.

'Shoo,' he shouted, and the golden striped moggy stared back unmoved.

'Damn cheek of it,' said Charles 'it's already left two dead birds on my lawn.'

Charles opened the back door, but the cat was gone. He soon followed, back to his lonely house.

Felix was trussed up on the bed like a Xmas turkey. Although the cage was a permanent annoyance, he actually felt more awake; no longer the subject of Dela's regular draining's. The lingerie still felt a ridiculous, partly because he was overweight, but he could get used to it - as long as it was their secret.

'Wear these darling,' and Dela stuck a pair of wireless headphones on his head.

Felix knew what to expect, and he was blindfolded with one of Dela's rather exquisite head scarves; perfumed too.

Their next door neighbour was another £100 short on the skin lightening creams she applied morning and night. Unfortunately her doting son, the croupier, was no longer in a position to slide some chips across the gaming table, due a rather unfortunate incident at a public convenience. So Dela left him in the bedroom with Felix, who was duly mounted like a horse.

'Oh my, Dela,' said Felix as the remuneration began, and the choristers on the CD sang 'Hallelujah'.

Dela heard them from the bathroom next door, and whilst admiring herself in the mirror. There wasn't even the faintest trace of a line; not on the forehead, around the eyes, or in the corners of her mouth. And cake was supposed to be bad for you!

Eventually there was a loud groan from the croupier, and the bedroom door opened. He looked sheepish, and Dela whispered 'let's keep it our little secret' as she let him out.

Now should she undo the padlock, and give Felix a reward? But he was so much more attentive. No, let him wait a little longer; perhaps even a month or two. She took out her camera to remember the moment, and who knows maybe she'd even post it online.

Joost was surprised how much time he was spending in church. Of course the delectable Bheki Ncube was the bait, or rather had been. But he felt a change. Perhaps it was Pastor Goodyear, or perhaps it was John, and knowing Stella and Hildy still existed. Or maybe plain and simple he needed help, and had nowhere else to turn.

Joost managed to fit his car in the last available space near The Church of Loving Saints, and began to walk the short distance up the street. It was nearly midnight; he was feeling tired, and hoped Bheki would to return to their hotel to sleep.

'That looks like him,' said Jimmy.

Dino grabbed the knife, but Jimmy grabbed his arm.

'Wait, I can't be certain yet,' said Jimmy.

Joost took a few more paces forwards.

'It's him,' said Jimmy, and they both stepped out of the van.

Joost could see them approaching in the twilight. He was on his guard, quick enough to dodge the blade. He kicked one of them in the groin before turning around, and Dino fell to the floor in agony. Joost ran, leading them away from Bheki.

When he turned the corner Joost realised it was a dead end. Two men lurched towards him, and he said a little prayer next to the fire exit, and a poster of Pastor Goodyear.

The side door opened, and a portly African gentleman stepped out. Dino was caught by surprise, and his arm was snapped like a pencil; his screams drowned out by the 'singing preacher'. Jimmy reached for the knife, but was kneed in the face for his trouble. Joost stepped over them both to thank his friend.

'Now that's what I call a miracle,' said Joost.

The African smiled, and tilted his trilby. The would be assassins were sprawled on the pavement, and Joost recognised Jimmy. He smiled; black eyes looked far better than black magic.

'Jimmy,' said Dino at the accident and emergency unit 'maybe it's time for you to look for another girl.'

'I couldn't agree more bro,' mumbled Jimmy, holding the icepack over his broken nose.

He'd never passed one exam back home. Then again he'd never sat an exam back home. He'd always been too busy herding goats, or looking after his younger siblings. But now Vankoni was trawling through the web for courses.

He twisted the pen Christine had bought him through his long bony fingers. But what interested him? Medicine? He'd spent so long taking life maybe he could start saving it. Then again Felix was a nurse, and he wasn't exactly the caring type. Physics? That's where Christine had started, but they weren't a meeting of minds, more like a collision of bodies. Heavenly maybe, observed definitely.

He scrolled down the page, stopping at chemical engineering; after all he'd helped Dilwood cut his latest shipment. He was about to hit the print button when Christine sent a text - 'b ready in 5'.

Vankoni raised his eyes to the ceiling, where was it this time? Dogging, some hotel with a morning show for the maid, or in Beaustead Park again, moaning for the tramps?

Chapter Thirty Eight

Some days were better than others for Frank Sleigh. Today the past was hidden under a layer of slap, and he had become another person. His driver placed his bags in the boot, and they headed for the hotel Mephisto.

His heart had nearly bled dry for Alison, but not for his ex-wife. His mother once asked why he always picked selfish women, but he was only copying the model she had given him. Anyway she no longer had to worry; he'd given up women for Herman, a Brazilian bartender, and he had a proposal to give during his show tonight.

There were a lot of comings and goings in the passageway outside their hotel room, and Joost could see from the window that the car park was full. It was Saturday night, and time for Madam Fang Fong's cabaret; it was her farewell performance.

'Is he, or she, here yet?' asked Bheki smirking.

She'd never been done by a tranny - yet.

'There's a Rolls-Royce arriving. I think that could be her,' said Joost.

There was a loud cheer as the car door opened, and out stepped the vaunted female impersonator that was the dear Madam.

'Looks like we'll be safe, at least for another night,' said Bheki.

She was missing her flat, her possessions, and Eudy.

'Joost I don't know if I can stay here much longer,' she said.

Joost could easily keep it up, but Bheki knew that.

'Let's give it a couple more days, and then decide,' said Joost.

That's if Bheki still wanted him; she did blow hot and cold.

'OK, but come and cheer me up,' she said lying back on the bed 'then I'll let you go and get a drink.'

Joost obliged, after all what was a man supposed to do?

He left Bheki purring on the pillows, and went downstairs for a bottle of bourbon. At the bar there was a big furore surrounding a blonde beehive. When their eyes met they both smiled in recognition.

'Darling I had no idea,' said Frank Sleigh AKA Madam Fang Fong.

She rolled back her eyelashes; after all, she had to camp it up for her adoring fans.

'I'm here with Bheki,' said Joost, pushing through the small crowd of admirers.

'Oh,' replied Frank, a little disappointed.

He held a pen for autographs underneath his false red nails. The mascara was deep blue, and the eyebrow pencil had drawn a swirl to his temples.

'Anyway handsome, see me after the show I've got something I want to share,' said Frank.

Mr Wheatley was admiring Frank's sequined dress, and smirked at Joost.

'Aren't you the lucky one,' said an envious Mr Crowley close by.

Holding onto his bottle of bourbon Joost fled back up the stairs.

The loud cheer nearly raised the roof, and Bheki and Joost wondered what was happening. Joost did like sexy clothes with a hint of sleaze but only women, and Bheki liked her men in trousers; I guess she was an old fashioned girl after all.

At the overcrowded bar Herman had just tearfully accepted a proposal of marriage from Madam Fang Fong, whom after singing her swan song handed out her new business cards 'Frank Sleigh, Medium and Clairvoyant.' This was no hoax. After seeing Alison at the pastor's house he could see Spirits, and not just the ones Joost was knocking back in his hotel room.

'Don't tell me you're going to get another bottle,' asked Bheki.

'No, I promised Frank I'd see him after the show,' said Joost on hearing several cars pull out.

'You mean Madam Fang Fong,' said Bheki smiling.

'Joost if you've got any more secrets you can tell me,' she teased.

He threw a pillow at her, before making his ways down the stairs. He didn't want to take the overcrowded lift.

The bar was thinning, and Frank shooed a jealous Herman away.

'It's business,' Frank said after him.

'Who's the guy with Madame,' asked the tranny in the lobby.

'Joost van Houten,' said Mr Crowley 'kind of cute isn't he.'

'Indeed, and tell me does he happen to have a girlfriend here?'

'Yes, she's upstairs. She's a knockout too.'

'And is she albino by any chance?'

Mr Crowley looked a little nonplussed.

'White with African features,' elaborated the tranny.

'Yes, now you mention it.'

'Hey where are you going Susie?' asked Mr Crowley.

'To the car, I need to make a phone call,' said Susie Chang.

'It's them alright,' said Susie.

'Well done my dear. Keep a watch, I'll tell Dela,' said Pandy.

'So Frank, what did you want to say? asked Joost. 'And don't worry I won't tell Pastor Abel.'

'My dear boy, he knows all about it,' said Frank, looking at his long and glorious nails. 'Anyway here's the news.' He looked up, staring into Joost's eyes. 'After attending the séance you provided, I can now see on the other side.'

Frank slouched back in his chair, waiting for the applause, but Joost looked sceptical.

'I have to put myself in a trance,' explained Frank 'not too deep though.'

Joost still wasn't convinced.

'I came across John Lacey,' said Frank. 'He told me to keep an eye out for you.'

'Thanks Frank,' and Joost got up to go.

'I've seen Stella and Hildy,' said Frank.

Joost grabbed the top of the chair he was passing, and nearly broke it in two.

'Sorry, I should have warned you first,' said Frank, as Joost collapsed back down in the seat next to him.

'Go on, please,' begged Joost.

'They miss you naturally, as much as you miss them, but they're fine'.

'Do you think I could hear them?' asked Joost.

'Hear, and see them, if you have the gift.'

And he shouted Herman.

'Get me the scrying glass.'

The glass orb sat on the table between them. Frank's face had turned pale, and it wasn't the foundation.

Bheki watched them from behind the long velvet curtains at the end of the bar, and saw the tears rolling down Joost's face.

'I miss you both so much,' cried Joost.

It was both grief and joy, for he could see them smiling again, before him in the glass.

'We miss you too Dad,' said Hildy.

'Stop blaming yourself Joost,' said Stella softly 'there was nothing else you could have done.'

'I wished I'd died instead of you,' said Joost.

'We know,' said Stella.

Bheki stepped away from the curtains, quickly running back to their room. She realised Joost would never be hers, and that she would never replace the ones he'd loved, and lost. Besides she didn't want to compensate, be his reparation. She quickly packed her bag, took the car keys, and fled into the night. Joost wasn't the only one dabbing his eyes.

'Anyway my darling Joost, you have a new love,' said Stella.

Joost felt guilty.

'You see things differently on this side Joost. Treat her well for she loves you as much as I did. And Joost, be kind,' said Stella fading away, with Hildy waving goodbye by her side.

Frank came out of his trance to find Joost sobbing before him.

'It's never easy,' said Frank consoling him.

Joost got to his feet, and they hugged one another.

'I must see Bheki,' said Joost, and he left to jump up the stairs, two at a time.

He opened the door, but it wasn't Bheki sitting on the bed waiting for him.

'Mr van Houten, it's nice to see you again. So this is where you've been hiding,' said Dela.

Before he could remonstrate a powerful hand was held tight over his mouth, and he breathed in the chloroform. He was too confused to fight back, even if Din was doing more sweeping than weight training these days. Never ask for what you wish thought Din. When he'd helped to kill Lance with the broom handle he'd hoped to be Mr Universe - instead he'd become Mrs Mop.

Susie Chang should have been watching the car park downstairs. If she had, she might have seen Bheki Ncube leave, but then again no one knew of her infatuation for James Middlemass, not even James; not until tonight that was.

James was in the lounge, and Bill was watching the back of the hotel.

'You know I've always had a thing for you James,' said Susie.

He looked a little flustered, and wished he'd never emptied Eve's locket at the pub.

'You don't know what you're saying,' said James.

'Far from it,' said Susie, standing closer, and looking deeper into his eyes.

'I need a change,' she continued 'that can't be all bad can it? Pandy is so selfish in bed.'

'It's a spell,' said James.

'I know, and you're my lucky charm,' said Susie.

From the look in Susie's eyes James knew he wouldn't get anywhere, but perhaps Dela could rectify things - later. Only that usually cost, and for now at least his funds were exhausted.

'Shouldn't you be watching the front?' asked James.

'Yes, but it's not really my fault is it? You're such a handsome devil, and you know it,' cooed Susie.

James did know she couldn't help herself; and he didn't want to get her in any trouble.

'Here let's go together. If we stay near the lobby I can still see into the lounge.'

'You just want to get me under the stars,' said Susie 'you're such a romantic.'

Finally convinced Bheki had flown the coop, Dela left with Joost soundly asleep in the boot of her car, although he would have a very rude awakening.

Joost was tied to the chair, when his face was slapped hard by Din. Vankoni would have enjoyed this much more thought Din, but he was showing Christine his telescope tonight.

'So this is how you do it,' said Dela, triumphantly holding the crocodile mask aloft.

Joost tried to break free, but Bill took the wind from his sails with an uppercut to the stomach. He really was regaining his punch.

'I have you, and I have the mask' said Dela 'there's just one thing missing isn't there Mr van Houten.'

Joost looked none the wiser; he just hoped they'd killed Bheki quickly.

'Bheki Ncube,' screamed Dela.

'She's not here?' asked Joost.

'Of course not,' said Dela.

'But don't worry we'll find her, and the tramp's little sister. And get this, you're going to help us.'

After an hour of punching, poking, and pinching, Dela was convinced Bheki had left without telling Joost, and could be anywhere. But she had one trick left up her sleeve.

'We'll throw this fish back in the water,' she whispered to Din as they left the room.

Bill, and James, watched over Joost; Susie Chang had returned to the jealous arms of Pandy long ago. He couldn't miss her for another minute.

The door of the vicarage opened.

'Good of you to join us Charles,' said Dela in the hallway. 'Did you bring you're scalpels?' she asked.

Charles nodded, although he was rapidly losing his appetite for Dela's sadism.

'Then you might like to watch this,' she said, and he followed her into the drawing room.

Dela untied the rolled up scalpels, and unfurled them on the deep mantelpiece. She carefully picked out a gleaming blade. And before approaching Joost, carefully rubbed a thick blue ointment on the tip. No one knew why, although they did know not to ask.

'Most men value one thing above all others. What's yours Mr van Houten?' asked Dela.

Din pushed a chair next to Joost, and Dela blessed the seat.

'These perhaps,' and she drew the scalpel slowly up his thigh towards his testicles.

Joost winced.

'Maybe,' said Dela. 'Or perhaps it's these balls,' as the scalpel rested dangerously close above his right eye.

He squinted. He really was between a rock, and what might no longer be a hard place.

'Or you could just tell me where Bheki's hiding,' said Dela.

Joost spat some blood out of his mouth.

'I've told you, I don't know. Look why don't you just kill me?' said Joost.

At least he'd be reunited with Stella and Hildy, eventually, and it looked like Bheki was safe.

'Fool,' shouted Dela, and she pierced his eye with the scalpel.

Joost screamed. He knew all about muti murders, and began to pray.

'How quaint,' mocked Dela 'he's found God. Charles, keep guard.'

On her way out of the room, Dela turned around.

'I'm going to give you one last chance to think about it Joost,' said Dela.

Joost and Charles were left alone, whilst the others could be heard laughing in the kitchen.

Everyone knew Charles was a weakling, so it was a surprise, not least to Charles, that Dela left him to oversee Joost; even with the scalpels for company.

After a few minutes Joost spoke.

'Did Lucy get the bicycle reflector?' he asked.

'You posted it?' asked Charles.

'Of course. Dilwood and me go back a long way.'

'So Dilwood did hit Lucy?'

'Much more than that; he wanted to kill her.'

'How do you know this?' asked Charles.

'I ran into them both that night, literally. I guess you could say I saved Lucy's life,' said Joost.

'Oh my, you really are a hero,' said Charles mockingly.

'You know, you don't really strike me as a killer,' said Joost.

'Nice try Mr van Houten, but I'm not about to lose my freedom.'

'Sorry to hear that,' said Joost 'but look my right eye's bleeding, couldn't you at least ...'

'Alright, although it won't make any difference. There's always plenty of blood at these things.'

Charles took a handkerchief from his jacket, and went to dab the blood around Joost's eye. Or rather he would have done if Joost hadn't head butted him unconscious. Joost heard the laughing down the hall, as he stretched for the scalpel.

'How long has he been gone?' asked Dela flinging the door open.

But Charles was still out cold, and in no position to answer.

'Perhaps it's time I gave you the heart to be brave' she said standing over him.

'You expected this?' asked Bill.

'Of course,' said Dela 'and by the way that ointment in his eye; whatever Mr van Houten sees, so do I,' and she put the crocodile mask to her face to watch the show. 'Magic isn't it.'

Dela took quite a delight in watching Joost's escape. First there was the stolen pushbike, then the taxi from the petrol station back to Steeple's End, before he did a runner from the cabbie. Finally he begged a couple of tired tranny's to drop him off in London. She couldn't hear a word, but silent movies could be fun too.

Chapter Thirty Nine

Joost hit the pillow exhausted, and with a makeshift eye patch thanks to Miriam Goodyear. Mai checked on him during the night, and Miriam and Abel said prayers for his health. The cook, Plackcedes Seka, made breakfast, but she was feeling marginalised by Mai, and her exquisite Thai dishes.

In the morning light Joost examined his bruises in the mirror. He put on the spare dressing gown hanging on the back of the door, and peeked under his eye patch. The eye was red and swollen, but he decided to let it get some fresh air. He was about to venture outside when the door opened. It was Plackcedes, the perky little grey haired cook from Tanzania, and she was delivering his clothes; washed and pressed.

'How's the eye Mr van Houten,' she asked.

'Much better Plackcedes, thank you,' he replied.

He was missing Bheki, but in her day Plackcedes must have been a real doll. It was just as well he was robed; or perhaps not he thought. She did look a little rough around the edges, battered even. Plackcedes fortunately left, before he made a fool of himself.

'Breakfast is nearly served,' she said on her way out.

She was pleased she still had it, but this wasn't the place for a quick meaningless romp; nice thought though, especially with such a fine specimen of a man, even with all the bruises, or perhaps because of them.

'Have you seen Bheki?' Joost asked at the breakfast table.

'No my son, I thought she was staying with you,' said Abel.

'Is she alright?' asked Miriam.

'She'll be fine,' said Joost hiding his concern 'that girl knows how to take care of herself.'

Joost was still at pains to reach out, and Miriam passed him the toast.

'I hope you're not thinking of going anywhere today,' said Abel.

'Well actually ...'

Abel cut him off 'impossible my boy. You're not nearly well enough.'

'Maybe tomorrow,' said Miriam a little more conciliatory 'when you've got more strength.'

Joost sighed, but he had a lot of respect for the pastor and his wife. He'd just have to be their patient for the day.

Dela was having a ball, watching it all through the crocodile mask, especially since Abel was her nemesis. And she had another spy in the camp, placed a long time ago, and by the name of Plackcedes Seka.

Joost's body was still tired, and he went back to bed after breakfast. Miriam wanted to phone her GP, but Joost didn't want to answer any more questions. And what of Bheki? Had she run away from Dela or him? Still there was one place he was sure to find her, at Kings' auction house tomorrow afternoon.

'Ha' scalded Dela 'he's asleep again.'

Felix turned around in his chair. He was much more attentive these days.

'Can I get you anything dear?' he said into the crocodile mask.

'Not at the moment, but keep this up and I might just unlock you for a few minutes,' said Dela.

Even a few seconds thought Felix feeling the strain. But he daren't ask, that incurred Dela's wrath, and more time in lock up. He just smiled dutifully.

Dela took off the mask, and stroked the chequered pattern. She stabbed her fingers through the three eye slits. It had much to offer, much more than Joost could ever know. But she had to know how to unlock its secrets.

The mask, thanks to the witless John Lacey, had connected with Joost, and by wearing the mask Dela could see through Joost's eye; the one she had sliced with her magic. But how could she see into the realm of the dead, and more importantly return them to the living?

Dela put on the mask again and again, invoking one Spirit after the other, applying this and then that potion and charm. But she was exasperated with her lack of success. She was about to fetch the whip for Felix when he said 'it's amazing what you can do with Joost's eye Dela'. Instead she kissed him on the lips, and unlocked him for some split second relief.

Chapter Forty

Joost had slept for a full twenty four hours, when he woke up the next day panicked. He looked at his watch and breathed a sigh of relief; the auction wasn't until later in the day; he just had to see Bheki.

Joost went across the landing to the bathroom, but through the bannister could see Plackcedes with her ear to the lounge door. He coughed loudly, and she looked up at him, startled. She quickly smiled back, and went on her way.

'I just know something's wrong with it,' said Miriam.

'But you can't expect the poor boy to have it removed,' said Abel.

'Perhaps not, but at the very least he should keep it covered up.'

Joost entered the room, and they looked uncomfortable. He didn't mention Plackcedes, and at the back of his mind he thought about blackmailing her - for sex.

'I might as well come out and say it,' said Miriam to Joost.

He hoped it wasn't a farewell from Bheki.

'Well go ahead,' he said.

'Something's wrong with your eye,' she said.

'You're telling me,' said Joost 'sore as hell.'

'There's something else, I just know it,' said Miriam, who was still trying to make sense of a dream from last night.

'Tell me everything that happened,' she said 'and I mean everything.'

Some of it was a little embarrassing for Joost, but he kind of hoped Plackcedes was listening in again. Eventually he mentioned the blue oil or tar on the edge of the scalpel, before it cut his eye.

Miriam decided to exam Joost a little closer, and Dela could see her staring right at her.

'Go ahead bitch, you won't notice anything' said Dela, but she was wrong.

Without warning Miriam held a serviette over Joost's right eye.

'Keep this in place whilst I get something a little more permanent,' she said.

She returned with a dressing and a bandage.

'Do you mind explaining Miriam?' asked Abel.

'I know the kind of magic Dela uses, as do you dear husband. That eye is infected.'

'It feels OK,' said Joost.

'No, not that way. Dela can see through your eye; where you are, whom you're with, and what you're doing,' said Miriam.

The last part was a little interesting, and had possibilities thought Joost. After all she wasn't particularly unattractive, and it sure beat hooking up on a webcam. But it was a lot more serious than that. What was he going to do?

'For now let's just keep it covered up' said Miriam, wrapping the bandage around Joost's head.

'Well one thing's for sure, Dela's had a good look around our house,' said Abel.

'I hope I haven't put you at risk,' said Joost.

'Don't worry dear boy' she'd never dare come after us,' said Abel.

Bheki was sat on the third row from the front, and doing her utmost to gain the attention of the auctioneer. Not because she was bidding, but because he was a handsome chap in a suit. He looked much taller on his plinth, and he had the room in the palm of his hand. He smelled of success, whilst Joost was losing the scent.

Joost was watching from the back of the room, at least one eye was, and even the sight of Bheki's cropped hair was intoxicating. After all, her head was one of the best things about her.

'Ladies and gentleman, lot number 21,' announced the auctioneer.

'A male and female pair of statues from the Ngbaka tribe circa 1750,' he continued.

'They really are a beautiful piece with a stunning patina,' went the spiel.

'Shall we say £40,000 to start?'

There was a pause much to Bheki's consternation, but eventually the bidding began in earnest. Bheki had reluctantly agreed upon a reserve of £110,000, but would have felt cheated on a price even slightly higher. For once in her life she wasn't to be disappointed.

At £200,000 there were only three bidders left in the hunt; the mysterious European lady in the fur hat and coat, a portly African gentleman who gave Joost a nod of recognition, which incidentally bumped up the price another 10 grand, and the phone bidder. The phone was held by a slim white woman, who looked the secretarial type. She had her hair done up in a bun, and wore a crisp white blouse, and pin striped skirt. In between bids she twisted a pen between her lips.

'It's with you Sir at £240,000,' said the auctioneer to Joost's African friend.

He looked at the furs, and the chinchilla hat shook its head. The secretary held up her number on the small white card.

'With the phone at £250,000,' said the auctioneer.

There was another flurry of bidding.

'With the phone at £380,000. Last and final bid. Sold,' and the hammer hit the desk.

Bheki was ecstatic; she'd probably be on the run again, but money opened a lot of doors. She got up to leave, only disappointed she didn't have the number of her auctioneer, but then spotted Joost and couldn't hide her joy. She rushed to him, before they went outside the bidding room.

'Oh my God Joost, what's happened to your eye?' asked Bheki.

'Dela. When I got back to the room she was waiting.'

'You mean they found you?' asked Bheki shocked.

'Yes,' replied Joost 'I thought that's why you had gone.'

Bheki had to come up with an excuse, and quick.

'I felt sick, and went outside to get some fresh air. When I couldn't find you, I made my own way back,' said Bheki, doing her best to look heartbroken.

Joost squeezed her hand tightly. If they'd have been married he would have been a little more inquisitive. If they'd been long time spouses he would have interrogated her.

'You did well to get away,' she said.

'But what about the auction,' said Joost, brushing over the pain Dela and her mob had inflicted.

Bheki tried to play down her excitement. She needed all the cash for herself, and heartless bitch that she felt, she didn't want a man wallowing in self-pity over a previous life. Joost was a great guy, but that was her bottom line. It was pointless hanging on.

Dela was wearing the mask again, and still no luck.

'He knows,' she said to Felix. 'Still this will make up for it.'

Dela picked up a small felt doll, and after dipping the pin in her bottle of blue tar she jabbed it into the right eye. Outside in the snow Joost screamed, collapsing to the floor.

'How's that feel Mr van Houten,' said Dela.

Bheki hailed a taxi as Joost staggered to his feet.

'I'd better get you to the hospital,' she said as he held onto her arm.

'No, to Pastor Abel's, and quick,' said Joost.

Joost was sitting in the study as Miriam examined his eye.

'It's too late dear,' said Dela, gloating over the scene.

Abel was holding one of his books on voodoo, frantically flicking through the pages.

'There's not enough time for that Abel,' said Miriam firmly, then suddenly everyone was staring at Joost.

'What is it? What's the matter?' he asked, seeing the look of dread on everyone's face.

No one could answer him, and Joost ran to the mirror. There was a blue worm growing out of his eye, but then it split in half, and then again. Tentacles were heading for his nose, and into his mouth. Miriam knew he had less than a minute to live.

'Sit down,' she screamed.

She tore the silk pendant, the one that said Victoria Falls, from the wall, and wrapped it around her hand. She grabbed the neck of the hydra, and pulled. But it fought its way back to Joost.

'Hold him down,' she said to Abel.

With Abel grabbing Joost from behind, and Miriam pushing her knee into the chair, she pulled with all her might on the wriggling nematode, before ending up on her backside. On the floor next to her was one eye, and a pool of blue oil.

'Joost are you alright?' asked Miriam, but it was pointless; he'd passed out.

'Oh my,' said Bheki.

'Dear Lord,' said Abel.

And they all began to pray.

Miriam put the eye on Abel's desk, and called Plackcedes to come and scrub the mysterious blue ointment off the carpet. Abel and Bheki dragged Joost to the bedroom; Bheki was left to undress him, reminded of what she had seen in Joost in the first place. But she knew she'd always be second best.

Plackcedes put down her mobile phone, and went to the study to clean up. With Joost tucked up in bed Miriam irrigated the wound, and applied a new dressing. In a previous life she'd been a nurse, and he was in good hands.

Abel was back in his study, when he called Miriam and Bheki.

'Has anyone moved the eye?' he asked.

They both shook their heads.

'Strange,' said Abel.

The window was shut, so that pesky cat hadn't run away with it.

'Where's Plackcedes?' asked Miriam.

Mai entered the room.

'Plackcedes has just left in a hurry,' she said 'she left you this note.'

Miriam unfolded the piece of paper.

'I quit,' it read.

She passed it to Abel.

'Quite curious. But whatever does she want with the eye?' he asked.

No one mentioned it, but everyone suspected Dela's hand somewhere in the brew.

'Felix answer that,' said Dela to the knock at the door.

He jumped up like the puppet he had become. The cage around his loins was a big motivator.

'Hello Placky. Do you have it?' asked Dela.

'Yes,' answered Plackcedes.

'Excellent, well come and put your feet up, we have a lot to discuss.'

Deal examined the eye, and placed it inside a small gold pot on her altar.

'Plackcedes my darling, perhaps you could even join us' said Dela.

Plackcedes beamed.

'I brought this as well,' she said almost as an afterthought, and handed Dela a well-thumbed calf skin address book.

'You've proven more than you're worth Plackcedes, and thanks to a rather unfortunate incident on Bonfire's night I do have a position to fill,' said Dela.

'You can stay here for a while, and don't worry about him,' she said pointing disparagingly at Felix 'I keep him all locked up, and out of trouble,' and she held aloft the key that always dangled so enticingly in front of her bosom.

'He's quite useless, but if his urges get the better of him, and he becomes a pest then just swat him with this Placky,' and Dela held up the leather paddle she delighted in keeping at arm's length.

They both laughed as Felix stared forlornly at the floor; Plackcedes hitched up her tatty grey stockings. She could sleep with Dela for the moment, with Felix on the floor at the foot of their bed; who knows he might come in use.

Dela liked Plackcedes, she could be obedient or stern, depending on the setting, and for an old timer she had a kinky grin that was quite bewitching. One of her middle teeth was missing, and probably knocked out by an over arduous lover.

Later that night in her temple, Dela put on the crocodile mask with trepidation. Joost's eye had been dried and coated, and was resting in its new socket; looking out from the forehead of the mask, in the third resting place.

Perhaps you're not as useless after all she thought, acknowledging Felix's albeit misplaced comment. She could see into the other realm for the first time. Quickly she learned how to track the Spirits, and was rapturous, but one puzzle remained; how could she bring them back to life?

Chapter Forty One

Joost was eating ravenously, and wearing an eye patch. He could have passed for a pirate, except this wasn't fancy dress; there was too much pain. He checked the last packet of John's heroin in his pocket. If Miriam's painkillers didn't do a better job, he might be using it anytime soon.

'Have you seen my address book Miriam?' Abel shouted into the kitchen.

'No, check the lounge,' she answered, as she helped Mai wash and dry the dishes.

Lucy didn't really need to hear it, although she was glad of further confirmation.

'How much is true I don't know,' said Charles referring to Joost's proclamation on Dilwood, and his benevolent intervention.

But ever since the packet had arrived Lucy was having flashbacks, and in them Dilwood's face was a clear as the light from a car headlight.

'What does he hope to gain from telling us?' asked Lucy.

'Payback maybe,' mused Charles.

And maybe the chance of driving a wedge between them they thought, although they were all up to their necks in blood.

'Are you ready Lucy?' asked Charles.

'As I'll ever be,' and she pushed her hands down on the kitchen table, lifting herself up out of the wheelchair.

James and Christine should have been here, but she knew where her mother was, with Vankoni, and James was having another midlife crisis.

Lucy walked to the window, and looked outside. Charles watched the clock; five, ten, fifteen minutes, and her legs still refused to buckle. He hooked his arm underneath hers.

'Shall we?' he asked, and they walked out of the vicarage to take in the crisp fresh air of Bishopsfield.

As they wrapped themselves around one another, and underneath the deep blankets at Abel's house, Joost thought he had won Bheki back. The softness of her caress, and the tenderness in her voice, felt like he had captured her heart. But Bheki had already written a goodbye letter, ready to leave on her pillow in the morning; she needed more. As the wind rocked the window frame they were both unaware of the approaching danger.

Abel slept lightly, as usual, and alone; Miriam and Mai were at church tonight. Bheki was supposed to have joined them, but wanted one last night with Joost. She'd surprised him, and he just had time to put the last of his heroin into his striped linen pyjama pocket. For one morning at least, Bheki would find something completely different nudging into her night dress.

A cat, the striped visitor, he recognised the cacophony, was stranded outside. Abel went downstairs, passing Mai's room, to let him in.

Not even the words 'thank you' had time to sink in as Abel slumped to the floor. Din withdrew the knife and smiled; after checking the pastor's vacant pulse.

They crept up the stairs slowly, and exactly to the room where Plackcedes had told them they would be sleeping.

Chloroform was much more sanitised than a blow to the head, and the results were conclusive, without risking death. The sleeping beauties were taken to the car in their night wear.

For Joost it was déjà vu, but he was shocked and crestfallen to see Bheki by his side, for he knew what lay in store for her. They were each tied to a chair.

The Christmas candles on the altar had been lit early, and Charles had provided a couple of lanterns to illuminate proceedings further.

'Well Joost van Houten, I actually have to thank you for so much; the crocodile mask, and your eye for beauty, but this is where it ends. For you I shall make it as quick, and as painless, as I can. Unfortunately I cannot make the same promise for Bheki,' said Dela.

There was a thunder clap outside, and Charles nearly ducked underneath a pew. The rain continued to lash against the roof, and the gargoyle that guarded the religious bastion.

Vankoni looked at Joost and vice versa. Joost was going to have a quick death, for what it was worth; unfortunately Vankoni was to have the pleasure, and he brandished a pistol.

Joost looked at Dilwood, then Charles, and finally Lucy, but she couldn't help; she'd only just found her legs.

Pandy watched James, trying to understand what Susie saw him in. Plackcedes was the newcomer, and stood between Gasper on one side and the rather jealous Bill and Barbara on the other.

His hands were strapped by his sides, but Joost's fingers stretched into his pyjama pocket. When a small packet hit the floor there was curiosity but not alarm, and when Joost overturned his chair there was consternation but not panic.

When Din and Vankoni roughly brought him upright the packet, or rather the contents, were gone. Joost spat out the plastic, and hoped John could hear him, but then what good was a little crocodile, even if the mask was here?

The lightening rod hit the weathervane, illuminating the stone sarcophagus that was the gargoyle underneath. His claws seemed to stretch, and there was more tension in his carved muscles. His heavy eyelids finally creaked open, and the frown that pointed inwards slowly unfolded, unfurling like a banner, and proclaiming his return. The crocodile mask might be with Dela, but John Lacey was very much with Joost.

'What the hell was that?' asked James, turning to Charles.

Even the usually impassive Dilwood was taken aback by the crashing footsteps coming down the tower. Everyone looked in the same direction open mouthed, and then Joost smiled. But he knew he had a very short time to get free; this wasn't a laconic inhaled haze, and John's help would be swift.

The gargoyle opened his wings, and flew towards Dela. Din stepped in the way, and was immediately thrown to the ground. The draft knocked the candles flying onto the altar cloth.

John's talons sliced through Joost's and Bheki's ropes, cutting them free. Vankoni fired a shot, but it just ricocheted off the gargoyle's granite mantle

'Remember our promise,' John said to Joost.

Joost grabbed Bheki's hand, and they ran to the door whilst John kept the others pinned back. It was freezing outside, but they were too scared to care.

'Which way?' asked Bheki in the pouring rain.

'Over there,' said Joost, and they ran into the night.

The stones dug into Joost's feet, but Bheki hadn't seen a shoe until she was ten; she was made of sterner stuff.

The flames had taken hold, with the gargoyle now flickering on and off like a faulty mechanical toy. The pews were alight, and everyone instantly knew how poor Gladys must have felt.

A burning rafter fell and hit Bill on the back of the head. Barbara, who ran to his aide, was also consumed by the flames as her clothes caught light. Dilwood was only concerned for one person, and desperately looked for an exit.

'This way,' said Lucy, and she led him to the bell chamber through the smoke.

'Where do we go next?' asked Dilwood, but she'd already swung the door shut and locked it. She threw away the key with a smile.

First the smoke, and then the flames, took Dilwood Benson, and this was no accident; the bells had tolled. His last thought was of Mai, and how she'd escaped his grasp.

With one final roar the gargoyle's life was extinguished; the others ran outside as fast as they could. In the confusion and melee, James led all but one survivor back to the vicarage.

Christine searched frantically amongst the faces, first for Lucy and then Koni; at least her daughter was there.

Joost shoulder charged the door to The Crossed Heart; it flew open. The pain would have been too much to take, but the heroin was starting to kick in.

'Let's find some clothes,' he said, and they rushed upstairs.

The trousers were too short for Joost, and a floral dress wasn't Bheki's style, but beggars couldn't be choosers. They slipped on some Wellington boots and coats downstairs, and headed for the kitchen; Joost had a promise to keep.

They both looked at the freezer. On top was Themba's Bible, his watch, and Eudy's ear-rings.

'No,' screamed Bheki.

'I wouldn't worry too much about them,' said Vankoni from behind them, holding a pistol menacingly.

Joost could see his reflection in the large stainless steel pan that hung from the ceiling; the one Barbara used for peeling potatoes. Grabbing Themba's Bible he swung around, and chopped Vankoni in the throat. He hit the deck like a sack of spuds, and clutched his neck choking. Bheki grabbed the gun off the floor. Five minutes later Vankoni was dead from a collapsed trachea, and asphyxiation. In the end it wasn't a gargantuan battle but it was justice, and all thanks to the Good Book.

They heard banging from the pantry. Bheki unlocked the door, whilst Joost took aim. But they were relieved as much as the hostages to see Themba and Eudy tied up.

'Is the baby alright?' asked a worried Bheki as they untied their ropes.

'He's fine,' replied Eudy smiling.

'A boy,' said Bheki with delight.

Priorities first, and Joost needed a swig of brandy from behind the bar. He also loaded as many bottles of spirits as he could into an old crate. There were even two dusty bottles of champagne. But where had Bill put the car keys? Eventually they were found on a hook in the kitchen; hanging from a plaque that read 'I'm the boss when she lets me.'

Leaving everything upturned, they drove away from the pub. Every time Joost saw a blue flashing light ahead, through the myriad of country hedges, he turned off in the opposite direction. It was a maze, but eventually they were on an A road to London.

In the boot next to Joost's liquor, and a spade, were defrosting piles of meat wrapped in the finest linen Bheki could find. They were entombed in a long steel locker that Bill had carried on his worldly travels. Joost decided to stop in Steeple's End, at the cemetery.

In a little corner of the graveyard Joost patted down the earth as Themba said a prayer.

'Good bye old friend,' said Joost, 'and Lance,' as an afterthought.

They walked back in the rain to the car; they all knew how close they'd come to ending up like John and Lance.

Chapter Forty Two

Miriam was in pieces, wailing as the police took the body away; she hadn't prophesied this. She was too distraught to be questioned, and later she'd wonder what role Plackcedes had played?

They could see a body being carried out of the house as they approached, but this time their prayers weren't answered. They left Bheki with the inconsolable Miriam. Joost dropped off the others, then felt the gun in his breast pocket for assurance.

Miriam looked like a ghost, and couldn't believe Abel would no longer be by her side. In fact she half expected him to walk through the door at any moment, with that broad grin on his face.

Bheki sneaked up to their room, passing Mai on the stairs. She pulled the drawer open in the bedside dresser, and removed the goodbye letter, tearing it to pieces like confetti. Maybe she'd give Joost a little more time; after all he'd just saved her life, and Eudy's. And who knows with Vankoni dead he just might let go of the past.

Din and Christine were both disconsolate for their lost friend. His last port of call had been The Crossed Heart, and there he lay on the kitchen floor before them, lifeless.

'Leave him Christine,' said Din, and she finally put down Koni's hand.

'He's with the Spirits now,' he sighed.

'Shouldn't we give him a proper burial?' asked Christine.

At least she still had James, who was being more loving, now his cheap slut had left town.

'The police will see to that,' said Din.

But the words resonated in his head; St Agnes burnt to the ground with three bodies inside, and a murder in the pub. It would bring too much heat on the village, and someone might crack.

'You're right Christine. How careless of me, he deserves a send-off fitting for a warrior,' said Din.

Vankoni was loaded into the back of Charles' jeep, with the sleet bouncing off. Dela would perform the funeral tonight, in the woods; it as going to rain on a bonfire after all.

'Well, whoever it was, they've done an excellent job,' said the nurse in A and E.

'The scar tissue's healing nicely, and no sign of any infection,' she said.

'Wait here whilst I get you a proper eye patch, and not this costume one,' and she left Joost alone to look in the mirror.

Some may have found it a little grotesque. Bheki being Bheki found it a turn on, and I guess for that, amongst other things, he had to be grateful.

'He's got no ID, and says it was an accident. I think we should call the police,' said the nurse.

'I quite agree,' said the doctor.

'Here you are try this on,' said the nurse sliding back the curtain.

This was the deluxe model; a firmly padded black eye patch, with nice bold contours, and a thick strong elastic band around his head that secured it nicely in place. Although Joost could sense something was amiss, and the nurse kept checking her watch. It was time for an exit.

'Where's the toilet please?' he asked.

'Just down the hallway on the right. But don't be too long, I need to go through the aftercare.'

But the stranger with the name Kobus Jonker was out of ear shot, and he wasn't coming back.

There was an owl in the trees close by, as Din poured gasoline onto the makeshift pyre of twigs and brambles. The assembled survivors counted themselves lucky as Vankoni's body went up in flames. Dela said a few words, but no one was really listening.

It was a shame she couldn't bring the dead back to the living, but that was one trick eluding her - for now.

They all sat around the fire warming themselves, as Themba turned up the gas. They were watching the rubble, and smouldering embers of St Agnes on the news.

'The police have no explanation for the fire,' said the newscaster 'but have found at least one body.'

Everyone hoped it was Dela.

'I really don't feel safe staying here,' said Eudy.

It was a feeling echoed by them all, but where would they be safe? No one wanted to appear avaricious, but they knew Bheki had made a killing from the statues.

They needed to get away, if only for a short while, and Bheki was about to answer everyone's prayers.

'What about a holiday?' she asked them.

'Where too?' asked Themba, imagining exotic spots in the sun, far away from the frost.

'Let's all go the Christmas market in Cologne; it looks magical,' said Bheki.

She went to fetch the brochures she had gathered earlier, stamped Serpentine Travels, and handed them out.

'You mean it?' asked Eudy looking at the pictures in delight.

She'd also longed for a fairy tale Christmas as far back as their days in Mozambique.

'Why not?,' responded Bheki.

There was a whoop of delight from Eudy, and seeing her smile light up the room was enough to sway Themba.

Bheki kissed Joost on the forehead but he wasn't quite as convinced as the others; Christmas was a time for families.

'Don't worry, this treat's on me,' said Bheki 'you've done enough - for the time being.'

'This calls for a toast,' said Joost trying to pick up his spirits, and he went to open the champagne.

'To the future,' they all said as their glasses chinked.

But they still needed a new property when they returned, and there was a haunting feeling of remorse for poor Pastor Abel Goodyear, and his widow Miriam.

Chapter Forty Three

Joost looked in the mirror, and tentatively lifted the eye patch. The wound appeared clean and was pain free, but the change in appearance was drastic; much more than a new haircut, or a pair of spectacles. He felt different too, almost as though he was looking at someone else.

Bheki was a blessing because she actually liked it, though it did make him look heroic in a combative way. Still the lack of distance perception was annoying, especially behind the wheel.

'Joost come quickly,' shouted Bheki from her lounge 'it's on TV again.'

He rushed into the room, and sat next to a quiet Eudy and Themba, on the last beanbag.

'The fire at St Agnes has been put out,' read the newscaster 'but who are the mysterious bodies? Our reporter spoke to the vicar earlier on.'

In front of camera was James Middlemass, looking shocked with all his might, and with the ruins of St Agnes behind him.

'I'm completely horrified that someone would do this,' said James.

'So you don't think it was an accident? asked the reporter.

'Well the police have said there were three bodies inside,' he replied.

'And you have no idea who they are Reverend?'

'How could I, we don't open in the night,' James replied.

'And ...'

James cut him off.

'Look I don't really have anything else to say. I've already told the police everything I know.'

'Reverend, the police say the bodies were of two men and a woman. Any comment?'

'Not at all, I'm as mystified as everyone else at the moment,' said James.

'But ...'

'I really have nothing else to say on the matter,' said James, and like St Agnes before him he disappeared.

The police were next, appealing for information. As the camera panned from left to right one last time, they saw a striped moggy dancing across the coals.

'One dead female,' mused Joost.

'It could be Dela,' said Bheki hopefully.

'Maybe,' said Joost although he didn't really believe it. But he did hope it wasn't Lucy; she could still come in handy.

Themba sighed.

'Well at least they've learnt their lesson,' said Eudy optimistically.

But Bheki knew albino gangs never gave up, and so did Eudy in the pit of her stomach. What they didn't know, was that Dela was eyeing a prize much more valuable than muti, and revenge; one that would buy them some breathing space.

'Rooibos anyone?' asked Themba.

As the rain continued to pour, they chose a hotel in Cologne, and it wouldn't be another Mephisto.

'We can't take that,' said James almost hysterically.

'Why not?' asked Christine looking down at her grey woollen coat on the bed.

'It needs dry cleaning,' said James.

'Honestly James, what's got into you lately?' asked Christine.

'I can't help it,' he replied. 'You remember that guy Lance, the patient,' he said.

'Yes.'

'Well I helped to send him on his way with an iron.'

Christine burst out laughing, and for the first time in years he found it quite erotic.

'Yes, well I know I've always left the housework to you. So I thought if I used an iron perhaps I could be a bit more enthusiastic with the chores. Unfortunately ...' said James.

'James you're such a love,' and she kissed him on the cheek.

In spite of Koni's death, or perhaps because of it, Christine now felt happier with James. And she was looking forward to their trip with Lucy. As an early Christmas present they were taking her away. It had been so long since any of them had taken a holiday, and in her heyday Christine had been a globe trotter.

'Remind me to buy a travel iron before we leave, just in case the hotel doesn't have one,' said James.

'James they all have irons these days, it's not like when you went to Burundi all those years ago,' said Christine.

'What if it's broke?' asked James, looking concerned.

'OK, OK,' said Christine holding up her hands 'we'll get one.'

James was mightily relieved, after all some of his trousers were already creasing in the case.

Lucy and Christine were in the kitchen, talking excitedly about the trip. And Lucy could look her mum in the eye again, now her lover Koni was dead. James was upstairs in his study contemplating.

Burundi he thought. That's where it had all began, where he first met Christine the adventurer, and voodoo. After his ordination James' predilection for young boys was given full reign over the choir. He'd wanted to stop but found Jonathan Lacey irresistible; he blamed John, and not himself. The way the sun caught his blonde hair through the stained glass windows, the chorister's ruffled collar, and his sweet angelic voice.

When suspicions and whispers began to circulate in the cloisters the Bishop didn't see it that way. James was booted to Burundi, where he went in search of a cure.

A witchdoctor by the name of Augustine Tiberius made a special potion that in the ensuing fever nearly killed him, but drove out his paedophilic demons. Then he fell in love with Christine, the first woman he had ever kissed.

The Bishop may have saved the Church's reputation, and James too, but they left poor John martyred, and to carry his cross for the rest of his life.

James opened the letter on his desk; he recognised Eve's hand writing. Thankfully there were no embarrassing accusations, or worse, threats, just a short terse note to say she had officially resigned her post, and had left the area and the Church. He needed a drink, to celebrate.

Felix was sitting on top of the case, trying to get it to close. Eventually Dela could pull the zip around, leaving just one more case to pack.

They were leaving Plackcedes in the flat whilst they took a short break to see some of Dela's continental followers. Naturally they had gifts; it was Christmas. So in went Irena's atlas bone, and nine voodoo dolls which would help to fill Felix's Christmas stockings.

The atlas bone would fetch a pretty penny, being enhanced with powers from its position in the body; sitting between brain and body. Irena had sure had the body, but not the brains.

The voodoo dolls were all in the image of Santa Claus, in the spirit of the festive season.

Felix looked at Dela but was frightened to ask. If he wanted the chastity cage removed she would burden him with an extra week at least; but he was becoming painfully swollen by the hour.

'Go and take another cold shower,' said Dela sensing his frustration building.

Felix shrugged his shoulders.

'Unless you want Plackcedes to use the strap again,' she said.

He scuttled off to the bathroom.

Late afternoon, and they were sombrely dressed at the entrance to Miriam's house. It was jam packed, and you could barely squeeze your way in.

In the lounge Miriam was laughing. Her maudlin veil had lifted, and although not quite the merry widow she was reflecting on the good times she and Abel had shared. She beckoned Bheki and her suitor to join them.

'How's the eye Joost?' asked Miriam.

'It's fine, thanks to you,' he replied.

She smiled.

'Abel asks that you be careful Joost,' said Miriam.

Joost looked into her sparkling eyes.

'I still see him you know,' she said with a wry smile.

Joost acknowledged her feelings with a nod. He had seen Stella and Hildy too. Not just in every room after their murders, but in Frank Sleigh's scrying glass.

'He's settled in quickly,' said Miriam.

Then as an afterthought she added 'he probably misses his desk more than me,' and laughed.

'Nonsense,' said the singing preacher joining them, and carrying his donations bucket. 'You were the love of his life.'

For a brief moment Miriam's brave face looked sad, and Bheki hugged her.

They circulated at the wake, amongst the mourners. Most were from The Church of the Loving Saints, but some were from Africa, having caught a flight as soon as they'd heard.

Frank Sleigh tugged on Joost's sleeve.

'A truly great man,' said Frank, with a drink in one hand, and some nibbles in the other.

'Indeed,' answered Joost.

'I've seen him too,' said Frank.

'How is he?' asked Joost, as though they were discussing an old friend who'd moved abroad.

'He's fine. He misses Miriam naturally, but he's got plenty of friends over there showing him the ropes.'

'You know the dead seem so close,' said Frank 'almost as though they could step right back to this side.'

Joost smiled, and the thought warmed his heart.

'Now wouldn't that be something,' said Frank.

They stopped a little longer; it would have been impolite not to eat, and Mai was feeding the five thousand. Bheki made a contribution for them all, and the singing preacher happily wrote £5,000 next to their names. Once the police released his body, Abel would take his last flight back home.

Themba idled by the large lit window looking at the properties. It was the fourth estate agent they had passed on their way to the tube. He pointed at the house, but Joost and Eudy had already seen it, and Bheki was collecting the details inside.

Chapter Forty Four

As the plane made its descent, Bheki looked out of the window; the airport below looked like an ice skating rink. She said prayers to Jesus and Ayza the protector, and then held onto Joost's arm. Eudy was on her other side, with Themba behind them, fast asleep as the wheels touched down.

It was mid-morning, and after a taxi ride to the Four Star Radisson Blu Hotel they were ready to see the sights. Eudy was wrapped up like an Egyptian mummy, whilst Bheki was more conscious of keeping her voluptuous curves on show; she didn't have a wedding ring on her finger just yet.

There were half a dozen Christmas markets in Cologne, but they were drawn to the stalls by the Cathedral, and the giant Christmas tree that stood outside. It wasn't the warm blue sea Themba had imagined, but waves of humanity undulated in the spaces between the stalls.

The aroma of spicy mulled wine wafted by their noses; they bought a drink each. It warmed their hearts, and their hands. Most of the hundred plus stalls sold food, and they eventually succumbed to the bratwurst.

Bheki and Eudy stopped at the handmade candles, and painted baubles with their nativity scenes. Joost's eye was fixed on the Russian dolls. And there was another watching through the madding crowd; Lucy Middlemass stood open mouthed.

'Are you alright darling?' asked Christine.

'I'm fine mother.'

'Maybe it's too much,' said James.

'Yes, after all you've only just found your feet,' said Christine.

Lucy took one last glance at Joost, and decided to guide her parents away.

'Yes, you're right,' said Lucy 'it is overwhelming. Let's go over there.'

And she pointed to the stalls on the periphery, where there was space to breath.

The stall holder was still opening and closing the Russian dolls in front of Joost as Lucy gave her parents the slip. She hurriedly wrote a note in eye pencil on her gingerbread wrapper, and grabbed her purse.

Joost moved on undecided, disorientated by his vision, and the numbers pushing against him. Lucy caught sight of his head, as she quickly bought the dolls. She pushed her way through, no longer the cripple, and stood in front of Bheki and Joost. Immediately they were alarmed, but Lucy appeared alone.

'I'm sorry,' she said.

No one else knew what to say.

'Here take this' said Lucy, and she thrust the dolls into Joost's arms 'a present.'

Then she disappeared.

'How very strange,' said Joost.

'Is she alone?' asked Bheki, trying in vain to see where she had gone.

Joost shrugged his shoulders, and Themba put his arms around Eudy for protection.

'Let's go back to the hotel,' said Eudy.

'That's where you are,' said Christine mightily relieved.

'Where have you been?' asked James.

'Sorry, I got lost,' replied Lucy 'but I've found my way now.'

Joost put the wooden dolls on the bed.

'It must be a trap,' said Bheki.

Joost went to separate the first doll; a large Santa Claus.

'Be careful,' said Eudy.

They all knew Dela had a penchant for dolls.

The next doll was painted as a large Christmas tree, and still no bomb exploded. But there was a surprise waiting further down the line.

Between the snowman, and the penguin with the red bow tie, a note was sandwiched.

'Call me, I want to help,' and there was a number.

'No way,' said Themba.

'We can't trust her,' said Bheki.

They were right of course, but Joost placed the note back in the safety of the dolls, for now.

'Well for goodness sake let's not sit around dejected, we've only got tonight and tomorrow,' said Joost.

They tried to pick themselves up, and took in the sights, although it seemed they weren't safe anywhere. But they did have an appetite, and Joost needed all his strength for tonight.

Lucy was washing her hands again. She wasn't developing OCD like her father but they were covered in blood, and how much she regretted everything; now she could walk again.

Lucy's life now seemed perfect; she was as pretty as a picture, healthy with child bearing hips, romantic, and extremely bright. No longer deceived by bitterness she wanted to right her wrongs. She was praying to God once more, and not the Spirits, and whatever help she could offer Joost she would. Naturally there was one proviso; in spite of her parents' misdemeanours, their folly should be spared. She would wait all night for a call from Joost, but it wouldn't come.

Dela and Felix were standing in the hotel lobby across from two Russian Mafioso, a German steel magnate, and a Chinese immigrant who had restaurants across the continent. Felix held a briefcase.

The magnate hugged Dela, and why not. She had brought his son back to life from a coma last year. The Russians were more orthodox and shook hands. Mr Li went round greeting everyone.

'Where shall we go gentleman?' asked Dela.

Mr Li had recently opened a flagship restaurant in Cologne, but the Russians wanted some steak, rare. They too had seen their business prosper, although theirs depended more on execution than expediency and planning permission.

Ponchos Steakhouse was in the basement, and busy. They were shown a table, and ordered. Joost had been holding onto Bheki all day, and just had to get his mouth round a nice fat rump. The others ordered steak with gorgonzola sauce. It was organised chaos, as the waiters danced between the tables. Joost and

Themba were drinking steins of beer, as the volume raised the roof. Bheki was sipping a Malbec wine and knew what response she would elicit from Joost later, in the privacy of their hotel room. Eudy had apple juice.

The Russian stabbed his knife into the steak, pleased to see a trickle of blood. Through the comings and goings he caught a glimpse of a fellow gladiator with an eye patch. Felix saw his stare, and turned around curious, but the other party had just left.

With the plates gone but steins and glasses still full, Felix opened his case. He looked a little out of place between the Russian warriors, the devious Mr Li, and the German magnate with the full beard and striking wolf like features. But the others showed him the respect a husband of Dela's deserved. It wasn't that Felix didn't do menace or indeed murder, but it was always underhand, and that's how he looked - respectively sly.

'Christmas presents Dela?' asked Mr Li.

Vasily and the others were more patient, but hoped they weren't about to be duped with gifts from the Christmas markets.

Dela checked the other tables, and began to speak in hushed conspiratorial tones.

'First the atlas bone,' said Dela.

Gunther's eyes lit up, and Vasily nodded with approval to his colleague. They passed it around themselves under the table, before it returned to Dela.

'Only one bid each gentleman. I don't wish to be here all night,' said Dela.

And they each wrote a sum on a serviette before returning it to Dela.

The atlas bone was the most powerful of all muti, synonymous with favour and fortune, and Dela had promised its owner a path to power. Gunther Strauss was running for Mayor, and Vasily the Federal Assembly; one of them was about to be disappointed.

Dela dabbed the wine from her lips with the winning serviette, and handed the prize to Vasily which was a winner for everyone; at least he wouldn't have to kill Gunther on his way to the car.

Felix handed out the Santa Claus voodoo dolls like after dinner mints; there were two each.

'On the house,' said Dela lifting up her hand.

Mr Li wasn't the only shrewd businessman in town tonight, and there was a sting in the tail.

'Just fax me when you have a name, and I'll do the rest from my end,' said Dela.

For a price naturally, and putting the clause into Santa.

With the meeting over Dela decided to take Felix for a stroll. The waiter cleared the table. There was no tip but a solitary felt Santa Clause on the table. Still he would put it in the staff room; what harm could it do?

The stall holder wrapped the long red candle Dela had just bought. It was wide, and on the side was an image of Santa about to shoot off in his sleigh.

'I know exactly where I can stick this Felix, when we get back home,' said Dela.

But Felix was more interested in the atlas bone.

'So go on, tell me. How much did you get?' he asked.

Dela delved into her pocket with a smile, and held up a banker's cheque for fifty thousand euros. Not a bad night's work, all said and done.

Felix looked at his watch.

'The flight leaves in four hours,' he said.

'Felix whatever would I do without you,' said Dela.

And she meant it, but she couldn't wait to see Plackcedes again, and then they could both give Felix the souvenir from Cologne.

They ate a full breakfast, and left their bags in the foyer. The receptionist recommended they visit the ice rink on Heumarkt. If last night was anything to go by, Joost and Bheki would try anything.

'Are you alright?' asked Themba as Joost sat on his backside on the cold ice for the umpteenth time.

'I'm fine,' said Joost.

Bheki loved it, and was laughing in fits. The strong hero couldn't skate. Joost tried to blame his eye, but Bheki was having none of it.

'Hold onto me,' she said, as Eudy and Themba gracefully floated by.

He held her arm but it was no use. He stumbled, he fumbled, and he tumbled.

'It's just not me,' he eventually said after getting back on his feet.

'Throwing in the towel Joost?' said Bheki smiling.

'I don't recall you being that brave last night,' said Joost.

'That's strange because I remember you being just as useless,' said Bheki with a gleam in her eye.

They kissed, and if their lips had locked any longer they just might have frozen together.

Joost decided to watch from the side-lines, and Eudy and Themba were even skating arm in arm. But Bheki didn't mind, she had her man exactly where she wanted him; if she wanted him at all?

All good things come to an end, and they began their sojourn back to London. Joost had packed the dolls and their message, against Bheki's advice, but she wasn't complaining; he'd not shot off when she'd looked at the rings in the jewellers. It was worth knowing, that was if he was worth keeping?

Chapter Forty Five

In the corner of the room was a green glass paraffin lamp, lit and sitting on a small round oak table with a lace table cloth. It suited Frank Sleigh's aesthetics, but was added for theatrical effect. Though he was no charlatan, Frank really could see the other side, and already his diary was full. Herman was his personal assistant but there was no camping it up for this audience, the ball gowns unlike Frank were in the closet.

In the gloom was a much more revered table, and at its helm sat Frank hunched over his scrying glass. It was just ordinary glass, and if truth were told it was a novelty crystal ball, but when Frank touched it an aura would surround; sometimes frosty white, sometimes gold, and on occasion when a disturbed Spirit was summoned, black or red.

'Portia you're first,' said Frank.

'Ask him if he's alright,' said Portia.

It was always the same question but she worried terribly. Montague, her deceased husband, had been a consultant surgeon. But his suicide followed a litany of private lawsuits; he'd played God for too long and had started to believe in his own infallibility, until a much braver soul stood up to him.

'He's fine,' said Frank mildly entranced.

He held his hands over the scrying glass and trying to cover the deep black aura.

Portia smiled to herself.

'And what does he want me to do with Benjamin?' she asked.

Benjamin was their arthritic bull mastiff, and even from across the grave Montague's opinion held sway; she'd been under his thumb too long.

'It's time to have him put down,' said Frank solemnly.

'Is he sure?' asked Portia.

Frank nodded.

He connected with the dead, and could hear the voices no one else in the room could. Most who attended for the first time were a little sceptical, some even tried to catch him out, but Frank would soon provide indisputable proof.

'Larry it's your turn,' said Frank.

It was Larry's first time, and he could be a believer or an unbeliever in the afterlife and clairvoyants, depending on his mood. When he'd booked his place at the table he'd been a believer, now he was here he was an unbeliever. But he had ways of unmasking Frank, or so he thought.

'So Larry, whom do you wish to contact?' asked Frank.

'My deceased,' deceased sounded much better than dead, 'partner, Olivia Reynolds.'

'Olivia Reynolds are you there?' asked Frank.

Again and again it appeared that Olivia was being a little coy.

'Have you brought something along?' asked Frank.

Larry who was sitting two chairs down and next to Portia slid a ring across the table. It was Olivia's, though they had never actually married; it was something to which Larry was averse, but now he regretted it.

Frank held the ring, and eventually he said 'she's here.'

'Ask her if I should sell the holiday flat in France?' asked Larry.

'Olivia says by all means but don't you mean the caravan in Cornwall.'

Larry smiled but felt a little uncomfortable, he had been undone. But still, Frank could have checked him out; he needed something more personal, and now he had laid his cards on the table he showed his hand.

'Ask her what's the first thing she remembers me saying.'

There was a pause, and Frank was actually enjoying this game.

'Easy,' he said 'is this the train to Nottingham?'

'What's the first present she ever bought me?'

'A teapot,' said Frank.

'Why didn't she like my Mum?' persisted Larry.

'She made her get rid of the cat,' replied Frank.

Larry was shocked, and would never doubt Frank again. There were both laughter and tears over the next five minutes, with Larry begging forgiveness for his numerous foibles.

Next were a couple of grieving old timers, and some crack head punter who wanted next week's lottery numbers. Finally came Lycan, real name Kevin. It was with some hesitancy that Frank had let him return, and already he was wishing he hadn't.

Lycan was a mid-twenties Goth with long brown hair, pork chop sideburns, and a werewolf fetish.

'Yes Lycan' asked Frank 'what is it this time?'

'I wish to speak to Winston Churchill.'

Lycan had this strange theory that certain historical figures had either been werewolves or were killed by them. Apparently Winston Churchill had been murdered by a German werewolf.

Fortunately Winston saw the funny side, but a séance was not meant to be light entertainment, and Frank, as well as some of his more sober and salubrious customers, was not amused. Frank cut the interview short, and before the usual genteel cup of tea, Lycan and the hapless gambler were shown the door.

'You can't throw me out,' protested Lycan moving his long mac in an incongruous flurry.

'I could always tell the police about the horses,' retorted Frank.

'I wouldn't come back here anyway,' was the last thing Frank heard from Lycan as Herman slammed the door shut on him.

In the street the bedraggled and desperate punter came up to Lycan.

'So what do you know about horses?' he asked.

'Oh fuck off,' said Lycan, and they went their separate ways.

'Apologies for the kafuffle ladies and gentleman,' said Frank, and he clapped his hands.

'Time for a cup of tea,' he added.

Five minutes later and Herman brought in the china cups and tea pot for a most congenial review.

They collected their assorted coats, hats, brollies, and walking sticks and one by one bade farewell. Herman brought the sealed envelopes to Frank in the drawing room. He didn't like to set a fixed price because grief was immeasurable, and not everyone had deep pockets. But nonetheless he opened the sealed envelopes, collected before the séance, with interest.

Each envelope was named, and as usual the gracious Portia was the most generous. Larry had changed his mind at the last minute, and enclosed a fiver and not a fifty pound note. He regretted it on the way home but would more than make amends next time. Lycan had slipped a twenty inside, and the gambler an I O U. The others were predictably grateful, and Frank had the handsome sum of £700 pounds before him. He gave it to Herman to trouser, before sitting alone with the scrying glass, and Alison.

'Don't worry my dearest girl you'll come back to us,' said Frank into the orb.

He'd heard rumours on the other side from a couple called Bill and Barbara that Dela had something afoot. He listened to Abel too; but wasn't all fair in grief and war?

Chapter Forty Six

Detective Inspector Dirk Sellars spun the mobile phone on his desk in the empty office; everyone else was at his leaving party. He was making a timely exit; there was a new wave of police joining the Met, politically correct and idealistic. He was part of the old guard, a dinosaur, chauvinistic, and willing to bend the rules when it suited. And it had suited him quite a lot, right down to his houses in Marbella.

Sellars had waited a long time for this moment, and yet now, on his very last day, he regretted wishing his life away. He'd swap it all to be a twenty something again, back on the beat. He took another sip of scotch, and braced himself for all the usual cliché's awaiting in the boozer down the road. There was a knock at the door.

'Aren't you coming Sir?' asked the pretty WPC through the glass.

In his heyday, when he'd cut a swagger in his uniform, he'd have had a ribald reply waiting on his lips. But now there was no sparkle in his eyes, only lines around them.

'Five minutes Jackie, just clearing out my desk,' he replied.

He was doing more than clearing out his desk. Corruption and pay offs were addictive, like gambling, and he wanted a royal flush one last time.

Inspector Sellars had been Dilwood Benson's eyes and ears, but it looked like he'd retired too, without even a goodbye. His understudy, Din, wanted a meeting, to pick up where Dilwood had left off, but in this case Dirk was taking him a leaving present.

He put the notes in his briefcase, along with his bravery award, and memory stick porn collection. The police file on Tendai Mathebula was for Din. She was a hooker once booked for soliciting, and whose prints turned up at the most unfortunate places; the murdered drug dealer's bedroom a couple of years ago, and more recently in the deceased pastor's kitchen. He didn't know where she was nor did he care, but Din wanted all trace of her to vanish. Naturally it would cost; enough to buy a couple of bar girls whilst he recuperated.

They were coming up the stairs dancing the conga. He took a handful of tablets with the last of his scotch, and pressed the key. Now Tendai was gone from the police national computer, just like Dilwood's prints before her.

Susie Chang took one last swig of senna elixir from the bottle, and dashed to the bathroom. She looked sea sick but eventually the gristle digested at The Crossed Heart passed her by, and with it any thoughts she had for James Middlemass. But Pandy could be fiercely jealous, and her late obsession hadn't gone unnoticed. Her constipation wouldn't lead to her emancipation.

She looked at the bank statement, careful not to show her hand. She quickly flipped up the sheet a second time, but still had a poker face.

'Well?' asked Joost.

Her excitement finally boiled over, and she jumped into his arms.

'It's in I take it,' and for once he wasn't referring to his limitless passion.

'Three hundred and eighty thousand pounds,' she said, taking as long as she could to drool over the words.

'Thanks grandma,' she said, and Joost opened another bottle of champagne.

The handcuffs weren't covered in pink fur, and the whip hand wasn't forgiving. His head was in a sling beneath two sweet moons. Plackcedes was in the queening chair whilst Felix received another taste of African hospitality.

Dela was kneeling besides him, curiously watching his arousal push against the cage. Eventually she relented, and removed the padlock, and Felix sprang into life. But too much of a good thing could be a bad thing, and Dela wasn't about to make his day.

She stroked until the very last moment, and timed her removal to perfection. Just as he jolted the stimulus was cruelly whisked away, and his enjoyment ruined.

'Spitter spatter it doesn't matter,' said Dela nonchalantly before dabbing up the trickle, and locking him up once more.

Plackcedes had a bird's eye view, and smiled to herself at the slave's ruination. She could only imagine the look of loss and disappointment on his face as he continued his duty.

'Poor baby,' she purred 'have you spilled some milk?'

Joost looked in the side mirror as Themba beckoned the van back a few more yards. He squeezed in between the gate posts, and parked on the drive.

Joost and Themba lifted out the couch whilst their respective sweethearts decided what went where. The house was big enough for two sets of furniture. There were four bedrooms, more importantly two bathrooms, a front room, a lounge, a drawing room, and a kitchen to shame Dilwood. Joost and Bheki both had their flats up for sale.

'It's Miriam,' said Bheki holding out the phone.

Joost put down the large cardboard box, not sure how to answer; pleased to hear her voice, or despondent over Abel?

'Hi darling,' said Miriam sweetly and setting the tone.

'Just a quick word because you've probably got your hands full,' she said.

She was right but it wasn't Bheki in his strong arms just yet. And, although their bedroom was at the far end of the corridor, they would have to tone it down, for a while.

Joost sank into the newly arranged sofa, and nodded his thanks to Eudy who handed him a huge mug of rooibos.

'Abel says don't worry, but Dela is planning something big. He's not sure what, but I'll keep you posted,' said Miriam.

Before Joost could ask how she was bearing up she was gone. He looked at the Russian dolls on the window sill, and wondered; he wouldn't phone Lucy just yet, he wanted to hang onto his ace.

Chapter Forty Seven

Charles was making a fuss, as he had always did, but not even Dela noticed he was just going through the motions; she had something much more important on her mind - resurrecting the dead.

'I'll take your bags upstairs,' said Charles.

Dela and Plackcedes were staying for a couple of days. Felix was back at the flat all tied up, besides he could do with losing some weight.

Charles placed the luggage on the duvet, plumped up the pillows, and rearranged the cushions on the spare double bed. His guests were staying overnight, and happy to share sleeping accommodation

The kettle boiled just as Charles heard his mistress' voice.

'Charles it's freezing down here,' said Dela.

They were in the basement, and Plackcedes was blowing air through her hands.

'Sorry,' said Charles, moving the gas heater from the far corner, before turning it on.

'Cup of tea anyone?' asked Charles.

'Please,' said Plackcedes 'milk and no sugar.'

Dela just nodded.

Plackcedes was getting used to being Dela's most personal of assistants, and she had slipped into the role seamlessly. With the Goodyear's she always felt beholden and timid, but Dela encouraged her to show more confidence, especially in the bedroom.

Charles placed the teas on the wicker table he had moved from the conservatory. Already the crocodile mask was leaning against the wall, watching him, as Dela and Plackcedes fastened up their lab coats. If Felix had seen them he'd probably be foaming at the mouth like a rabid dog.

'Well Charles?' asked Dela sternly.

He looked mystified.

'The specimens,' reminded Dela.

Charles instantly threw the blanket back like a theatrical magician, and revealing the contents of the cages; six dogs all tranquilised and docile. Dela held out her outstretched arm, and Charles obediently handed her the keys; he had been trained too.

Leaving them in the laboratory Charles went into his back garden. The latest snowfall had melted away, and he diligently planted the tulip and daffodil bulbs. Deceased potted plants were hunted down, and the soil thrown onto the compost heap. The clay pots were allotted space in the greenhouse, where Charles proudly checked on his new Chinese elm, and Japanese red maple, bonsai trees.

Plackcedes had slaughtered enough wild animals back home not to be cautious, and the blood drained down the ceramic slab pooling at the bottom. Dela who was wearing the crocodile mask saw the mutt's Spirit lift. The hound happily bounded towards the light but then, almost as an afterthought, stopped and looked at Dela. The jaws opened wide, and the snarling beast sprang towards her. Dela ripped off the mask somewhat startled.

'Are you all right madam?' asked a concerned Plackcedes.

'Just a little fright Placky,' said Dela.

She quickly returned the mask, and saw the last spotted Dalmatian paw go through to the other side. Incredible; now all she had too was bring Chester back.

Chester was running through a meadow when Dela finally tracked him down. He was chasing after the pack. Charles, who was bringing a new bottle for the gas heater down the stairs, gave her the command words, but a panting Chester couldn't pass the threshold back to the surgery.

'Stupid hound,' said Dela 'let's try another one.'

Plackcedes had gone to freshen herself up, and Charles was about to do the honours; it was the first time Dela had seen him smile all day. He patted the powerful mastiff's head one last time, and sent the beast on his way with a cut and a thrust. Dela saw Midway's big brown eyes look sadly towards Charles.

There were no buttercups or sweet heather beneath his feet only burning coals to dance upon, and every time Dela whistled, Midway jumped in the air. Like a sheepdog he followed her towards the gate, and then suddenly he was there, back in the room.

Charles was in disbelief; the dog he had just killed was back to life before him on the marble altar, and with his neck miraculously healed. But Midway was growling and not wagging his tail. Fortunately the knife that Plackcedes held went straight through the demon dog's heart.

'I meant to ask,' said Plackcedes 'is this the cake knife?'

Hey presto Dela had done it, and she went to take a bath whilst Charles cleared up the mess. Plackcedes had a large slice of walnut sponge cake, and with her grey hair now dyed purple she looked rather delicious herself.

Felix was laced into a rubber body bag, and the heating was on. Grey canvas straps were buckled over him and under the bed; he was almost immobile. From the bedhead above his face hung a plastic phallus, and if he struggled to lift his head high enough he could suck out the orange juice, to stop himself dying of dehydration. Like a Ladyboy down on his luck he eagerly drained more sustenance, and glad to be alive.

They had to be quiet; none of them wanted the manimal next door listening in. Besides, in spite of finally being given Josh Templemead's heart, Charles could still be a little sensitive; at least when it came to people.

Plackcedes fastened the nipple clamps onto Dela's plump breasts, and the chain hung in between. The butt plug was soft and flexible, and Dela always encouraged her to ram it home. Plackcedes obliged and Dela stifled a gasp. Waves of emotion were washing through her, and Plackcedes quickly stifled Dela's moans with a warm invitation. They needn't have worried about Charles listening in, getting his rocks off, he was at the front of his house admiring his Christmas tree. He skirted the last of the fairy lights around the bottom and flicked on the show.

Charles knocked gingerly on the door.

'Breakfast is served,' he announced.

Plackcedes went downstairs, with Dela still resting. Later, as Charles' Christmas carols played through the house, Placky would bring her breakfast in bed.

Plackcedes found the duplicity exciting, the maid who was mistress, and to whom Dela would often bow down.

'Well done Charles,' said Dela 'but I think we'll be warm enough.'

He had left the heater on since morning, and the cellar was warm as toast; he turned off the gas.

Dela thoroughly expected to reproduce her trick with the very next canine, the lame poodle. She easily found her on the other side, but, in spite of the pawing and pining, Lassy couldn't find her way home. Dela removed the mask, and scribbled some more notes. Despondently, Plackcedes reset the stopwatch.

Another specimen was slaughtered in the name of pseudo-science, but still only Midway had made it back. They broke for tea.

In the middle of a snowstorm it didn't take long for temperatures to plummet, and the gas heater was back on. Dela realised having the body at her disposal was not a luxury she could take for granted. So Charles did the honours, and the two remaining animals were buried quickly in the snow-capped compost heap. Later, Everest didn't make it back, but Hercules couldn't wait for Charles to fasten the spiked collar back around his neck.

'Thank you Charles,' said Dela at the train station.

He attempted a smile.

'Get me more specimens,' said Dela 'I'm almost there.'

'Of course,' replied Charles.

'You can trot off back home now Charles and do whatever it is you do,' said Dela 'and don't dare lose that bloody mask.'

'Put my bags up there,' said Plackcedes on the train to Dela who humbly obliged.

It was exhilarating to experience the orders she usually dished out, and with it came a hitherto unknown freedom, a subjugated invigoration from the abdication of responsibility. Dela was the magician, but Plackcedes was quickly learning some tricks of her own.

A couple of podgy middle aged manimals in suits sat close by, and were ready to try their luck, but Dela gave them the evil eye, and their guffaws meant to impress those around were silenced.

'He must have been a good boy mistress,' said Plackcedes, reversing their roles for the benefit of Felix.

'If he's still alive,' replied Dela, prodding the rubber bag.

'Let's check,' said Plackcedes.

Plackcedes undid the zipper, and Dela unlocked the cage, but before his freedom could swell too much she quickly locked him back up.

'He's still with us,' said Dela.

'Poor thing,' said Plackcedes, mocking his torment.

They peeled off the rubber suit, but before Felix could thank them he was gagged and blindfolded. Still, perhaps he could illuminate them on the role of a slave. With the headphones playing Charles' festive carols, Dela gave the doubled over Felix an early present, the Cologne Christmas candle.

As they sipped rum on the sofa Dela was becoming annoyed with the bent over Felix's whimpering. The candle was burning bright, and the wax running onto his behind. But as she watched the flame flicker it suddenly hit her; that's what was missing, and the reason only Midway and Hercules had made it back. They needed fire. She hugged Plackcedes, who quickly shoved her tongue down her mouth. As for Felix, well candlelight was quite romantic.

Dela checked through her notes, she was right. And another thought crossed her mind; if the body wasn't there could a memento suffice? After all Hercules was mightily drawn to his collar, unlike Everest who'd had a mountain to climb.

Felix was sore but at least his beloved Dela was back, and in spite of her imperialistic frostiness she was just as glad to see him. Plackcedes was in the kitchen making him a supper to remember.

'Felix we're almost there,' she said.

'And you think this is the gift the Spirits have spoken of?' he asked.

'Undoubtedly,' she replied.

'And what are we to do with Joost?' asked Felix.

'I think we'll let him play for a little longer,' said Dela. 'He may have escaped for now, but I hardly think he'll come looking for trouble.'

'I guess you're right,' said Felix, but he wished they'd finished the job, he didn't like loose ends.

Plackcedes brought him the most magnificent pie with roast potatoes and gravy. Plackcedes had been taught never to waste food, but they didn't tell him it was Midway.

Dela was feeling torn between lovers, but it made her heart feel young. Whether or not Felix sensed Plackcedes' jealousy was neither here or there, he had always been Dela's staunchest advocate, and deserved his moment of attention; uncaged.

Leaving Felix in his slumber, Dela couldn't resist phoning Din, and telling him the good news.

'Hello brother, where are you tonight?' she asked.

He might be a thug but Dela always worried about him.

'At the warehouse,' he replied.

'So you're still going it alone?'

'Kind of.'

'Meaning?'

'I've roped someone in to help,' said Din.

'Anyone I know?'

'Yes.'

'Can you trust them?'

'You tell me sis, it's James Middlemass.'

'Well I don't think he'll do you over that's for sure, but do you think he's up to it?' asked Dela.

'He says so, and at least he can make the business look respectable.'

The business Din was referring to was the import side of the operation. James would be well out of his depth dealing with the drug pushers and the runners.

'Well that's good,' said Dela.

'But that's not the reason you're phoning is it. So tell me what's happened?' asked Din.

'I've done it. I've brought one pooch back to life.'

Although Midway wasn't exactly a pooch, he'd been marked for destruction after carelessly savaging three hikers in a bloody rampage.

'That's excellent news sis, but don't bring Dilwood back just yet, I quite like running the business.'

'On that point my dear brother I think we can both agree - best to let sleeping dogs lie.'

Chapter Forty Eight

The book of condolences was full, and the eulogies exhausted at The Church of Loving Saints.

'Aah, there you both are,' said Miriam to Joost and Bheki.

'It's so sad to see him leave,' said Bheki.

'He's not leaving, he's going home,' said Miriam.

The police had released Abel's body as soon as they could, and he was due for his final flight. Everyone whose heart he had touched was either here, or in Zimbabwe waiting for his coffin to touch down.

Eight of his closest friends carried the oak casket on their shoulders to the awaiting hearse.

The singing preacher who would love Bheki to call the tune came by her side to talk.

Everyone wanted a word with Miriam, so Joost was rightfully honoured when she whispered in his ear.

'He was always fond of you, from the moment you first met.'

Joost was taken aback; after all, he'd not exactly led the life of a saint.

'Oh he knew more about you than he ever let on, but he was like that,' said Miriam.

'Thanks Miriam, but you know there's nothing special about me,' said Joost.

'We shall see,' said Miriam 'we shall see.'

'What did Miriam say to you?' asked Bheki.

'Just how special I am,' said Joost smiling.

Bheki pinched his hand.

'Just joking,' he said

'So?' asked Bheki.

Joost didn't like this possessive side of her nature, and surely she couldn't be jealous of a widow's whisper.

'She was saying that Abel liked me quite a lot.'

'That's all?' asked Bheki.

'Of course,' he replied.

He was wearing the new black suit she had bought him, he had eyes only for her, as did half a dozen other men in the room, and she behaved like this! He might not have bought her an engagement ring but only because she was unfathomable. Perhaps he should take a good look around; there were plenty of other women on show.

Themba rushed up beside them.

'It's Eudy,' he blurted out 'I think she's about to give birth.'

They went to see for themselves; Eudy was sitting down and breathing heavily.

'Have your ...' said Bheki.

'Yes. I knew I shouldn't have come,' said Eudy.

'Make way,' shouted Themba 'my wife's about to give birth.'

A middle aged woman stood in front of them.

'By the look of her she's about to drop any minute.'

Themba looked annoyed.

'Gracious Brooks, midwife at your disposal,' said the woman holding out her hand.

'Let's get her upstairs quick, and you,' Gracious looked at Joost 'bring us some hot towels.'

'And bring me a drink,' added Eudy.

'Tea?' asked Joost.

'Gin,' said Eudy before disappearing with Gracious.

Joost rushed back from the off-licence, and followed Eudy's wailing up the stairs to the Goodyear's bedroom. Then he and Themba went outside for some fresh air. Themba looked like a ghost.

'Don't worry it gets better,' said Joost.

'That's what Bheki just told her,' said Themba.

'I meant for you,' said Joost smiling.

Joost couldn't find any glasses so he had given Bheki the gin on its own, which was just as well for Eudy as she drank straight from the bottle.

'I guess you've thought of a name,' said Joost trying to distract the restless Themba.

'Noah,' said Themba.

He would have been inside the room, but Eudy didn't want him there until all the bloody mess was over, besides Bheki was holding her hand.

Little Noah was born on a day without rain, which was good for Abel's cortege. As one life bid farewell another had just begun its journey.

'A healthy baby boy,' said Bheki smiling, and joining them outside.

'You can go up now,' she said to Themba, and Joost and Bheki followed him inside before the singing preacher could get any closer.

Gracious stayed a little longer, making sure mother and baby were fine. As she came down the stairs Joost asked her 'when should we take them to hospital?'

'I wouldn't if I were you,' said Gracious 'the place is full of germs.'

'And I thought we might keep them awake at night,' said Joost with a grin.

'Oh don't worry,' said Bheki 'we can still practice making babies of our own.'

Miriam couldn't help but perform a spontaneous christening. It was kept low key by everyone, but the singing preacher sang a delightful refrain that had everyone in tears.

'Hi,' said Mai.

'Hello,' replied Joost.

'Have either of you seen Plackcedes lately?' asked Mai.

'No, why?' asked Bheki.

'The police want to see her,' said Mai.

'Probably an unpaid parking ticket,' said Joost.

'But she disappeared after Abel's murder,' said Bheki.

'I know, I was just kidding,' said Joost.

'Well don't,' said Bheki.

'Plackcedes is definitely involved, and I guess with Dela too,' said Joost.

'Quite the Detective aren't you,' said Bheki sarcastically.

'Anyway guys I'm going to find Miriam, I'll catch you later,' said Mai.

'What's got into you?' asked Joost.

'What do you mean?' replied Bheki.

'You know, Miriam can't speak to me, you don't like what I say. I thought you were even going to accuse me of wanting to screw Mai.'

'You mean you haven't already,' said Bheki.

'You see, that's exactly what I mean.'

Eventually Bheki gave in.

'I'm sorry Joost, I guess I'm just broody.'

'Oh,' he said.

'Are you angry?' she asked.

'Yes.'

'Do you want to make me pay?' she asked.

He looked at her high heels, and black seamed stockings underneath the sleeveless turquoise dress and red raincoat.

'I guess so.'

'So why don't you fuck me then hero,' she taunted.

'Where?' he asked 'the place is packed'.

'If you really wanted it you'd already know by now.'

He escorted her to the kitchen, and the small broom cupboard.

At first it seemed a bit strange with the prayers only a few feet away, but soon he lost himself in the ardour as Bheki's svelte body rubbed against his.

In the evening they called a taxi, and after Miriam had made an endless fuss over little Noah. With her new hairdo no one had noticed Plackcedes Seka standing in the crowds outside.

'For goodness sake Felix, I can't have you panting like a dog every time we walk by,' said Dela.

'It's for your own good,' added Plackcedes.

'Honestly Felix, Plackcedes is nearly in her sixties' said Dela.

It was true but there was that gap in her teeth, her purple dyed hair, and those thick suspenders she always wore that silhouetted under her skirts; the same skirts that seemed to struggle to stretch around her big fat ass. Was it really his fault he looked? And it was Dela who'd left his cage off.

'I'm going to very busy until the new year, so I'm going to make damn sure you stay out of mischief,' said Dela.

Felix was on all fours on the bed, and grateful the candle had been put safely away. But there was something entertaining his butt as Dela milked him into the draining tray. Eventually his prostrate was expunged, and after his ablutions he was locked up. He actually felt better for it, with no more unruly urges crossing his mind, at least for now.

'You see Plackcedes,' said Dela 'men really are quite simple animals.'

Plackcedes nodded in agreement.

'Where are you now?' asked Frank into the scrying glass.

'In the hearse dear boy, on the way to the airport,' replied Abel Goodyear. 'I hope the air stewardesses are fit, I do love a woman in uniform.'

'What about the other side?' asked Frank 'what's it like?'

He was less interested in the living world, and even less in lip-sticked attendants, at least of the female variety.

'It's beautiful, unimaginable. At times I feel like I'm floating, and the hymns rain down, much more than music, you can physically feel them.'

'And the other Spirits, do you see them?' asked Frank.

'Naturally,' replied Abel. 'And there's no petty rivalries here, no envy,' he said.

'Is everyone you knew there?'

'Only the dead ones,' said Abel.

'I know that,' snapped Frank.

Abel knew Frank could become a little terse, and really didn't want to become his inside man. He would make this there last meeting.

'You know I really don't have to come if I don't want,' said Abel.

'I'm sorry,' said Frank 'I haven't had much sleep lately.'

'Alison?' asked Frank.

'Yes.'

'I've told you before dear boy she's having a ball. After all, you've seen her.'

'I know. I just wish she'd had more of a life,' said Frank.

'Well this life lasts forever so I wouldn't worry, and there's a good chance you could join her, see her again.'

'A good chance?' said Frank.

'Remember what we used to talk about Frank, your dark side,' said Abel.

'Yes.'

'Well you must keep it at bay, otherwise there could be unfortunate consequences.'

'I'm trying Abel.'

'Perhaps more prayer,' said Abel 'some charity work perhaps. And less heat under the collar over unimportant things.'

Frank could be a monster, using any excuse to vent the anger that flowed underneath his skin like lava. And he had seen the 'consequences' of inner turmoil in his scrying glass. The other side wasn't a bowl of cherries for everyone, but when the black dog of depression bit him he wanted to feel bad, anxious, and lost; he needed it, drowning in a pit of despair, self-pity and loathing. Feelings of emptiness, hollowness, were sometimes all he ever craved. Perhaps he was beyond redemption? After all where did the masochist live in a benevolent land?

'You're right Abel, I need to shed my melancholy,' said Frank.

'I understand Frank. Before you could hide from yourself as Madam Fang Fong,' said Abel.

He was absolutely right, but one day he was bound to face himself in the mirror.

'I don't like what I see,' said Frank honestly.

'Then now is the time to take action, is it not?'

'Yes,' said Frank.

But the more he saw of the other side, the more he realised to which side his disposition was suited, and it wasn't the land of milk and honey.

'Look Frank I wish you well, but this is the last time we shall meet,' said Abel.

'I understand,' said Frank.

'But let me tell you this as a friend, you are not beyond redemption. There was a man much like you who has now been saved.'

'Who?'

'Joost van Houten. Seek him out Frank, and tell him this from me, God help us all because Dela has found a way to bring back the dead.'

Before Frank could ask a million and one questions Abel was gone, and for Frank at least he wouldn't be coming back.

Chapter Forty Nine

They should have been un-wrapping the latest shipment, instead they were fighting over the broom.

'You've missed a bit,' said James.

'Where?' replied an indignant Din.

'Over there, in front of the office.'

Din grabbed the brush off of James, and rushed towards the last of the dirt. Suddenly he stopped and laughed, and James joined him.

'Look what she's done to us,' said Din referring to his sister.

'It's not really her fault, after all we did wish for it,' said James.

It was all part and parcel of Lance's rather protracted death, and no one had been able to look a gift horse in the mouth, but perhaps they should have been a little more careful. Din wasn't so much bulking up these days as sweeping up.

'Well I guess when Dela's not so busy she'll undo the spell,' said Din.

'What's she up to these days anyway?' asked James.

'Resurrection,' said Din, and then he held a finger to his mouth.

It could have been worse, sometimes he drew the finger across his throat.

'Is that why she spends half her time with Charles and his poodles?' asked James half joking.

Din nodded solemnly, and from the look in his eyes James knew not to push the subject any further. But he did grab the broom back and run towards the office. Din tripped him up, and as James went flying he picked up the broom once more. He swept the dirt into a neat little pile, but James was crouched behind him, and with a smaller brush of his own gathered it into a dustpan and the bin. Din snapped the broom in half, and looked murderously at James.

'I couldn't help myself,' said an apologetic James, wishing Dela wasn't quite as busy.

Din suddenly came back to his senses 'sorry,' he said.

'Let's un-wrap the shipment,' said Din.

There was a pallet in the warehouse, delivered from the docks this morning. Din sliced through the shrink wrap, and threw a box to James. Inside there were packets, jars and cans of Ratip pepper, oyster sauce, curry paste, dried lemon grass, dried chilli, fried garlic, and chilli mushroom paste.

'We were never sure if the pepper helped with the sniffer dogs, but of course we have an inside man,' said Din.

'We' used to be Din and Dilwood, now it stood for Din and James.

'What we're after is on the third row,' said Din.

They stacked the first two rows against the wall, and then Din starting from a corner handed every third box to James.

'You can open any packet you like,' said Din 'they all contain heroin. The jars have amphetamines inside, apart from the shrimp paste that's ecstasy.'

'What about the cocaine?' asked James becoming quite excited with his new career.

'We'll swap some of the horse with the African Group,' said Din.

James looked lost.

'Heroin, and they're an outfit on the other side of the river,' said Din referring to the Thames.

James nearly jumped out of his skin as Din's mobile rang.

'I'm outside,' said Dirk Sellars.

'It's him,' said Din to James.

'Good morning gentlemen, working late I see,' said Sellars.

He placed his burgeoning briefcase on the floor.

'Thanks for coming,' said Din.

'Not at all. But before we begin whatever have you done with Dilwood?' asked Sellars.

'He had an accident,' replied Din.

'You haven't been a naughty boy I hope,' said Sellars.

'No, like I said it was an accident,' repeated Din.

'Hey look it doesn't matter to me, I'm retiring. I brought the file you requested.'

He handed the briefcase over to Din who checked the contents.

'What about the whore's computer records?' asked Din.

'All deleted.'

'How can I be certain?' asked Din.

'Would I lie to you. After all you could always turn me in, and disappear back to Africa with your money.'

'True,' said Din.

'Anyway my man, I've got a plane to catch, so that's thirty grand if you please,' said Sellars.

'James fetch my case from the office,' said Din.

'You know with you and Dilwood gone there's something else I need,' said Din.

Sellars smiled as he counted the thirty large. He'd been waiting for this.

'The name of the inside man at the docks,' said Din.

'I was wondering when you'd ask,' said Sellars.

There was a pause.

'How much did you have in mind?' asked Sellars.

Din looked a little exasperated.

'I was kind of hoping you'd give me the name for free.'

'Nothing in life is free Din. You of all people should know that.'

'So what's your price?'

'Considering the value to the business shall we say a hundred large ones?'

Din rubbed the top of his head.

'It's too much, way too much.'

Then I guess we don't have a deal,' said Sellars pocketing the last of the 30K.

Din pulled a gun and aimed at Sellars head. Dirk tried to pull one himself from his mohair coat but James knocked it out of his hand. Perhaps he was better than he thought.

'You know I'll do it Dirk, and I'm counting. Ten, nine, ...'

'It's Lars Anders the deputy manager.'

'What's his cut?' asked Din.

'Ten grand per shipment.'

'But we paid you twenty,' said Din.

'That's business,' said Sellars.

'May I leave now?' he added.

'Yes go on,' said Din 'enjoy the money.'

This last sentence was the code for James to act.

'I will, but just remember Din without me there would never have been any operation,' said Sellars before turning around.

As he did James cut him wide open with the pallet knife.

'Why?' asked Sellars as he lay dying on the concrete floor.

'Just balancing the books Dirk, after all that's business.'

'Well done James,' said Din 'and by the way the money's yours.'

'You know what Din, he was making all that cash and couldn't even have his shirts ironed,' said a disgusted James rifling the dead man's pockets.

They'd fight over cleaning up later on.

Susie had been a little slut, but what was good for the goose was good for the gander. Good old Pandy was trawling the shemale websites for a replacement, and he didn't feel that old. He took another rainbow blotter from the locked drawer in his desk. The brightly coloured LSD tabs were next to a sealed gold envelope. Inside was an antique pearl necklace. He'd bought it to celebrate their anniversary, before Susie decided to make her intentions towards James Middlemass known.

The door creaked open, and Pandy quickly tried to close down his laptop.

'Have you forgiven me yet?' asked Susie.

'Forgiven you for what?' asked Pandalay.

'My infatuation of course.'

'Oh that trifle, I'd almost forgot,' lied Pandy.

'You know we never slept together,' said Susie not believing him.

'And besides he's not even into the third sex,' she said.

'Let's not talk about it Susie, besides I have a present,' said Pandy, and he opened his drawer once more.

Susie tore the envelope open, and was speechless.

'Go on try it on,' said Pandy.

'Are they real?' she asked.

'Of course, and happy anniversary,' said Pandy.

'Here you do it,' screeched Susie 'I'm all finger and thumbs.'

'Girls eh,' said Pandy and there was a look of sadness in his eyes.

He stepped behind Susie who was now seated in his 'Captain's' chair.'

'Careful,' said Susie.

But his hands were wrapped around her neck, and the thumbs were digging in. Mr Pandalay may have been an old timer but Susie was too fragile to fight back. Besides she'd always loved him with all her heart, until that ridiculous fantasy for James Middlemass; she stopped struggling.

Pandy was in tears, she'd broken his heart, and he'd stopped hers. The phone rang and he slowly picked it up.

'Hi handsome,' squealed the Ladyboy 'I'm Mona and we gotta a whole lotta moanin to do.'

Oh my thought Pandy, and he wrote down Mona's bank account details.

Mr Pandalay needed his inhaler, and once recovered looked at the lifeless body. He got a chiffon scarf to cover her bruised neck and kissed her on the mouth one last time. Dela's antics had made him feel invincible, untouchable even, but he couldn't dispose of the body alone.

Din and James were wrapping Sellars in shrink wrap; Din once had boxes full of the stuff but Dela for some reason kept asking him for more. The phone rang.

'Hi Din,' said Pandy 'I hope I'm not disturbing you.'

'Go on,' said Din.

'Susie's had a bit of an accident,' there was a pause.

'How bad is she?' asked Din.

'She's dead'.

'That's pretty bad,' said Din.

'Yes. Look I was wondering if you could help me get rid of the body?'

'Funny you should ask,' said Din 'I was about to get rid of one myself. I'll be round later'.

'Thanks Din. Chow,' said Pandy.

'It's Pandy,' said Din to James 'he's just killed Susie.'

James looked very terribly guilty.

Frank thought he could trust Joost, but he didn't really expect him to defeat Dela, especially if he helped her. Dela was the one who could bring back Alison, and that's all he wanted.

'Herman I'll be gone for a day or two, look after the house,' said Frank.

'Be good, and if you can't be good be ...' said Herman.

'Careful,' they shouted together.

Frank caught the train to Bishopsfield. According to Bill that's where Dela had honed her latest skills, on the local vet's animals. He took his scrying glass, maybe the witch would be interested in his own powers?

The knock at the door caught him by surprise. Charles Carney had at last baked Josh Templemead's heart into a pie, and was just taking his first bite. Perhaps a little more mint sauce he thought.

'The surgery's closed today,' said Charles to the stranger.

'I haven't come with a pet, I've come to see Dela Eden Obi.'

'Who?' asked Charles.

'You don't have to pretend with me. Look I know what goes on here, and I have a proposition for Dela.'

'I still don't know who you're talking about,' said Charles.

'Look I'm not the police, and I have information that Dela would be disappointed to miss.'

'About what?' asked Charles.

'Whom actually,' corrected Frank 'Joost van Houten.'

Charles finally conceded.

'Come on in, but she won't be here until this evening.'

Frank hung his coat in the porch, and was shown the lounge.

'Can I get you a drink?' asked Charles.

'Scotch on the rocks if you have any,' said Frank.

'Undoubtedly,' replied Charles 'I think I'll join you.'

And he had one more scoop of pie before covering up the casserole dish.

They sat in front of the burning logs in Charles' fireplace, as Frank loosened up.

'This Joost fellow, I believe he's been quite a thorn Dela's side,' said Frank.

'You could say that,' said Charles.

'I can nip him in the bud,' said Frank.

'Well it's not me you have to convince, but what makes you say that?' asked Charles.

'I can take you to Joost, or lead him, and his whore, into a trap.'

'Interesting,' said Charles. 'By the way, can I get you some cherry pie and vanilla custard?'

'A man after my own heart,' said Frank.

Perhaps thought Charles, but not just yet.

With more whisky washing down the second helping, Frank elucidated on his own clairvoyant gift, and how he had stumbled upon Dela's latest trick.

'I'd be a good man to have on your side,' said Frank.

Charles had no doubt, but the last thing he wanted was an even more omnipotent Dela. On top of that he wanted to help Joost, not betray him.

'Let me take these into the kitchen,' said Charles picking up the dishes.

He had one more bite of Josh's pie, picked up his sharpest knife, and returned to a restful Frank.

Frank caught a glimpse in the mirror but he really was too slow. Nonetheless Charles caught him in the throat and not the heart, equally deadly but Frank spun around with blood gushing everywhere.

There was a terrible mess, but perhaps James would give him a hand shampooing the carpet.

'Hi Din I've got a bit of a problem,' said Charles down the phone.

'Let me guess,' said Din.

After all wasn't three the magic number?

Chapter Fifty

It was bitterly cold outside, and dark, although Charles did his best with the flashlight.

'My I have been blessed,' said Dela 'I guess I won't need your hounds of the Baskervilles after all Charles.'

Back home in Africa, Dela had only had one set of books to learn English; the cases of Sherlock Holmes.

They were looking at the three bodies stacked up in Charles' shed; one wrapped in cling film and reminding Dela of Felix, one rolled in a rather exquisite rug, and then Charles' victim - the conundrum.

'Thank you Charles, we can join the others now,' said Dela looking rather pleased with herself.

She watched Charles trudge back ahead of her, and illuminating the path; she couldn't wait to hear a more detailed explanation of his indiscretion.

The logs were roaring in the hearth, and Charles had made gingerbread men for everyone. It reminded Lucy of Cologne, and she wondered when Joost would get in touch - if ever.

'Well you two have really surprised me,' said Dela to James and Charles 'especially you Charles, have you eaten the heart already?'

'Some of it,' he said.

Christine was standing by the white tinsel Christmas tree.

'Charles where did you get this?' she asked holding one of his baubles.

'I gave it to him mother,' said Lucy.

It was one of a nativity set Christine had bought at the Christmas fair in Cologne.

Plackcedes brought drinks and vol-au-vents in from the kitchen, and Charles was a little peeved she had intruded into his domain without even asking.

'So Charles why did you ever kill Frank Sleigh?' asked Christine.

James had removed his wallet when helping to move him on top of the others, and Christine was looking at his driver's licence.

'I caught him snooping around,' said Charles.

'That's all?' asked James miffed that Charles had stolen some of his limelight.

Dela was carefully listening; she had found it a little strange that Charles had resorted to murder, even with his new found courage.

'Not exactly, I invited him in and he kept asking about Dela, and if I knew anything about voodoo.'

'Which naturally you denied,' said Din stifling a yawn.

'Of course,' said Charles looking a little hot under the collar.

'Well go on,' said Lucy, trying to prompt Charles into a more convincing yet elaborate tale.

'Oh yes, he said he was a clairvoyant who knew Joost van Houten, and when I left the room temporarily to make a cup of tea he tried to make off with this.'

Charles grabbed the crocodile mask off the top of the sideboard, immediately earning his reprieve and Dela's thanks.

'Thank you Charles but be careful how you handle the mask,' said Dela, and she bit down on a prawn canapé.

She then gave Felix a playful slap on the wrist as he went for another bite himself.

'Careful Felix you're trying to lose weight,' she reminded him.

Felix put it down, and looked around the room smiling. He noticed James looking jealousy at Charles.

Dela was in party mood, and it was time for a game of truth and dare.

'Your turn Pandy,' she said.

Mr Pandalay was already regretting his crime of passion, and looked very uneasy indeed, especially with James standing next to him; he took a puff from his inhaler.

'A lovers tiff,' he eventually said.

Din laughed out loud.

'Surely not Pandy,' said Dela, looking sad on his behalf.

'I just snapped,' he said.

'Obviously,' said Dela.

'Like Susie's neck,' added James.

'Quite,' said the sober suited Mr Pandalay.

'Well never mind; easy come easy go. And at least we don't have to worry about the police in Susie's case,' said Dela whilst staring at Charles.

'I truly am grateful Charles, but how do we know that Frank Sleigh won't lead the police straight to us?' she asked.

'But he did come to steal the mask,' said Lucy jumping to Charles' defence.

'True,' said Dela 'but perhaps he told someone where he was going.'

'He would only tell one person,' said Pandy.

'You know this Frank?' asked Dela inquisitively.

'In a way yes; Susie was a big fan, and went to his leaving party. He used to be a drag queen.'

Now he was just a drag.

'And?' asked Dela.

'He lives, or rather he lived, with his boyfriend Herman.'

James was already getting ready to hand over the wallet, and the diamante encrusted mobile phone.

Din scrolled down the numbers, and then held a finger to his mouth. Everyone was silent.

'Hello is that Herman?' asked Din.

'Yes it is,' replied the voice.

'I know you don't know me, but I'm a friend of Frank's. Unfortunately he's plastered, is there any chance I can bring him back in my car?'

'Please do,' said Herman 'I hope he hasn't made too much of a nuisance of himself this time.'

'Well he has made rather a mess of the carpet,' said Din.

'Sorry about that. Look here's our address. How soon can you bring him home?' asked Herman.

'I'll be there in an hour,' said Din, and he closed the call.

'Well sis looks like you'll have another specimen by tonight,' said Din smiling.

'You coming James?' asked Din, fully expecting his protégé to join him.

'James not so fast,' said Dela as he prepared to leave 'we haven't heard your story yet.'

He was getting quite a taste for assassination; it was up front and personal. And Christine was becoming quite proud of her man too.

'Well Din was there, obviously,' began James.

'Not so bashful James, you did it on your own,' said Din.

'Thanks. Well basically it was a business dispute, and I needed to protect our interests,' said James proudly.

'So you cut him open, quite the Jack the Ripper aren't you,' said Dela smiling.

'Sis we must go,' said Din, and he kissed Dela on the cheek.

James was hanging onto his tailcoats as they brushed by Charles' tinsel on their way out.

'Go on then,' said Dela to Felix, and he crammed another mushroom vol-au-vent in his mouth, before washing it down with the local breweries special festive beer.

When Din and James returned with their present everyone was feeling a little tired. The Middlemass' and Pandy soon returned to their respective homes, but Din couldn't face another long drive. He decided to crash out on Charles' sofa; the one not stained by Frank's blood.

Dela and Felix were tucked up in bed whilst Plackcedes had the other spare room. Dela left the curtains open so she could see the snow falling outside.

'Are you alright?' asked Felix.

'I'm fine darling,' replied Dela, and she could see the love in his eyes.

'Felix do you think that sometimes I'm a little too hard on you?' she asked.

He smiled, and thought carefully about his response.

'Definitely,' he replied 'but you know what, I absolutely love it. After all I'm a manimal,' and he growled.

Dela couldn't stop laughing, and it felt like their early days when Felix was always making her laugh. She took the key from the chain around her neck.

'Can I trust you?' she asked.

'Of course,' he replied 'there's not much I can get up to here.'

Dela unlocked him. He was right; after all there was only Charles, Din, and Plackcedes in the house.

Early morning and Din let himself out of the house. Felix was watching from the window, and later saw Charles heading to his car and the 24 hour supermarket; he needed some stain remover.

With Dela sound asleep Felix crept along the landing, pillowcase in one hand and knife in the other. He silently turned the brass door knob to Plackcedes' room.

She was wearing a scarf around her head as he hoodwinked her with the pillowcase. He pressed the knife against her throat, and after a few grunts unburdened himself of his lust. He lay on top of Plackcedes as she removed the hood.

'You know Dela would flog you half to death for this,' said Plackcedes.

Felix went to grab the knife, but it was already in her hand.

'Don't worry I won't tell,' said Plackcedes smiling.

'But first you got to do a lot better than that. Now do me again, and make it real slow this time,' she said.

Finally Felix got up to go.

'Better, but longer next time,' said Plackcedes.

Her teeth bit into his ear as she whispered 'you owe me.'

The manimal slinked off with his tail between his legs.

'Morning darling where have you been?' asked Dela, stretching in the bed.

Felix put a pot of tea, and the leftover vol-au-vents, on the dresser.

'I just thought I'd do something I haven't done in a long time,' he replied.

'How sweet,' said Dela 'breakfast in bed.'

Eventually Dela finished her poached eggs, and looked pitifully at Felix. In her outstretched palm was his chastity cage.

'Sorry darling, but you have been much better behaved since you started wearing it,' she said.

He looked down at the floor.

'Alright,' relinquished Dela 'take a shower first but then I'm locking you up. Besides it will soon be Christmas.'

The first specimen was hauled onto the slab, with the gas heater on maximum. The orange candescent flames flickered, and just for good measure Dela had lit six of Charles' Christmas candles along the back wall, on his hostess trolley.

Charles and Felix, the attendant morticians, were allowed to stay and watch the proceedings; some of the victims might be aggrieved, if they returned. Felix glanced nervously at Plackcedes, but his secret was safe, for now.

Dela wore the crocodile mask, searching for her prey. Herman couldn't wait to return. Unfortunately his Spirit flickered in and out of view, before finally disappearing, but at least he was dressed.

Charles went to get his other gas heater from the advertised surgery, and James Middlemass was ordered to collect every candle he could find. He decided to stay for the show, and like Charles and Felix, held a machete.

The near reappearance of Frank Sleigh was actually solid, and was both much better, and worse. Everyone in the room could see his strong Spirit hovering above the corpse. Unfortunately two pairs of extremely hairy arms dragged him back by the ankles. For a moment James was shaking.

Dirk Sellars did a no show; such were his sins only a cloud of hot brimstone and sulphur could be seen, and smelt, in the cellar. It seemed that the afterlife, like the world, was a melting pot.

James was beginning to wish he'd never become involved with Dela, and wondered how many years of atonement in a monastery could save him from such an equally ghastly fate.

Charles hoped even more to do the right thing when given the chance, and kept his fingers crossed.

They staggered out of the cellar, leaving Charles to use the pole and open the old coal hatch, hopefully removing the stench.

'We'll try again another day,' said Dela, convinced the trick was to increase the power of the flames.

And next time she'd try Susie Chang; surely her life must have been a little more serene, if not Saintly.

Dambala, the great cosmic equaliser, had spoken, but even Dela was surprised to see the affirmation of a Christian belief - especially one so hellish.

'Don't look so worried James,' said Dela 'I'll protect you.'

He bit the head off a gingerbread man.

Eventually the three unwise men were bagged up, awaiting a less than Christian burial.

As soon as everyone had left, Charles rushed into the kitchen, pushing the last of his pie in the microwave; he'd finish off a hearty meal tonight.

Chapter Fifty One

He stepped onto the bus, holding the six foot pine Christmas tree in front of him.

'You can't come on with that,' said the driver.

Joost put the tree to one side, stared at the driver with one eye. The driver quickly looked him up and down, and gulped.

'Alright, but keep the tree to one side,' he said.

It was a bit tight, and a few passengers went home with pine needles in their shopping bags, but it was snowing, and the pavements were slippery.

Joost made it back to the house just before Bheki, who unloaded bags of new baby clothes from the taxi. Themba made them a cup of rooibos, whilst Eudy rocked Noah in his cradle.

'Where would you like me to put it?' asked Joost holding the tree, and looking at Bheki's ass.

'Wherever it goes it's going to be a tight fit,' she replied, and there was a knowing pause between them.

Joost place it in the corner, and opened a box of coloured lights, carefully wrapping them around the tree. He hadn't done this in years, and he could almost hear Hildy asking to help whilst Stella wrote the Christmas cards.

'I'll have to get some baubles now,' said Joost.

'And a star to put on top,' said Eudy.

Joost tried to put on a brave face, and forget about the past, but it was hard, especially at Christmas time. He kept Bheki's present in his pocket, unsure whether or not she'd like it. I guess it would depend on her mood, and his too; it was an engagement ring.

The icy wind blew through the doors at the police station as the courier delivered an envelope to the duty sergeant. He put it to one side, and finished booking in the two drunks; the festive season had begun.

He looked at the letter on his break. It was addressed to him, and looked like a Christmas card not a bomb, but it could still contain anthrax. He broke the seal carefully in front of his mug of coffee, and iced doughnut. Inside, the card read Merry Christmas from Dirk, but there were no glad tidings; it was posthumous.

'Hi Mike, hope you and the wife are well' began the message 'but if you're reading this I'm dead. I wasn't always what I seemed but ask the boys to protect my memory if they can. Anyway to cut a long story short ...'

Mike turned the card over to the back.

'I was involved with a drugs gang run by Dilwood Benson and Din Obi. Dilwood's done a runner, but his partner has killed me. You can find Din and maybe my body at ...' and there was a long address for a warehouse.

'P.S. You always did wonder where I got the money for all those holidays haha.'

Mike put the letter under his saucer, and went to get another doughnut. He'd like to protect his friend's reputation, but Dirk sought revenge from the grave. But the whole station could be put under investigation, and Mike's hands weren't exactly lily white either.

Eventually he handed the letter to his superior, one of the new boys who thought he was a knight in shining armour, until his zealous aspirations would be ground down like Mike's coffee.

James was doing a lot of praying lately; ever since he'd caught a glimpse of the darker side, and perhaps his future. And it wouldn't be temporary, eternity was just that. He could still smell the sulphur in his nostrils. He hadn't eaten since, and couldn't get those long hairy arms with the gnarled hands and claws out of his mind. He could hardly atone for his sins with a charity fun run. Christine interrupted his meditation.

'You still look worried James,' she said entering the spare room come chapel.

James had initially converted the room for appearances sake. But recently he'd found two pieces of charred timber from the burnt out church, and fashioned them into a cross; rising from the ashes and all that. And there was a brass bell the Bishop had asked him to return.

The fund to replace St Agnes had already begun, but it would be bereft of the services of the Reverend James MIddlemass. He wasn't duly concerned; right now he was deeply worried about his future, not his past, which was no longer intertwined with St Agnes.

'It was nightmarish Christine,' he said, once more referring to the demonic ghouls.

'All right James, I've heard the story a hundred times already, there's really no need to keep going over it,' she said.

Neither did she want scaring half to death.

'Anyway how long have we got left in the vicarage?' she asked.

'Until February,' said James.

'After all we've done for the dozy beggars around here,' said Christine referring to James' congregation.

'I'm afraid so,' he said, still on his knees.

'Well let's hope you start earning some money from your latest venture,' she said.

'Oh I've already begun,' said James smiling 'how does thirty grand grab you?'

It grabbed Christine quite a lot, and she grabbed and hugged James too. But she had to see the shoebox to completely believe it.

'It looks like this change in direction could work out rather well,' she said flicking through the banknotes.

Perhaps it could. With their respective lovers no longer around, and with Lucy recovered, they'd found a new energy, and it wasn't the passion of Christ.

'But for god's sake James do cheer up,' said Christine 'and keep the faith.'

Faith in voodoo and Dela she meant. Christine had no doubts herself; she'd never really been a fan of hymns.

James decided to cover his bets, and returned to prayer. After all like the tenet proposed, ten minutes of prayer a day was a worthy gamble for paradise. James prayed for another hour.

They drove past the site where Irena was buried, into the woods as far as they could go. There were three bodies to bury now, and probably a fourth later. Charles and Felix took the pick axes to break up the stony ground, and Din and James followed with the shovels. Pandy sat in the car next to Christine, puffing on his inhaler.

James looked exhausted and Christine took him, and anyone else who asked, a mug of hot chocolate from the flask.

Six foot down and Frank, Herman, and Sellars, were thrown unceremoniously into the pit; it was left open for now.

Din swung Susie's corpse into Lucy's old wheelchair, and they prepared to find a clearing. Pandy was consumed with guilt, and asked to stay behind in the car.

'This will do,' said Dela.

The place looked familiar to Din, and he nervously twisted the gold ring that Irena had given him before throwing deep into the woods.

Dela marked out a large circle, broken branches were laid around the circumference, and doused in petrol. Susie was thrown in the middle, with her head and neck contorted, and the fire was lit. There was no need for a familiar item when you had the entire body at your disposal, and Dela soon found Susie washing her hair in a brook next to a large, but not enchanted, castle. She seemed happy enough but needed no encouragement to join them.

Before you could say shampoo and conditioner Susie Chang reappeared alive, although naturally she appeared dazed, and her clothes weren't going to keep out the cold.

'Has he forgiven me?' asked a bewildered Susie.

Din, who was regretting the murder of Irena, lowered the gun and whispered in Dela's ear.

'Let's ask him,' said Dela removing the crocodile mask.

Pandy's phone rang.

'Are you lost?' he asked.

'No' said Dela.

'Look we've got Susie here,' she said.

Pandy took in a gulp of air.

'How is she?' he asked.

'Fine considering she's just come back from the dead,' said Dela.

'Look, are you sure you want her to leave you again?' asked Dela.

She could be a romantic too. The phone was on loudspeaker, and Din got ready to squeeze the trigger.

'No,' replied Pandy.

'Then what do you want us to do?' asked Dela.

'Bring her back to me,' he said 'I made a terrible mistake.'

Din put the gun back in his trouser pocket, and gave Susie his thick woollen coat to wear. Christine handed her a cup of hot chocolate.

'Love's a funny old game,' said Din.

Susie ran back into his outstretched arms.

'Can you ever forgive me?' Pandy asked her.

She kissed him on the cheek and mouthed 'yes' as the tears ran down their faces. They had more than made up, Pandy could ditch the terrible Mona, and it was true - you only did live twice.

Dela let Pandy and Susie stay in the car, as the earth was thrown over the three who didn't make it back.

As they drove off the bracken was crunching underfoot, and someone was wandering about. It was an old friend of Din's who had a story no one would believe, but nonetheless was grateful for a second chance, and who knows a spot of revenge - hell had no fury like a woman killed.

No one was happier than Pandy and Susie, but everyone was pleased, apart from the remorseful Din. He decided to drive to the warehouse, and console himself with work.

'I'm going to do some stocktaking,' he said to Dela, who was busy reading the Christmas cards on the vicarage mantelpiece.

James wasn't in party mood either, and decided to follow Din. It was better than listening to Dela, and the lesser of two of evils.

'Where are you off to?' Christine asked him.

'I thought I'd give Din a hand,' he replied.

'Well you'd better get going,' she said 'Din drives like the devil.'

Christine had only just realised what an astute businessman James could be, and with his recent earnings it was all she could do to encourage him.

It was kind of habit forming, and no one could blame Din for reaching for his gun; he was rushed by three guys in black body armour as soon as he flicked on the light. And they only had one response - Din was shot dead.

James had wanted to turn his car around, and avoid the flashing blue lights but he was caught in their trap.

'Step out of the car sir,' said the police officer.

'You're out late sir,' said the policeman as his colleague went to check on James' driving licence.

'I often come out at night,' said James.

The policeman smiled.

'Not a vampire are you sir?'

'Goodness no, I'm a vicar.'

'He's right,' said his colleague returning James' ID.

'It still doesn't explain what you're doing out so late in this neck of the woods does it sir,' said the policeman.

'Look I know it's silly but it's the only time I get to myself, to contemplate,' said James.

'Really sir, and what are you contemplating tonight?'

'Eternity, paradise, and hell,' replied James.

'OK sir you can save it for the sermon, but be careful, there's some real demons on the roads these days.'

They let him go, but if they'd followed him home they'd have found a house full of monsters.

'Another vicar looking for hookers,' said the officer shaking his head.

James pulled Dela to one side; he'd heard the gunfire, and seen an ambulance take Din's body away. She didn't take the news as badly as he thought - well she could bring back the dead.

Chapter Fifty Two

Dela had a list in front of her, it wasn't a Christmas list, but if your name was on it you might receive the best ever present. She wanted something from Din's flat, including Koni's pen; the one Christine Middlemass had bought him. And then there were her loyal servants Bill and Barbara, who'd never brought her as much joy as Plackcedes, but nonetheless needed rewarding for their dedication.

Dela had ordered Charles to grab something from The Crossed Heart, before a lifetime of knick knacks were carted away. The missing publicans were rightfully considered victims of the church fire, with the third body unidentified.

Felix was out shopping for one last present, and Dela looked at the collection he hated so much - the shrunken heads. There were four in all, and she tried to keep them out of sight, but it wouldn't be easy with Plackcedes just as fascinated.

'Do you know who they all are?' asked Plackcedes.

'That is my great grandfather,' said Dela with pride.

'That one is the man that murdered him, that's a rival witchdoctor, and that head belonged to an explorer,' she said.

They were all crammed together in a shoebox, and if it wasn't for Felix they would have become as much a part of their Christmas decorations as the flashing Santa Claus in the front window, high above the ground.

'They are truly magnificent,' said Plackcedes twisting her hair.

Dela looked at her, and instantly knew what was on her mind.

'What do you want me to do?' she asked.

'I thought you could try something new to keep me happy, that's what you want isn't it?'

'Yes, with every breath,' answered Dela.

'Come along then,' said Plackcedes grabbing Dela's arms from behind, and pushing her towards the bedroom.

Christmas had come early.

The elderly married couple dropped her off in central London still worried, even though Irena had done her best to placate their concerns. But they had found her alone on the edge of the woods, in the middle of the night.

She passed the rows of stores packed with shoppers. Not so long ago she would have joined them to please her new beau, but now she knew she'd been duped, and worse. She walked into a bar for a stiff drink.

'Can I get you this one?' asked the pin striped youth with lewdness in his eyes.

'Not unless you want to hear what awaits you after death,' said Irena.

He quickly scarpered.

Upon Dela's instruction Felix had drilled a large hole between the bathroom and the bedroom. He wore his headphones, and had to guess who was pleasuring him from the other side - Dela or Plackcedes. Unfortunately he couldn't hear the door open, and the neighbour's son enter.

'Tell your mum the debts cleared,' said Dela, as Plackcedes helped pull the twitching Felix through the gap.

'He's all yours,' she said.

The neighbour dropped to his knees, and Dela and Plackcedes couldn't stop laughing.

When it was all over Dela gave their guest a drink of cola; the one with Santa on the bottle.

'And don't worry,' said Dela 'I promise I won't tell your mum about our little secret.'

After all he was engaged to a girl from their village back home.

'I don't know which one of you did it, but that was the most explosive experience ever,' said Felix.

Dela and Plackcedes gave each other a knowing look, and smiled.

'Hey look you two,' said Plackcedes 'it's Christmas Eve, why don't you go out for a meal?'

'Brilliant idea,' said Felix.

'Are you sure you'll be alright on your own?' asked Dela.

'Don't worry about me,' said Plackcedes 'I'll be fine, now go the both of you.'

Even from the height of their flat Plackcedes could see them leave the block arm in arm. Now was her chance.

Joost looked over his shoulder to check Bheki had left the room, and answered the call.

'Hi Joost,' said Irena.

'Where have you been stranger?' asked Joost.

'You won't believe me,' said Irena.

'Try me,' said Joost.

'Well it's about life and death,' said Irena.

'Go on,' said Joost, and he was poured an appetizer.

'Wait, don't say any more,' said Joost 'I need to see you in person. I'll be there in under an hour.'

'Where are you going?' asked Bheki.

'Oh just some late night Christmas shopping,' said Joost.

He hated to lie, but Bheki had been more than jealous of Irena.

When everything had been revealed, Joost couldn't help but hug Irena. Before he could leave her flat there was a knock at the door.

'I hope I'm not interrupting anything?' said Bheki looking at Irena.

'You followed me,' said Joost thoroughly disappointed.

'And you lied, or did you get lost and think this was a shop?' retorted Bheki.

Joost sighed. He was in no mood for a fight.

'It's not what it looks like,' he said.

'And what does it look like? asked Bheki.

'Look sit down and we can explain,' said Joost.

'This I can't wait to hear,' said Bheki sarcastically.

Two hours later and Bheki had been convinced Joost had been on his best behaviour. But one thing did concern her; he seemed terribly excited that people could be brought back from the dead.

Plackcedes had understood Joost's heartache, she had one of her own. Her husband had been cruelly taken from her over twenty years ago, in an accident at work. He'd died in a blast at a gold mine, in a place where life was cheap and compensation unheard of.

Plackcedes had never forgotten her first love, and now she had a chance not just to see him again but to bring him back. She removed the wedding ring from her finger, and placed it in the middle of four lit candles. With her hands shaking she donned the mask, and was looking at his handsome face again.

'Join me,' said Plackcedes.

'But I am happy here,' he replied.

'For loves sake,' begged Plackcedes.

'But you are old my love, and I am forever young,' he said.

'Please, the window is closing,' said Plackcedes 'come back to me.'

'It is not possible,' he replied staunchly 'it would anger the ancestors.'

Plackcedes removed the mask with tears streaming down her eyes. When she had dried her sorrow, she heard a commotion coming from the bedroom, and in that awful moment realised the shrunken heads had come alive - full bodied.

Old adversaries remain just that, and Dela's great grandfather and the warrior who'd killed him were taunting each other with their spears. The explorer was in a fight to the death with the witchdoctor, and the tussle soon spilled over into the lounge.

Plackcedes hid behind the sofa. When the noise had died down she saw Dela and Felix standing in the upturned room with their mouths wide open.

After they'd found a drink to give her, it was up to a trembling Plackcedes to explain.

'As soon as you left there was a knock at the door,' said Plackcedes 'it was Joost van Houten.'

'He must have waited until we left,' said Felix fighting her corner.

'Go on,' said Dela.

'He forced his way in, and grabbed the mask,' said Plackcedes.

Felix and Dela looked at one another and nodded, so far it made sense.

'He tried it on saying he'd got his eye back, but the heads came back to life.'

'Great grandpa,' said Dela smiling.

'The mask was knocked from his grasp in the fighting, and Joost fled empty handed' said Plackcedes.

'Where are they now?' asked Dela.

'I'm not sure. Maybe they're still in the block?' said Plackcedes.

There was a loud scream from outside, and Felix went to check the window.

'They're outside,' said Felix as he saw four men in fancy dress disappear behind the garages.

Plackcedes did her best to look mortified, whilst Dela just looked mournfully at her empty shoebox.

Later in the evening Felix passed Plackcedes in the kitchen.

'I found this on the floor,' he said with a knowing look on his face, and handed her a wedding ring.

Plackcedes looked shocked.

'Don't worry,' said Felix 'I won't say a word. But now we're even,' and he returned the plain gold band to her grateful outstretched hand, enjoying the moment as he felt her warm flesh.

Chapter Fifty Three

Joost un-wrapped another Versace sweater, and thanked Bheki; not the way he would have liked, but Eudy and Themba were there, as well as little Noah.

Bheki tried to look pleased with her perfume although Joost had another present in his pocket, and it wasn't what she would normally expect from that direction. But there was still an unpleasant mood between them, and Themba and Eudy decided to take little Noah for a ride in his pram, so they could clear the air.

'You can't still be upset about yesterday,' said Joost.

'You lied,' said Bheki.

'Well I could hardly tell you I was going to see Irena, you hate her.'

'She started it,' said Bheki.

'The poor woman was killed by Din,' said Joost.

'So now you're feeling sorry for her,' screamed Bheki.

This was intolerable.

'Look I know what you need,' said Joost, and he grabbed her arms.

'Get off of me,' shouted Bheki, and she bit his neck as they wrestled on the floor near the Christmas tree.

Joost ripped her corduroy trousers down, and as he pummelled into her she dug her nails deep into his back. Eventually they were both done.

'Merry Christmas,' said Joost.

'Now that's what I call a present,' said Bheki, 'perfumes ha.'

James and Christine were dressed in their evening wear, circulating amongst the guests. It could be there last chance to party in such beautiful surroundings.

Dela placed the opal ring ripped from Herman's finger between the lit candles on the hearth. She wanted to remove all doubts concerning her new powers, besides in for a penny in for a pound of flesh, and she put on the mask.

Soon a hand was seen reaching out from the void, and it had to be Herman's, the fingernails were painted alternate black and electric blue. Before it could grab the ring back James hit the unfortunate hand with a poker, and it returned to whence it came.

'Beggars can't be choosers,' said James by way of explanation, and then he looked at Dela who had removed the mask.

Fortunately there was no scornful look, and he pocketed the ring.

'He wasn't going to stay around long, but Din, Vankoni, Bill and Barbara will,' said Dela.

There was a ripple of applause, although James didn't want to see Vankoni return, and prowl around his wife like a hungry wolf.

'That's great news Dela,' said Lucy. 'When can we expect to see them?'

'New Year's Eve.'

At least he'd have Din back thought James; he wasn't making any headway in his crumbling drugs empire, although he hadn't told Christine.

'Do you have it Charles?' asked Dela.

He looked a little flustered, and he could see Plackcedes grinning at him with that gap in her teeth. Finally he remembered.

'Of course,' he said, and he handed Dela a photo of Bill and Barbara from his jacket pocket.

'I thought that would be most appropriate,' he said.

'Excellent,' replied Dela. 'And for Din I have his favourite watch.'

It was a Rolex, diamond encrusted - naturally.

'And for Koni?' asked Christine making James feel a little nervous.

'This delightful pen he was quite fond of,' said Dela holding up the article like a clerk in a courtroom with the exhibit.

Christine smiled, and fortunately James didn't notice.

It was nearly midnight, and everyone else had gone to bed. Joost opened the wooden dolls until he had Lucy Middlemass' number in his hand. Tentatively he sent a text 'I'm ready to talk. Joost'.

He was sat on the sofa with a glass of scotch in his hand when the phone vibrated.

'Is that Mr van Houten?' asked Lucy.

'Please call me Joost,' he said.

And they had a long and thoughtful discussion about redemption and resurrection in warm hushed tones. Lucy was grateful for his role in Oxford, and he for Dilwood's death. Din's demise was the icing on the Christmas cake.

'Where have you been?' asked Bheki as Joost got underneath the bed sheets.

'I was having a drink,' he replied.

'No more secrets I hope,' said Bheki.

'Not at all,' replied Joost.

Bheki had never seen him with such a wide smile on his face. Obviously she was keeping him happy, but could he do the same for her?

Boxing Day and they went for a walk in the park. There were lovers, couples with families, and singles. Which if any, thought Bheki, would she and Joost become? Although she was proud to be holding such a handsome man.

The ring was burning a hole in Joost's pocket, £10,000 worth from the sale of his flat. But for now, after speaking with Lucy, he was holding back. He kissed Bheki on the cheek.

'I thought you had something for me?' she asked.

'I have, but I can't give it you whilst everyone is watching,' he replied.

Bheki laughed, and they walked arm in arm, down the hill into Greenwich.

Chapter Fifty Four

They were paying a visit to Miriam Goodyear, to see how she was coping, but Joost had an ulterior motive. After visiting the bathroom he quietly swept into Abel's study, and opened the top right hand drawer of his bureau. It was exactly where he'd seen the pastor leave it the last time they talked - his watch.

On their way back Joost was dying to see John Lacey's old flat, but he didn't want to visit until he'd shook Bheki off.

'I'm going to get some more booze,' he said as Bheki got out of the car.

'Well don't be long, Eudy and Themba have taken Noah for a check-up, and the house is empty,' she said with a glint in her eye.

Joost felt even guiltier, but drove as fast as he could.

Bheki couldn't figure him out. One minute he was terrified to drive alone, the next he was OK, one day he wanted to get engaged, the next day he stalled. He'd bought her a massive rock she wasn't supposed to see, and then he stole the pastor's gold watch - whatever was he up to she thought?

Joost was shocked to see the removals van being loaded up outside John's flat, but perhaps he'd made it just in time. He left the screwdriver in the glove compartment, passing two guys carrying a fridge freezer on his way in.

'He's gone,' said the old lady.

'I know,' said Joost.

'I don't just mean he's left, I mean he's dead,' said the woman.

'I know,' said Joost again.

She didn't even bat an eyelid, such was her sorrow.

'A mother always knows,' said the craggy faced woman with sadness drawn on her face.

'Are you another of his so called friends looking for drugs?'

'No,' said Joost.

'Well don't just stand there then, come and tell me what you know.'

The old lady came to the conclusion that Joost was as high as a kite, but at least she had someone to talk too, someone who listened.

'He had such a sad life really,' she said 'but I never knew until it was too late.'

'Knew what?' asked Joost.

'The goings on at the church,' she replied 'with that priest.'

'I had to bring him up alone' she continued 'his stepdad didn't want to know, hated kids.'

Joost didn't explore the church scandal; he could tell it would be heart breaking from the look in the old woman's eyes. But he did lend a shoulder to cry on.

'I'm looking for something,' Joost finally said.

'Go on,' she replied.

'A souvenir to remind me of John.'

He'd said enough about the afterlife.

'Take your pick,' came the reply.

Joost rummaged from box to box, but couldn't find a pen.

'Where does he keep his gear?' he asked.

The woman looked disappointed.

'It's all gone,' she said 'and I thought you were different.'

'Trust me, I am.'

'Look under the sink, that's all you'll find,' said the woman.

There were no drugs, but Joost did find what he was looking for, a metal pen with no ink that John used to snort his coke.

'This will do just fine,' said Joost.

'Alright son, I think you'd better go now.'

'Sure, and you know something, John turned out to be a great kid,' said Joost.

She smiled.

When he got back Bheki didn't even ask; something was afoot, but she was no longer sure if she cared.

Joost checked his phone every half hour, and eventually got the text he was waiting for 'Harrods 10 tomorrow morning'.

Joost caught a glimpse of Lucy with her mum near the designer bags. With his back to hers, surrounded by frantic shoppers, he slipped a small package into her coat pocket. Before he could go, and with Christine in the next aisle, Lucy grabbed his arm, and thrust a piece of paper into his hand. 'Thieves wood 11 p.m. New Year's Eve' it read.

It looked like he wouldn't be counting down the clock with Bheki after all.

Chapter Fifty Five

She'd been asleep when he'd quietly got dressed, and Bheki knew what the letter left on Joost's pillow was, even before she opened it.

'Sorry but I can't be here tonight. It was wrong to keep you hanging on, but tomorrow's another year. Thanks for loving me, Joost.'

She tore up the letter, and threw the bedside vase at the wall. Eudy came rushing in.

'I saw his car leave this morning with his bags packed,' she said. 'I'm sorry sis.'

'Hey the world's full of one eyed handsome men,' said Bheki as her tears began to fall.

Joost arrived in the evening at the reference point on the map - soles point. He was on the high ground above Thieves wood, wearing army surplus camouflage and boots. He checked his night scope and revolver, and poured himself a black coffee.

Four cars stopped on the perimeter of the wood. Someone opened a gate, and they slowly drove in. Joost ran down the hill to his car.

It was best to be around people, and they were spending New Year 's Eve at Miriam's. The house was packed, and Miriam had just finished reading the last sermon written by Abel. It was only half finished, but poignant nonetheless; it was about love, loss, and carrying on the good fight in adversity.

'Where's Joost?' asked Miriam.

Bheki was tongue tied for once.

'He's indisposed,' said Eudy on her behalf, before noticing something else. 'Have you seen Themba anywhere lately?'

It was Dela's rogue's gallery, and everyone was there. They cleared a sufficient area, making a large circle on the ground with branches. Mr Pandalay and Susie Chang splashed over them with petrol from two large jerry cans, and all that remained were the tokens.

'May I do the honours?' Lucy asked Dela.

'Be my guest,' said Dela handing over the mementoes.

She was about to wear the crocodile mask.

Lucy stepped up to the ring, and threw in a photograph, a watch, and a pen. Joost was watching from a safe distance through the trees.

'It's nearly time,' said an excited Miriam, and along with the television everyone got ready to count down.

'Stand back everybody,' said Dela, and Plackcedes lit the fire, quickly stepping back from the flames.

'Ten, nine, eight,' they counted, with Bheki and Eudy holding hands.

Little Noah was sleeping through it all, and Themba had vanished into thin air long ago; but he'd received a vision from the ghost of Pastor Abel Goodyear.

Plackcedes saw something fall from Lucy's pocket next to her, and picked it up. She was shocked, and handed the photograph to Dela as quick as she could. But before the high priestess could ask 'then who ...?' four unexpected figures appeared in the circle.

'Three, two, one,' they shouted, and 'Happy New Year sis,' said Eudy.

'Thanks Dela,' said Joost stepping from behind the bushes, and pointing the gun at her chest.

'Oh and in case you're wondering about the photo, it was Stella and Hildy van Houten.'

The flames were dying down, but fireworks lit the skies.

'Well let's not just stand here,' said Pastor Abel to the others, and they made their way to Joost, stepping over the dying flames.

Joost couldn't take his eyes off of Stella, and Gasper Owido tried to grab the gun. In the struggle a shot rang out, and the weapon dropped like a hot cake.

'Nobody move,' said Themba holding a gun of his own.

Joost picked up his smoking gun from Dela's feet.

'Get to the car,' he said to Stella and Hildy.

'Make that cars,' said Themba.

Joost made sure the others had a head start, and then ran after them.

'Quick stop them,' shouted Dela, but no one else's car would start; they'd stolen the keys.

Dela fell to the floor, wounded and bleeding. Plackcedes was first by her side, and then Felix.

'I've been hit,' said Dela, and there was a pool of blood forming on her chest.

She was about to see Din after all.

Abel had taken a ride with Themba, but they all made it back to his house in one piece.

'For once I'm lost for words my son,' said Abel to Joost whilst standing outside his front door, on the threshold of a miraculous return.

'I don't know how to thank you,' said the pastor.

'Thank Bheki,' said Joost 'and Themba'.

'By the way how did you know?' Joost asked Themba.

'The pastor told me.'

'And the gun?' asked Joost.

Themba pressed the trigger, and a flame shot forth.

'Mai's cigarette lighter,' he replied.

As Abel walked into the house the crowds parted leaving a path to Miriam. Many fell on their knees making the sign of the cross. Bheki was both laughing and crying; instinctively she knew Joost had got his wife back.

'OK John you're next, where too?' asked Joost.

'My mums,' he said.

'Joost?'

'Yes John?'

'How can I ever repay you?'

'That's a question I should ask you,' replied Joost.

'Anyway if you ever need me, just come knocking,' said John.

'And vice versa my friend,' said Joost.

The old woman was home alone when she opened the door, and simply put her arms around him. Her son was home, and she could tell; he'd left the demons behind.

Eventually they were alone, the van Houten family.

'I don't know how you did it Joost, but Hildy said you'd never give up,' said Stella.

Joost tried to act strong, but the tears couldn't help themselves falling from his remaining eye.

'What's happened to your eye?' asked Stella.

'It's a long story,' said Joost.

'Joost we need to talk,' said Stella.

'Of course,' he said.

'About Bheki, and alone' said Stella, nodding her head towards Hildy.

'Oh,' he said.

'Let's join the revellers in Trafalgar Square,' said Hildy 'I've only ever seen it on TV.'

In the early morning he left them on the doorstep of the South African Embassy.

'What are you going to say?' asked Joost.

'Don't worry I'll think of something,' said Stella.

They looked exactly as they did on that fateful day.

'Keep in touch dad, I love you,' shouted Hildy after him.

He waved back before turning the corner, and four squabbling figures rushed by him on their way from a party; three Africans in tribal dress, and an English explorer.

'Where's Bheki?' Joost asked Themba back at the house.

Eudy answered.

'She's gone Joost,' she said.

He sat down on the sofa, head in his hands.

'She did leave a message though,' said Eudy.

'Go on,' he said expecting to hear a final rebuke.

'I'll be at my favourite restaurant,' said Eudy.

'That's it,' said Joost.

'That's it,' said Eudy.

'So what is her favourite restaurant?' asked Joost.

'You tell me,' said Eudy.

'Themba?' asked Joost.

'Sorry, I can't help you on this one.'

Joost looked dumbfounded.

'What took you so long?' asked Bheki.

Joost tucked his chair under the table at the Blue Samurai, and smiled. The waiters were still clearing up from the previous night.

'It's over,' he said.

'I thought as much,' said Bheki 'so why have you come?'

'Because it's over between me and Stella; she doesn't want me, and I don't want her, it's you I love.'

Bheki looked at him in disbelief.

'It's true Bheki, honest to God.'

Bheki pulled a Bible from her bag.

'Swear it,' she said 'and be careful, you know there's an afterlife.'

He swore.

'But why?' asked Bheki.

'Two reasons,' said Joost.

'One, we'd grown apart years ago, and two you mean more to me than anything else in the world.'

'Prove it,' said Bheki.

'I've got something in my pocket' said Joost.

'Haven't we been there before?' said Bheki grinning.

'Not exactly,' he said, and he pulled out the engagement ring Bheki had already secretly seen.

'You're certain Joost?' she asked.

'Yes,' he replied.

'In that case I accept, we're engaged' she said.

The owner and his staff burst into applause, and for once they both looked rather sheepish.

Back home there was more good news, and Joost showed Bheki the text message.

'Dela was hit by the bullet. She's dead. Good luck. Lucy.'

Chapter Fifty Six

James Middlemass was feeling glad to be alive, when the doorbell rang.

'Who is it dear?' shouted Christine from upstairs.

'It's just some old acquaintances,' James shouted back.

John Lacey and Abel Goodyear stood before him. They'd waited until Lucy had gone for a ride on her new bike, a present for Christmas; there was no point in traumatising his daughter too much.

'Remember me?' asked John.

'How could I forget,' answered James solemnly.

'I hope you're still not angry John, it wasn't entirely all my fault was it,' said James smirking.

'Now gentleman let's not have an unseemly argument,' said Abel.

'James the good news is, it's almost never too late to redeem oneself,' said Abel.

'Precisely,' said James 'but what's the bad news?'

'This,' said John, and he stabbed Reverend James Middlemass right through the heart.

'Or let me put it another way,' said Abel to the dying devil at their feet 'an eye for an eye.'

As they were about to turn and leave in Abel's car, he noticed one last thing, and dragged it off of James' wrist.

'Would you believe it,' said Abel 'my gold watch.'

The new nurse, fresh from college, looked out onto the beautiful snow topped gardens. Freshly crunched on top were a set of paw prints.

He looked around at his new office. This is what he'd always wanted to do, care for the elderly in a nursing home like Greenpastures.

There was a cat pawing at the window, and he lifted it up. The golden striped feline immediately jumped onto his desk, and began purring, arching his back. It was all the fresh faced nurse could do but sit him on his lap, and stroke him.

'My you are a friendly one aren't you,' he said.

But his own thoughts were becoming strangely less friendly, and by the time the cat had left they were distinctly homicidal.

Joost was behind the wheel of his brand new sports car. It was early morning, Bheki was by his side, and he was determined to master driving with one eye.

With his foot over the accelerator Joost took a packet of cigarettes from his pocket, removed one, and lit it from the car lighter.

'Another secret honey?' asked Bheki.

Joost pulled onto the motorway.

'It's no secret baby, and you should know, I'm always smoking.'